Air Guitar And Caviar

Jackie Ladbury

Typesetting, Fabrian Books - fabrianbooks.com. Cover Illustration by Berni Stevens © 2017.

For my wonderful Write Romantics, for having faith in me and making this book possible.

CHAPTER ONE

'I will ask her out, I will ask her out.' Dylan Willis reassured his reflection in the sports shop window.

Ignoring Beanie, his singing partner, he checked out his stance. His battered guitar was slung low, his legs akimbo, and his brown, leather cowboy boots were suitably scuffed and worn. He intended to look every inch the Rock God he was destined to become. Admittedly, it made it bloody hard to play, but, hey - serious cool came at a price.

Dylan had hoped stardom would call a little sooner, seeing as he was pushing twenty-four, but he was still pretty confident, despite the evidence to the contrary. He just had to pick the right moment to shine.

But that day, he was on a different mission. That day, he was going to shine solely for the beautiful woman who had caused a spike of pure lust and unlikely possessiveness to snake through his veins. He just prayed she'd walk by again, her silky, sunshine coloured hair blowing in the breeze, her huge green eyes watching him with interest.

When she did, he was going to ask her out, and she would say yes, and they would fall in love. He didn't think it would be too hard to engineer, but it would certainly further his plans if she actually showed up.

He hadn't anticipated being rained on, either. He peered up at the grey clouds closing in over the tiny square of blue sky, a steady drizzle misting his face and blurring his vision. He squinted down the road, shoving a wayward curl out of his eyes, as it slid, damp and irritating, down his forehead.

He rotated one foot and then the other to stop the numbness from setting in.

A raindrop dribbled down the back of his neck.

He was not having fun.

He also had a bad feeling that the steady trickle was going to turn torrential, and that the gorgeous woman destined to be his one and only wouldn't show.

He refused to consider that possibility, though. He wanted – no, he needed to see her today. That minute, in fact.

Strumming a song that he could play in his sleep, he shivered inside his flatmate's leather jacket, praying it wouldn't shrink in the rain. He'd be a dead man if it did. Rain dripped off his hair, down his nose, and on to his guitar, which he swiped at with his sleeve every now and then. It wasn't his best Yamaha, so he wasn't too worried about it warping, but even so.

Beanie pulled his thin coat over his head in a pointless attempt to stop the flow of water dripping down his chin. 'Do you think we should call it a day?' he asked.

'Ah, Beanie boy, I can feel a song of heartbreak coming on.' Dylan twanged a couple of low chords to demonstrate his misery, as he took in the rapidly emptying street as rain darkened the dingy paving stones.

Beanie nodded and continued doing what he did best, namely shivering and looking ill. Stood as thin as a rail, his complexion would have put any ghost to shame – because he was pale, as in a how long have you got left to live kind of way, and his straggly dog, part terrier, part Hound of the Baskervilles, looked as if the Grim Reaper would claim him at any minute.

Beanie's musical instrument of choice was a metal triangle, which he attacked with random diligence, the tune in his head apparently being a different song to Dylan's. They were a sad looking trio, but it made them money.

Dylan took it all in his stride, preferring to spend his time on the streets, rather than in the dump of a rented house he shared with three other mates who hadn't quite got the hang of working for a living.

But still The Vision hadn't showed.

'Sure, they say all the best songs are written when you're at heartbreak hotel.' Beanie pulled on his damp cigarette, cupping his palm around it against the rain. 'This one's not far off being suicidal, so you're on the right track.'

Dylan played a melancholy riff to prove Beanie's point. 'Thanks, I think.' He unhooked his guitar from around his neck, but at a flash of blonde hair swinging in the distance, his stomach lurched. 'Oh, my God, it's her. Quick, sing.' He threw the guitar strap back over his head and feigned nonchalance.

Beanie peered out from beneath the shelter of his coat, his neck elongating as he shucked it off like a snail welcoming the rain. He started to harmonise, his head bobbing up and down to the music, tinging his metal triangle indiscriminately, with great concentration.

Staring at the woman heading his way, Dylan faltered. An emerald green, fluffy jumper skimmed her thighs over figure-hugging jeans, tucked into long brown boots. She threw her head back and raked her fingers through her hair, swishing it about, while her lips, a pearly pink, were just on the right side of pouting without making her look sulky. Dylan groaned, imagining his own fingers lacing through that silky hair as he kissed those soft lips, puckering up just for him.

She tilted her umbrella back and appeared to be enjoying the cool rain on her face as she meandered towards them. Pausing as she neared, she threw a coin into his cap on the ground.

Dylan's imagination orbited way past overdrive as he caught a flash of her bright red fingernails and wondered if it was possible to die from the ache in his groin. He flashed her his best smile and tried to stop his tongue from lolling, as she turned into Starbucks, disappearing from view.

He let his left hand drop, his mournful song dying on his lips. The smile that was known to melt the hardest heart had fallen on stony ground. She'd looked straight through him.

'What do I do?' He turned anxious, puppy dog eyes toward Beanie.

'You can wait for her to come past again next week, which of course, she might not do. Or you can go in there –' Beanie inclined his head in the direction of the coffee shop, '– and get her?'

'I can. Of course I can. Can I?'

'What have you got to lose?'

'Everything?'

'I think you'll find the answer is nothing,' Beanie replied, pulling his coat up around his ears once more.

Dylan ran his hand across the back of his neck and twisted his guitar around his body to rest across his shoulders. He breathed in. 'Maybe now is not the best time – with it raining, and all.'

Beanie glowered. 'You've talked of nothing else since you first set eyes on her.'

'Okay, you're right. I'll do it.' He smoothed his hair down with little effect. 'How do I look?'

Beanie looked him up and down and sniffed. 'Wet. You look very wet.'

'Thanks – remarkably perceptive.'

Dylan picked up his soggy cap from the pavement, fished out some coins from the pile, most of which he'd put there himself to nudge the punters in the right direction, and passed them to Beanie. 'If you see Stanley, make sure you buy him breakfast.'

'Course I will.'

'And not the liquid sort, yeah?'

'You can rely on me, you know that.'

'Right.' Unconvinced, he shoved his cap into his battered rucksack and pocketed the rest of the money. 'Off I go, then.' He faltered, pushing his hands into his pockets and rubbing the toe of his boot against his calf. 'I'm too scruffy aren't I, for someone like her?'

Beanie widened his eyes. 'I'd shag you any day.'

'Thanks. Might hold you to that, if I get desperate.'

Beanie whacked him on the back. 'Just go, will you? I'll be right behind you, okay?'

Dylan dragged his heels and prayed he was doing the right thing, as he stepped inside the cafe, feeling way out of his comfort zone. His happy disposition and laid-back manner usually charmed people easily, but for once, his ready smile morphed into a tongue-tied rictus as his mouth dried with nerves and his lips stuck to his teeth.

Across the coffee shop, The Vision flicked through the newspaper stand and picked out a colour supplement, before heading to one of the booths, unwinding her scarf as she sat down with her latté. She smoothed out her napkin and placed it at the side of the coffee cup, adding the spoon diagonally across it. Dylan watched in amusement as she angled her phone precisely next to the napkin, lining it up vertically. She was light years away from his bumbling, scruffy self, and he was being ridiculous even contemplating asking her to go out with him.

For a moment, he almost legged it, but he knew Beanie would be waiting outside to shove him back through the door. At least he was out of the rain, he thought, as he ordered a coffee and steeled himself to head her way.

After pretending to look around the café for somewhere to sit, he edged over to her table. 'Do you mind if I sit here?'

She looked up, and he caught his breath at her perfection, as she gazed directly at him and waved her hand towards the seat opposite. She glanced around the almost empty café, frowning slightly. 'Feel free, although it's hardly the best seat in the house.'

'I think it is.' He pushed his guitar into a corner and sat down a little too quickly, almost knocking his chair over.

Her brief smile of politeness brightened her face, but she quickly looked away, staring into her coffee.

Dylan watched, mesmerised as she stirred her drink mechanically, until the chocolate powdered star shape on the top dissolved in the froth. He didn't know what to say next, as he gazed into his own muddy-coloured coffee, stirring it and tapping the spoon on the side of the cup.

She glanced up sharply, and he froze mid-tap. Resting the spoon on his saucer, he cleared his throat, meeting eyes that were questioning. She frowned as her hand hovered over her drink.

'I just wondered ...' he began, shoving his hair out of his eyes.

'Yes?' She took a sip of her drink, then directed her clear eyes toward him once more.

‘Err, I just wondered, do you come here often?’ Yeah, great line Dylan, really original.

The Vision spluttered into her coffee, grabbing a napkin when the splutter turned in to a cough.

‘Sorry, sorry!’ Dylan lunged forward to thump her on the back, but she waved him out of the way, her eyes flashing.

‘I’m fine. Stoppit!’ She stood up, her chin jutting out. ‘Really? I’m trying to have a moment’s peace, and you march in, plonk yourself opposite me, when the place is almost deserted, drip rain on the seats, and spout one of the corniest lines ever to have been uttered. You think that’s going to swing it, do you?’ She huffed out a long breath and sat down again, her eyes still flashing enough for Dylan to see the intensity of the deep green in her irises. She raised her hand before Dylan could respond. ‘I just get really sick of it. It’s bad enough at work.’

That threw him, although her unexpected outburst had already rocked his confidence. ‘What is?’

‘People coming on to me all the time.’

‘Really? That happens at work?’

‘Yes.’ She ran her fingers through her hair, a ring she wore catching in it. ‘Mostly the same man, but it’s just as irritating.’ She glared at Dylan as she untangled her hair from the ring.

He stood up. ‘I’m so sorry. You’re right, I shouldn’t have bothered you.’ How could he have been so crass to think it was acceptable to launch himself at a woman who was a stranger to him, even if she’d been more than intimate in his dreams? It was so unlike him, anyway. He wanted to explain that she had made him lose his sensibilities, but he thought that might not go down too well, either. He stood up to leave, reaching for his guitar and shifting his rucksack higher up his shoulder, mortified that he had upset her.

Her demeanour seemed to change, though, when she spotted his guitar. 'Oh, it's you, the busker. You usually have a hat on.' She looked at him squarely for the first time and smiled tightly, almost apologetically.

'Yes, it's me.' His full-on smile re-appeared as he wiped his hand on his jeans and held it out, seizing the moment. 'Dylan Willis,' he added.

She looked at his hand as if she wanted to Dettox it, but nevertheless, shook it briefly. 'Sorry again, I'm just a bit stressed at the moment.'

Dylan's hand tingled at her touch - he decided he might never wash it again. 'Nice to meet you.' He paused, waiting for her to introduce herself.

She didn't.

But faint heart never won fair lady, he thought, and that was his one chance to win her over, although, so far, he'd made a total balls-up of it. 'It's just that I've seen you around, but I don't know how often you come here, so I thought I'd check, in case you didn't plan on coming back again? I'm not a stalker, or anything.' He cringed. Why did he have to add that?

'Right, that's good to know.' She peered upwards at him from under her thick fringe. 'There's a reason why you think I should tell you my plans?'

He groaned. 'I'm so sorry. I do sound a bit stalkerish, don't I? I'm really not.' He ran his hand around his neck, totally unable to drag his eyes away from her face.

The Vision stayed silent.

'Well, I'll leave you to your coffee.' He picked his guitar up. She clearly didn't want to speak to him, but still he gazed at her.

No, actually, he couldn't just leave it. He sat down again, placing his hands flat on the table. 'Would you like to come and see me play?'

She frowned. 'Sorry. Play?'

Dylan wanted to wipe away her frown with a trail of tiny kisses. He wanted to melt away her prickly outer layer with the heat of his longing. He wanted to prove to her that they were made for each other.

Of course, he did none of those things. He just willed her to say yes while trying not to show his desperation.

She eyed him warily.

He stared at her some more. His little speech hadn't gone quite the way it'd played out in his mind. 'I don't just play on the streets. I do gigs, as well. I'm really good.' It came out in a rush and sounded as if he was scraping the barrel in trying to prove his capability. He probably was, but it was the best he could offer.

'I don't doubt it.' Her smile almost reached her eyes.

He waited, rubbing the toe of his boot against the back of his leg again, his smile wilting.

'What am I supposed to say to that?' she asked, tucking a strand of hair behind her ear and glancing at her phone as if she hoped it would ring and rescue her.

'Say yes,' he said. 'You'll make my day, and I'll take you for a pizza afterwards.'

Her almost smile faded, her full lips pursing. She slid her hand across the table, the neat fingers and perfectly painted nails making Dylan want to withdraw his hands from view, even as his hopes soared.

Before they made contact, the woman withdrew her hand, apparently thinking better of the move. 'Thank you for your kind offer, but I don't date at the moment. I really don't have the time.' Her smile was regretful and polite. 'It's nothing personal,' she added.

His own smile faded as he took in her words, his shoulders slumping as the sharp pain of rejection hit home. He glanced upwards, through his eyelashes, hiding his disappointment. To his surprise, he saw genuine regret tinged with unhappiness behind her smile.

Pushing abruptly to his feet, he stepped away from the table. He'd intruded when she clearly needed to be alone. 'That's okay.' His voice was thick with disappointment and he couldn't seem to walk away as he should. 'If you change your mind, I'm in the Dog and Duck every Sunday.'

'I'll remember that, thank you.' She smiled sadly and shook her head, her actions belying her words.

'Well, good, because that's where I'll be.' He turned away, shrugging with resignation, casting a regretful look at his much-needed coffee as he closed the door behind him.

Beanie was waiting for him, his ready thumbs-up drooping, as he took in Dylan's dejection. 'Bad luck, mate.' He slapped him on the back. 'She looked stuck up, anyway.'

If he'd hoped to cheer him up with his words, he'd done a pretty useless job of it. Dylan shook his head. 'Maybe, but she still needs me in her life.'

'Yeah, well, whatever. You'll be all right, will you?' Beanie shifted from foot to foot, uncomfortable in his unlikely role of agony aunt. 'Do you want to keep Scrappy-doo for a while, you know, for company?' he volunteered.

Dylan, barely glanced at his friend, just studied the damp pavement, lost in thought. 'Nah, you're all right, mate. I'm not about to top myself, but ... you know.' He shrugged and tried out a weak smile. 'It's cool.'

'No worries, then. Come on, Scrappy.' Beanie drifted away, taking the straggly dog with him.

***

Scarlett watched their exchange through the window of the café, blinking in surprise at how rude she had been. Yes, the man had been trying it on, but he hadn't been arrogant, or pushy. He'd simply asked her out, politely, with no obvious hidden agenda.

He had nice hands, she thought, with fine blonde hair dusting his long fingers, his nails square and perfectly trimmed. Ideal guitar playing fingers, she supposed. His blue eyes had pierced hers, as if he could see into her heart and was prepared to forgive its granite-like qualities, offering her a chance to redeem herself. But she didn't want her heart mended, didn't want redeeming. She just wanted to be left alone.

She put her hand up to her brow, sad that she was so broken, she couldn't even take a harmless chat up at face value and had managed to embarrass the poor chap so cruelly. If she'd been at home, she would have put her head in her hands and wept.

The familiar feeling of falling into an abyss of unfathomable emotions swept over her. The dull ache it caused was no less painful, for all its familiarity, but she had learned to cope with it. Occasionally, though, a new, raw pain thumped her in the gut, overwhelming her. One hit her then, and she pushed her chair back, anxious to leave, knowing that full on sobbing would be the next phase, if her erratic emotions hitched up a notch. She needed to focus on something else.

She grabbed her handbag and rushed out of the café, pulling out her car keys on the way, as if she'd suddenly remembered an errand she had to do. RADA would have been proud to take her on, she thought, as she kept up the act of being someone in a hurry, until she reached her car door.

The legacy of Sky, her ex-boyfriend, ran deep and barbed and she hated what he'd turned her into, knowing she was no longer the woman he'd left behind. She needed to be strong but didn't have the energy or the desire to carry on and she cursed the man she'd loved, even as she hated him for abandoning her.

CHAPTER TWO

The driving rain had soaked Dylan in seconds, but he didn't care. He just started walking and, eventually, wound up at the park, one of his favourite places, where he could write his songs in peace.

Finding a seat on a bench, he watched the mallard ducks by the lake, waddling in the mud, fighting their corner against the Canadian geese. He was lost in thought as he kicked at the stones in annoyance, knowing he should have handled the embarrassing chat up scene so much better. Hadn't he been singing about such things since he was a teenager, for God's sake?

But then was not the time to be dejected, it was the time to be positive, to move his game plan forward. And he would do exactly that, as soon as he discovered what his game plan was.

Biting at his thumbnail, he tried to think of a solution.

It was cool, he decided. He'd win her round once she heard how talented he was. His only problem was that he'd never played a gig on his own before. He was used to messing around in his home town with his old band. And rather than being a brilliant performer to the masses at the Dog and Duck on a Sunday, he actually served the beer and washed the glasses, so Mac the landlord would feed him. But hey, that could be changed, he thought – no worries.

He stood up and slung his guitar over his back, determined to hold on to the positives. Mac would be bowled over by his talent, and the Dog and Duck would be forever grateful that Dylan put them on the map when he became a household name. He just needed to sort it out with Mac on a hangover-free day, when he wasn't being an evil son of a bitch.

So, no time like the present, he thought. A drink might cheer him up, and he could handle Mac. He meandered back to his shared house, side-stepped the dirty trainers, bicycle wheels, and piles of junk mail that tripped him up at every turn, and after changing into dry clothes, wandered over to the Dog and Duck.

The babble of drinkers, cheap music, and the chink of glasses soothed him, as he sat down on a barstool in the snug, skimming sticky, half-dried liquid from the counter-top with a beer mat before depositing his elbows on it. The snug was the only part where the old regulars felt comfortable, since the rest of it had been turned into a gastro pub, done out in pseudo Art Deco and unwelcoming glass and steel. The menu had become unrecognizable, too: chips were only ever seen stacked up on top of each other as if the chef was once a tidy log cutter, and noisettes of unidentifiable and mostly unappetising food were the order of the day.

Stanley, wearing grimy trainers and an incongruous cream suit, shuffled up to him.

'Hey, Stan.' Dylan nodded toward him. 'I like the bib and tucker.'

Anya, the new Hungarian waitress, sniffed in Stanley's direction from behind the bar, as if he'd brought a bad smell in with him. 'It can't be worse than that dreadful coat that looks like a dog blanket. Even the dog discarded that.'

'You like it?' Stanley's gravelly voice conjured up smoky nightclubs and whisky chasers. He fingered the huge lapel of the smart suit, which looked as if it belonged on the set of Grease. 'I found it in one of the charity bags outside the hospice shop. Fits a treat, and what a bargain, when you cut out the middle man.' Stanley flashed teeth that looked as if he'd sucked on coal for the last twenty years.

Dylan looked away quickly.

'Wondered if you were eating in here, later?' Stanley's bloodshot eyes pleaded an unspoken question. His brown, chewed-up toffee looking face crinkled with gratitude as Dylan patted his pockets.

'My turn again, is it?' Dylan joked.

'Jesus, you're a saint ...'

'Yeah, yeah, I know.' Dylan cut Stanley off before the thanks became too ingratiating. 'What shall we have, treacle baked gammon and julienne frites?' He studied the upmarket menu and wondered when he'd turned into his mother, feeding the homeless. It must be a genetic thing. He'd be doing a charity cake bake next, if he wasn't careful.

'Ham and chips, is that?' Stanley asked, screwing his eyes up.

Dylan nodded as he replaced the menu in its fancy silver-plated holder.

Stanley never strayed far from Dylan, who'd mostly fed and watered him on a full-time basis, since he'd found him shaking in a doorway one night. Whether from a lack of, or too much, substance abuse, Dylan had never discovered, but his fate had been sealed – he was bonded to Stanley.

He gave his attention to Mac, as Stanley contentedly slurped his beer. 'I'll bet you'd let me set up a stage and play a gig in here, wouldn't you, Mac?'

'Why would I want to do that?' Mac's permanent scowl deepened.

'Because I'm brilliant,' Dylan replied, terrified that Mac would say no, but equally terrified he might say yes. Despite that, the desperation in his own voice annoyed him, especially as his words earned him a curled lip from Anya, who mostly prowled around the place squirting air freshener while declaring My nose is not used to the stench of an English pub, to anyone who would listen.

Dylan emptied his pockets of loot onto the counter, and Mac sifted through the detritus, throwing out the occasional Romanian Leu or metal button with a smirk, as if it was proof of Dylan's lack of talent. He piled all the ten pence pieces up, until there was enough money to buy a pint, and shoved the Euros back at him, along with the rogue coins and sweet wrappers.

Dylan put them back in his pocket with a resigned air, aware that some people just saw him as a singing dustbin. 'I've got all my own amps and stuff, and I'll tidy up afterwards, I promise.'

Mac dragged his gaze away from Anya's bottom and looked at Dylan, his eyes wide as if he hadn't been expecting Dylan to be that organised. He polished another glass, a half smirk on his lips. Dylan knew that look. It said, I'm listening, but I'm going to tell you to piss off, anyway. It was a normal response from Mac, and wasn't necessarily a bad sign.

Dragging out the standoff, Mac took a swig of his tomato juice and grimaced; it was no doubt drowning in vodka again. He threw a handful of peanuts into his mouth and chewed.

Dylan almost decided that Mac had forgotten all about their conversation, when Mac said, 'This is my little empire, and I don't want you tarnishing its reputation, okay?'

Tiny bullets of chewed peanut shot out from Mac's mouth toward Dylan as he spoke, and Dylan dodged out of their way the best he could, wondering why higher management hadn't replaced Mac, along with the ancient Axminster carpet and dirty leather chairs. Although, since Anya had started, he had at least ditched the brown corduroy jacket that he'd always sported and generally tidied himself up a bit.

Mac stared hard at Dylan, as if evaluating his worth, before eventually saying, 'You write your own songs, do you? I don't want two hours of bloody Ticket to Ride and Abba putting everyone off their Tiramisu.'

‘Of course, I’ve written some sublime songs.’ He didn’t add that no one had actually heard them yet, which made it purely self-conjecture.

Mac stopped rubbing at a twenty pence piece that looked as if someone had taken an axe to it. ‘Sublime songs, eh. That’ll be interesting. You won’t want paying, will you?’

‘Err ...’

‘No, I didn’t think so,’ Mac said firmly. ‘You weren’t thinking of paying me, were you?’

‘Mac, you know I’m always broke.’

Mac chewed thoughtfully. ‘Oh, go on then, but if you’re crap, you’re out on your ear,’ he said, shooting more peanut bullets at Dylan.

‘I’ve told you, I’m brilliant,’ Dylan said, tempted to cross his fingers behind his back at such a claim, but then again, he was pretty good, in his opinion.

For a street busker.

‘We’ll see about that on Sunday.’

‘Cool. Can I borrow your phone? I just want to call a mate of mine who does graphic design. If I’m going to do this thing, I might as well do it right and put out some flyers.’

‘Why haven’t you got a mobile? Even ten-year-old school kids have mobiles these days.’

‘I left it in my hat when I was busking, and it got nicked.’

Mac shook his head. 'I don't know. Whatever happened to honour among thieves, eh? Go on, then. It's around the back.'

CHAPTER THREE

Scarlett pulled the duvet cover over her head, as her phone gate-crashed her dreams. She stuck out her arm, feeling for her alarm. 'Please, no, I'm too tired.' She opened one eye. It felt gritty and sore, as if she'd forgotten to take out her contact lenses again.

Her brain came alive, when she realised her feet weren't hindered by crisp hotel sheets, flattening her, like a letter pushed into a too small envelope. Pulling herself up, she sighed with relief as she took in her surroundings and slid back into the silky warmth of her own bed.

She was home.

As her mobile started ringing again, she dragged it under the duvet, groaning at a picture of a Great White shark flashing up on the screen and the sinister tune from Jaws that blared out.

Todd, the chief pilot of StarJet. She didn't dare ignore it. What a start to the day.

'Todd, good morning, you're up bright and early.'

'Scarlett. A thought. I'm taking the Frog-eyed Sprite out for a spin to Stapleford and wondered if you fancied coming with me. The Piper needs a turn over before the winter, so we could fly out to Le Touquet, if you fancied it. Partake in a bowl of mussels and some garlic bread, before heading home.'

Scarlett sighed. No way! He was doing it again – blurring the lines between their professional and personal life. She took a deep breath, gearing up for another battle. She really didn't want to trundle down the motorway at half speed in his ancient sports car, teeth rattling and hair whipping around her face. Not to mention, the darn thing broke down more times than a sinner on death row. Add on a lunch date, and a flight in a tiny, scary aeroplane, and the whole day would be hell.

It wasn't the first time he'd tried to persuade her into doing something she didn't want to do, afterward using her refusal as an opportunity to sulk, or to exact revenge later. He was so wearing.

Focusing on his voice again, the cut glass accent that she used to admire so much, but had now, simply become grating, she crawled out of bed and opened her blinds, putting her mobile on speaker.

The tops of the trees outside her window swayed gently, the maple leaves turning russet red, and white clouds shimmied across a magical blue sky. A bright new day unfolded before her: England at its best. All doubts disappeared.

'I'm sorry, Todd, but I'm babysitting my sister's daughter.' She focused on the dust motes swirling in the sunlight and drew a smiley face on her bedside table, idly wondering how her flat could get so dusty in five days when a pot plant was the only animate thing in there. 'It is my day off, remember?'

'Suit yourself. I'm sure most people would love such an opportunity.'

'And I hope you find that perfect someone to fit the bill. Have a lovely day. It looks like ideal flying weather,' she added quickly as she pictured the mask of disapproval on the other end of the phone.

Todd almost always used a tone of voice that bordered on an order, rather than a request. She'd put it down to his RAF background at first, but she'd since come to recognise him as a bully, using his position and history as leverage to behave badly. Because of that, she'd soon learned to hate him, but keeping him at arm's length was as exhausting as the job itself.

Waiting for his response, and knowing she would pay for refusing, she wondered when the status of their relationship had changed so markedly.

'Fine. Oh, I'll need you to fly tomorrow. Expect Simon from Ops to call you.' The clipped tone said so much more than his words, but she wouldn't let him rattle her.

She'd spent the last five days flying over the freezing wastelands of Russia, from one oil field to the next, as obnoxious passengers drank the bar dry and chain-smoked foul smelling cigars until her eyes streamed. They must have paid well over the odds, Scarlett decided, as even Todd made no comment on their smoking, just slammed the flight deck door closed and feigned ignorance. Fighting over the phone with Todd was a breeze in comparison, but she was wiped out and needed to relax and recover, and she wouldn't let Todd ruin her day, even if he did manage to rule her life.

'That's great,' she said, trying to inject pleasure into her voice. 'I need the flight pay.'

'As much as you need your job, I'm sure.'

It took her a moment to recognise the veiled threat, and she held her breath, determined not to give him any more bait. She forced a smile to maintain her equilibrium – it usually worked when she'd rather speak her mind.

The silence lengthened, but she knew she could wait it out better than he could.

'Right, then,' he eventually said. 'I'll bid you good day.'

Her smile was for real that time. She'd won the battle, even if winning the war was a long way off. 'Bye, Todd, enjoy your day.'

She exhaled loudly, her hand shaking, as she put her phone back on the bedside table and sat down heavily on the bed. She stared at the wall for a moment before regaining her composure. 'A shower, I think.' Her words sounded forced, but she determined to put Todd out of her mind and make the most of the day.

She showered and dressed quickly, sliding a black cashmere jumper over her head and pulling on her jeans, tucking them in her long leather boots. She grabbed her jacket and keys, and slung her bag over her shoulder, giving her flight bag, sitting on the floor, a determined kick, as she let herself out. The unpacking and washing could wait.

Elsa, her five-year-old niece, stood waiting by the door when Scarlett reached her sister's house, and on seeing Scarlett, she squealed. 'Can we go to the park and take Buster with us, please?' she begged. 'Mummy has to go out, and he gets really lonely on his own.'

The dog's lead had already been clipped to his collar, so it looked pretty much like a done deal. Scarlett smiled and tickled the mongrel's ears. 'Of course we can. I know you can keep him under control.'

Elsa beamed at the compliment and didn't even make a fuss when Scarlett plucked her coat from the banister and held it out, knowing that Elsa hated wearing it.

Louisa, Scarlett's sister, rounded the living room doorway wearing a grey suit, her hair in a neat chignon. 'Hi, darling, how are you today?'

'Yeah, fine, nothing much to report. Knackered, as usual.'

Louisa smiled in sympathy, and rubbed at her sister's arm. 'You look pale. Are you looking after yourself?'

'I know what the subtext here is, and yes, I am, thank you.' She tried a brave smile, even though she suddenly felt weary and lonely.

Louisa hugged her. 'I just worry for you. You have hardly any social life.'

'But on the upside, I do get to serve some pretty good food to some pretty amazing people, even if they are the only ones who think they are amazing.' Her smile was self-deprecating. She knew she should try to regain her zest for life, but that particular tunnel had no pinpoint of light burning bright at the end of it.

'Yes, well, we'll talk when I get back from the interview.' Louisa looked ruefully at Scarlett as she slipped on high heels.

Elsa stood on tiptoes for a hug, and Louisa kissed the

top of her head, smoothing down her soft curls, as she picked up her coat.

'Good luck,' Scarlett said, folding Elsa's pliable body into her own, in case she made a fuss over her mother leaving.

'Thanks. I think I'll need it. You do have your keys to get back in, don't you?'

Scarlett nodded while fishing the spare keys out of her bag, which she waved in front of her sister's face.

'Great, see you later.' Louisa opened the front door, her keys rattling, and recognising the signs, Buster thumped his tail on the parquet floor, waiting impatiently and staring at Elsa with his big brown eyes.

'Come on, Aunty Scarlett, Buster wants to go.'

Scarlett picked up her bag, slammed the front door, and together they scrunched through the autumn leaves, heading for the park.

She breathed in the crisp air, as the breeze lifted and twirled her hair. England had never looked so good after the barren tundra of Russia, where the wind had frozen her cheeks and nose, instantly turning her eyelashes into icy spider legs. Even so, there was a definite chill in the air that she hadn't felt last week, and she pulled the sleeves of her jacket down over her hands, wishing she'd worn her gloves.

'There's the man who sings songs for Mummy. Come on.' Elsa pointed at someone in the distance, and Scarlett recognised the outline of the busker, his wild corkscrew hair fighting its way out of a peaked cap.

She grabbed at Elsa's hand. 'Shall we walk the other way to the park, darling? The ice cream man is often on the corner of the street.'

'No, I want to see the singer. He's my friend.' Elsa skipped ahead, leaving Scarlett no choice but to follow.

As they drew closer, Dylan broke into such a smile of welcome, it made Scarlett's normally formidable exterior melt. She smiled back, relieved that he wasn't bearing a grudge at the way she had turned him down.

He managed a little wave for Elsa, as he wound down the song he was singing, and when he'd finished, he rested the base of the guitar on his foot, casually holding the neck. 'Hello again.' His blue eyes pierced Scarlett's once more, the intensity of them making her feel as if he was trying to read her thoughts.

She broke eye contact and took an involuntary step backwards, afraid he might hypnotise her with his eyes.

Elsa did the opposite and stepped forward, grabbing his hand. 'This is Dylan. He's my mummy's friend – and mine.' She beamed up at Scarlett. 'We give him money.' Elsa swung his arm, her small hand engulfed in his. 'And he watches me dance, don't you?'

Dylan winced. 'Ouch, that sounds really bad. Hello, Elsa, Buster.' He reached down and stroked the dog, while beaming at Scarlett.

'You know each other?' Scarlett asked, stating the obvious.

'We have form together, don't we?' He winked at Elsa and raised his hand to be high-fived.

'Give him some money, and tell him your name. He'll make up a song with your name in it, honest he will.' Elsa slapped Dylan's palm with her own and danced a little jig around him.

Dylan raised an eyebrow. 'Well?'

Scarlett hesitated. 'I'm Elsa's Aunty.'

He gave her a look that said Elsa's Aunty would have to do better than that.

Scarlett sighed. 'My name is Scarlett, but you'll have a hard time coming up with something that rhymes with it.'

'That's a lovely name, and don't worry, I'll write a song especially for you.'

'It's true, he will. He did one for me.' Elsa looked delighted as she danced, drawing them closer together, circling around both of them and wind-milling her arms.

'Really?'

'Don't sound so surprised. It'll cost you, though,' Dylan said, his eyes challenging.

'Give him some money, Aunty Scarlett.' Elsa pulled on Scarlett's sleeve, her face shining with excitement.

'I don't want money, Elsa.'

Elsa looked from Dylan to Scarlett, a frown creasing her smooth forehead. 'Would you rather an ice cream, then?' She peered up at Dylan. 'That's where we were going, to the ice cream van parked all the way around the corner of the other street.' She enunciated clearly, dragging out the word all, while gesticulating with her hand. 'But I said we could get one at the park café afterwards, as I wanted to see you.'

Dylan gave Scarlett a sidelong glance that said she'd been rumbled, but he kept his smile in place. 'They do a mean latté at the café by the lake, too, if you fancy one?'

The sincerity of his smile seemed to pull at Scarlett, but she shook her head, not wanting to offend him, but equally not wanting to spend time with him.

'Come on, Dylan, I've got bread for the ducks.' Elsa picked up his hat and shook it carefully. 'And you've got lots of money in your hat. You could buy me a milkshake, too.'

'No problem, beautiful girl.' Dylan winked at Elsa as he wound his guitar strap around his neck once more and pushed his guitar around to his back. He slid the coins from his hat into his pocket and plonked the cap on Elsa's head as he fell into step beside Scarlett.

If she didn't know better, Scarlett would have bet Dylan's last purloined pound that the whole thing was a set up, but as she glanced suspiciously at him, was unable to think of a single reason why he shouldn't be there.

CHAPTER FOUR

'So, do you come here often?' Scarlett quipped, once they'd settled by the park lake, a coffee each and a large milkshake for Elsa.

'I apologise unreservedly for that comment the other day, and yes, I do come to the park quite a lot. It helps my concentration, when I'm composing. I bring Scrappy-doo, my singing partner's dog, sometimes, so I don't look like a sad weirdo, or like I'm up to no good. Not that I am up to no good, of course,' he added quickly, slapping his forehead. 'What am I saying?' He turned big eyes toward Scarlett. 'I do myself no favours. I'm really not weird, trust me.'

She waved her arm, dismissing his comments. 'You write songs, though? That's pretty weird in my world.'

'Yes, I already told you that. Didn't you believe me?' He turned his attention toward Elsa, who pulled at his arm, having noisily sucked her glass dry in seconds.

Elsa passed him a lump of crusty bread. 'Here's your bit.' She obviously wasn't going to be fobbed off, and Dylan started to break his bread into tiny lumps, as if buying time. 'Dylan, stop messing around and come oonnn.'

'I'm coming. Keep your wig on,' he laughed, as Elsa tried to pull him up.

'We'll let Aunty Scarlett sit here a while, because she gets very tired being a hostess for foreign men,' she said, giving Dylan big, sad eyes.

Dylan's own eyes widened as he took stock of Scarlett. 'That sounds too interesting to pretend I didn't hear it. Actually, it sounds so much worse than me watching Elsa dance.'

Scarlett put her hand to her brow, pushing back her fringe. 'No, it's not half as good as it sounds. I'll tell you when you get back. Go.' She pushed him away, as Elsa hopped from one leg to the other with impatience, until Dylan stood up and headed down to the water's edge.

They messed about by the lakeside, Elsa splashing about in her red ladybird-covered wellingtons, laughing as she waddled in the mud mimicking the ducks. She put a lot of effort into throwing the bread out into the water, and the two of them cheered when the moorhens outswam the geese to get at the bread. When her wellies got stuck in the mud, Dylan scooped her up before plonking her down on the grass, afterwards braving the duck poo-smeared mud to rescue the wellingtons.

From her spot on the bench, Scarlett enjoyed watching their antics and found herself touched by Dylan's consideration of Elsa. After a while, though, she realised she was focussing more on Dylan than Elsa. A lot more.

His long legs were encased nicely inside very faded denims, and his thin tee-shirt, with a weird logo on the back, showed off a nicely honed torso. His hair was unruly and probably not the best fashion accessory although cute curls crept around his neck, drawing her attention to his broad shoulders. Luckily, his face more than made up for any deficiency - or more particularly, his smile and his blue eyes. All in all, he was an exceedingly attractive package covered by very scruffy clothes.

Beyond that, she couldn't really work him out. His manners were impeccable, and he spoke well, although she had a feeling that his idea of wining and dining would be a Big Mac and a swift half in the Dog and Duck.

She hoped he understood that she wasn't on the market for romance, despite her giving in to the park visit, and that he wasn't hanging around thinking she would change her mind.

Since Sky, Scarlett had become a rock and an island, and she managed very nicely on her own, even if a twinge of loneliness crept in occasionally.

Tuning back in to her surroundings, she half listened to Dylan and Elsa's conversation, as they headed back up the grassy slope.

'Most of them have three leaves but if you can find a four leaf one, you'll have good luck,' Dylan explained to Elsa patiently. He held Elsa's wellies in one hand, and a clump of grass and leaves in the other, and they inspected the likely candidates they'd plucked from the grass.

Elsa opened her hand and dropped her squashed clovers on the bench, then concentrated on counting their heart-shaped leaves. Spotting a buttercup in her collection, though, she soon lost interest and began pulling off its petals, instead.

'Come on, Elsa, you have to find at least one four leaf clover for me.' Dylan threw her a smile, and she dutifully trotted off to search among the grass once more.

As soon as she'd gone, Dylan sat back down next to Scarlett. 'That'll keep her busy, while we have a chat.' His eyes levelled with hers. 'Looking for a copy of the Big Issue sticking out of my back pocket?' He narrowed his eyes. 'I can see you're trying to place me.'

'Not at all,' Scarlett lied, blushing at her transparency.

'It's okay. An understandable reaction, though, actually, I busk mostly for the experience, rather than the money. Although surprisingly, I do earn a fair bit. Mind you, it's often Mickey Mouse money. If I ever make it to Zimbabwe, or Vietnam, I'll be rich as a king. And people feed me - all the time - but let's not get side-tracked by my uninteresting career path. What's this about your job as a hostess for foreign men?'

'I'm an air stewardess - cabin staff, hostie, whatever it is people call us these days.'

Dylan's mouth drooped. 'That's a shame. I was hoping Elsa had exposed a grubby little secret, and you'd have to go out with me to guarantee my silence. I guess your job's not altogether unlikely, thinking about it, though, given the proximity to the airport. EasyJet, or Ryanair?'

'I work for a private airline.'

'Oh, bad luck.'

'Not everyone holds that opinion, actually.' She knew she sounded prissy and sharp, but she'd worked hard to get to where she was, and he was hardly in a position to judge.

'Maybe not, but you must miss out on all those holiday destinations.'

'That's true. I so wanted to go to Benidorm every year. I'm gutted.'

Dylan pursed his lips. 'You don't sound gutted.'

'I'm being facetious. Sorry. I do travel to some interesting places, and meet some great people.' Her annoyance showed in her tone. She often downplayed what she did for a living, and he'd beaten her to it. Ridiculous to be miffed, but she couldn't help it.

'Met many famous people, though?'

'Yes, tons. Although met is a bit ambitious. Mostly, I serve them food and drink, and they fall asleep – though I am sometimes invited to go along to their shows, and suchlike, especially if they do their whole tour with us. Sometimes, I ...' Her voice cracked, and she pressed her lips together to stop them from wobbling. She closed her eyes momentarily, her eyelashes fluttering as she fought back tears.

'Sometimes, you ...?'

She shook her head. 'Nothing.'

His stare was piercing when she opened her eyes, fixed on her face. He nodded, as if deciding not to push her. 'So, you're coming tomorrow?'

He changed the subject so abruptly, she had to backtrack in her mind to follow its path. 'Oh, gosh, I forgot all about it .... Umm.'

‘I know. I blindsided you, so you wouldn’t get a chance to think up an excuse. Come along. It'll be fun.’

‘I'll try,’ she said, knowing that she probably wouldn’t. ‘Do you have a card?’ she asked. A business card was always a good cop out, when she didn’t want to commit to anything, and it usually put paid to further advances.

‘A card for what?’

‘A business card.’ As soon as she’d said it, she knew how foolish her words sounded.

‘I don’t. Do you have a business card?’ He seemed amused and disappointed in equal measure, but he held out his hand, his eyes boring into hers.

She stared back. ‘Why do you want my business card?’

‘I might want to hire an aircraft,’ he said, deadpan.

She was struck once again by the intensity of his stare, and his tenacity. She also saw, in those dimmed, bluebell coloured eyes, that he knew he’d been snubbed, and she instantly felt ashamed. She dug out her business cards and passed one over. ‘I’ll try and make it – to hear you sing,’ she said, suddenly meaning what she said, but fearing it might be too late.

‘It’s okay. You don’t have to. I’m going to go now. I should be working.’ His words sounded flat with disappointment, and his shoulders drooped. He stared at her business card, before sticking it in his back pocket and holding out the remains of his bread to her. It felt like he was returning his offered friendship along with the stale crusts.

She took the bread, and he plucked his guitar from the bench, threw the strap over his shoulder and the guitar around his back. 'See ya,' he said.

'Bye. Maybe see you tomorrow.' She tried out her best air stewardess smile, wishing she hadn't been so standoffish again, while wondering why she had.

He didn't smile back. 'No worries.' He offered up a small wave as he trampled across the grass taking a short cut. He whistled a trill tune, and Elsa looked up just in time to see him leave.

She waved manically, abandoning her search for good luck among the clover.

Scarlett wandered over to her. 'How did you know that was Dylan whistling to you?'

'Oh, he always does that for the scruffy dog he looks after, and now I recognise it. Mummy uses a similar one for Buster.'

'That's how you know him, through walking Buster?'

She nodded. 'I thought he might want to be Mummy's boyfriend, because they often chat when they meet up at the park, but she says she only has eyes for me, whatever that means.' She gazed toward Dylan's retreating back. 'Our dog is much nicer than his, though,' she added proudly, before stuffing a large piece of the bread meant for the ducks into her mouth.

Scarlett extracted the rest of the stale bread from Elsa's fingers. 'I'm sure you're right. Come on, let's get back to your mum. She should be home by now.'

They wandered back, and once they'd reached Louisa's house, Scarlett flopped gratefully onto a battered sofa.

Louisa was happy with the way her interview had gone and seemed to want to talk about it. Feeling unsettled, Scarlett was more than happy to let her chatter on as her mind drifted.

'I think they called me up on a Saturday, knowing I was a single mum. I'll bet they wanted to see if I could handle it, so thanks ever so, for helping me out. I know it was your day off.'

'No problem. We had a great time, didn't we?' Scarlett bit her lip, remembering the hurt in Dylan's eyes. 'Elsa says you know the busker who stands on Forrest corner. Dylan?'

'Yes, I know Dylan. What about him?'

'She seems to think you should go out with him?'

'What? Oh, good grief, no. He's not interested in me. I'm far too mumsy and staid. He's just a really friendly guy.'

'I think he asked me out. Well, I know he did, but it was in such a roundabout way that I was a bit off with him. He sings in a pub, too, doesn't he?'

'I don't know about that. I know his guitar is practically welded to his body, but maybe he wants more than just a guitar to keep him warm. Ah, bless him. He's lovely, Scarlett, a really decent guy.' She peered at her sister. 'But you said no?'

'I don't date, do I?' For a moment, she had to fight back the mixture of panic and despair that assailed her all too often. She could change things if she wanted to. Move on. It was her choice.

'I wouldn't presume to say that you should go out with someone you don't want to, but Dylan is one of the good guys. I hope you didn't do your Precious Princess act on him.'

Her sister's words weren't exactly a surprise. Scarlett almost wished she hadn't mentioned Dylan. She'd hoped talking to her about him would help. Fat chance. 'So, a total stranger comes on to me, and I'm supposed to go and eat pizza with him?' Scarlett thrust out her chin, challenging her sister to retaliate, but deep down she knew she was in the wrong. She should have been kinder.

'Oh, Scarlett. You are what you are, but I hate to think you would give up the chance of loving again, if it came your way.' She picked up their coffee cups and walked them over to the sink, dumping them in the dubiously coloured washing up water and grimacing as they sank. 'Ooh, I think I washed the frying pan up in that last night.' She turned back to her sister. 'You'll know when it's time, because the right man will come along, and you won't give it a second thought.'

'Pretty sure it's not going to be any time soon, even though the dastardly Todd isn't taking no for an answer, either.'

'I've warned you about him. You should report him in case he gets out of hand.'

Scarlett sighed. 'I know, but he has the power to fire me if he chooses to, and he owns half of StarJet. It would be a bit like reporting him to himself.' She stretched out her legs and stood up. 'I should go. I don't know what time I'll be needed to fly tomorrow.'

Louisa sniffed and crossed her arms. 'It's not right in this day and age.'

Scarlett sighed and shrugged into her jacket. 'Which bit?'

'All of it. You not getting a proper rest, and having a slimy man breathing down your neck that you can't do anything about.'

'I know, but that's the private sector for you. You take it, or leave it.' She opened the front door slowly, reluctant to be on her own. 'Call me if you need me to look after Elsa again.' She blew Elsa a kiss and closed the door behind herself, the familiar rock of misery settling once more into her heart.

Reaching Forrest Road, she found herself dawdling, in the hopes of seeing Dylan so she could apologise, tell him she'd try very hard to hear him perform. Try being the operative word, as she worked for an airline that had her around the throat and could make her dance to any tune it wanted.

Dylan, nor his side-kick, were anywhere to be seen, though, and she dragged her heels, unwilling to return home, knowing her black mood would just worsen with the re-surfaced memories.

Dylan didn't know what a lucky escape he'd had, she thought, as she let herself into her flat. The silence and cold air smacked her in the face like a rebuke, reminding her of her chosen solitude. Not for the first time since she'd met Dylan, she wondered if maybe it was time to start again.

CHAPTER FIVE

Since being turned down by Scarlett in the park, Dylan had rather gone off the idea of playing in Mac's pub, but he turned up anyway, helping himself to a shot or two, of Dutch courage, as he set up his microphone and amps.

Anya tried to jolly him along, but when that didn't work, she resorted to making him feel guilty about his lack of enthusiasm. 'Mac has put his nose on the line for you,' she said, making Dylan think of something shady like cocaine sniffing, rather than risk taking. 'You must not be ungrateful and take his hospitality for granted. Why have you changed your mind?'

'I've had my mind changed for me. There was a girl I really liked, and I invited her to my gig, but she didn't want to come.'

'A girl who doesn't want to hear you sing – is she mad?' Anya instantly won Dylan over with her outrage on his behalf, even though, as far as he knew, she had never heard him sing. 'You like this girl. Why?'

'I suppose it boils down to the fact that I fancy her.' Dylan scratched his head, uncomfortable with such candid talk. 'Really, though, I don't know what hit me. I mean, I'm normally a take it, or leave it, kind of guy, but – I don't know, she just walked past me in the street, and I felt this incredible surge of …' He puffed out his cheeks, trying to nail the emotions that had steamrolled him into believing in love at first sight. 'It was like being electrocuted, but in a good way, I guess.'

Anya's forehead creased. 'A good feeling, yes?' She seemed unconvinced.

He shrugged. 'Yes. Have you ever thought you were made for someone, and you just needed to wait until they turned up? Well, that's how it felt. She turned up, and I knew.' He took another slug of his vodka shot and slammed it back down on the counter with more force than necessary.

Anya moved the shot glass discreetly out of his reach. 'And she feels it, too?'

'Sadly, she wouldn't care if I stopped breathing.'

'That is a problem.'

'Yes, that is, indeed, a problem.' He laughed sharply and rose to his feet, a little unsteadily.

Anya pushed him back down again.

'Wow, I didn't think my story was that interesting.'

'I'm getting you some coffee and a sandwich. You have a long night ahead of you.'

'You mean I'm getting pissed?'

'Pissed.' She enunciated it slowly. 'That is a good word, no?'

'It is a very good word, and it's a very good feeling, until it hits you that you can't walk properly.' He nodded in agreement, wishing he could have just a drop more vodka to ease his pain.

Thankfully, by the time Anya had fed him Mac's Bacon and Cheese Special, usually reserved for Mac's hangover mornings, and had coffee poured down his throat until he was buzzing, he felt heaps better. But it came nowhere near to the feeling that hit him when he glanced up to see a swish of blonde hair and the almost shy, pink-lipped smile of the very girl he'd been waiting for.

***

'Hi, Dylan, I told you I'd try to make it.' Scarlett pushed a lock of hair behind her ear, inexplicably nervous. Her flight had run smoothly, and she'd arrived back in plenty of time, and so had decided spontaneously to come and watch Dylan sing, having felt bad for being offhand with him.

Unfortunately, she'd mentioned her plans to Todd, using it as an excuse to turn him down, when he started dropping hints about going for dinner after the flight. He'd immediately Googled the Dog and Duck, found out they served food, and more or less invited himself along. She'd reluctantly agreed, thinking she could kill two birds with one stone and get him off her back for a while. A decision she was already regretting.

'Wow, you look great. I can't believe you've made it. It is you, isn't it, under all of that stuff?' He peered at her made-up face, and Scarlett was hit with another adrenalin inducing shot of his blue eyes.

'Sorry, I've just finished work, hence half-uniform, half-me.' She had no idea why she was apologising for her pencil skirt, topped with a loose jumper she kept in her car for such eventualities. 'We're not allowed to wear our uniform to pubs, in case people think we intend to go to work after drinking alcohol. My flight was a quick there-and-back to Nice, so – here I am.'

'Nice, eh? And how was it?'

'Nice was very nice,' she quipped, as she always did.

Dylan smiled. 'And you came straight here to be at my gig. That's brilliant. Come and sit at the bar. Mac will keep you company, while I'm on stage. I'll get you a drink. Wine?'

'Umm, thanks. Sauvignon Blanc, please.' She wondered whether she should mention that Todd was coming, too, but didn't have enough time to decide, because he walked through the door and spotted her immediately.

Striding over to her, he greeted her rather more effusively than she thought it merited, embracing her and kissing her cheek. 'Scarlett, looking as lovely as ever.'

'Todd, you saw me half an hour ago.' She felt the usual rush of embarrassment, as he ostentatiously unbuttoned his pilot's epaulettes from his shoulders, just too late for it to be a useful thing to do. In effect, it told everyone close enough to see: look at me, I'm a pilot, but I'm not allowed to show everyone how important I am, in a pub.

Scarlett heartily wished she'd put up more of a fight to stop him from coming with her.

Dylan returned from behind the bar at that moment, bearing a glass of wine and a bottle of beer. Scarlett caught his eye, as he stopped dead, looking at first perplexed, then indecisive. Although he faltered, he soon rallied, straightened up and smiled at Todd. 'Hi.' He placed the drinks on the bar.

'Hello. We'd like a table for two, for supper.' Todd glanced around the pub, his mouth turning down at the edges. 'Good grief, Scarlett, is this the sort of place you frequent?' He flicked at his sleeve as if he'd already been contaminated by its sleaziness.

'I said you wouldn't like it,' Scarlett hissed out of the side of her mouth, praying he would leave and find a restaurant more suited to his snobbish tastes.

He tapped his watch, frowning, as if he'd already spent more time than he was willing to, on such an establishment. He glanced at the drinks Dylan had placed on the bar. 'You ordered drinks. Great.' He picked up the bottle of beer, read the label with interest and took a sip. 'Beer's fine, for now. I'll have wine with supper. Thanks, not bad.'

Dylan raised his eyebrows and folded his arms, his head cocked to one side.

'Dylan, meet Todd. He's ... umm, a colleague.' She turned toward Dylan, hoping he would understand, although it didn't look promising.

Todd nodded across at Dylan. 'Captain Carrington,' he said briefly, before gazing around the pub. Dylan obviously wasn't important enough to waste any more energy on.

For a second, Dylan looked as if he might salute, before pulling a what the hell? face at Scarlett. In return, she tried to convey an apology with her eyes. She really shouldn't have brought Todd with her.

'You say there is entertainment tonight?' Todd looked down his very Roman nose as if the thought of it made him shiver.

'Yes, it's me,' Dylan said, carefully. 'And I'm just on the right side of drunk to be looking forward to it.'

'Oh. Good for you,' Todd replied, lifting his Roman nose into the air once again in a way that allowed him to look down the length of it, at Dylan.

Anya appeared at Todd's side at that moment and offered to take them to their table, and Todd took Scarlett's elbow possessively.

'Good luck,' Scarlett threw over her shoulder toward Dylan, hoping that she could redeem herself again, once she'd managed to shake Todd off. She knew she would have had a better time if she'd stayed at the bar, but she turned brightly towards Todd, ready to play the dutiful hostess role that came so easily.

Except, Todd, having finally managed to get her alone, appeared to think that she had signed up for more than her duty, and alarm bells rang in Scarlett's head, when he said, 'We'll order a bottle of wine, and I can sober up back at your place.' He took the wine list Anya brandished at them. 'It is walking distance, isn't it?' Todd asked, as he studied the wine list.

'Erm, yes,' was all she could manage, although she cursed under her breath for not immediately putting him right. The last thing she wanted was to fend him off, and once he got inside her flat, it would be harder to get rid of him.

He closed the wine menu with a flourish. 'We'll have a Macon Villages. That one.' He stabbed the wine list with his finger, dismissing Anya, and turned his rather bulbous eyes towards Scarlett. It didn't seem to have crossed his mind that Scarlett might like to have had some say in the choice of wine. 'So, about this offer to Le Touquet. We happen to have two days off together next week, and I could do with testing out a King Air that's going up for sale. What do you reckon, shall we make it a date?'

Her heart thumped with panic. He was moving fast all of a sudden, and it scared her as much as it horrified her. 'Work and pleasure, what an ideal combination.'

'Really? Is that a yes, then?'

Her mind worked quickly. She couldn't believe he was being so blatant. 'No, not really. And you know you'd be the first one to condemn it. In fact, I think it's in my contract that I can't fraternise with the staff, or clients, isn't it?'

'Yes, but I part own the company.'

'Oh, I see. So, it's do as I say, not do as I do.'

Todd reached over the table and trailed a finger down her arm, making her shiver, but not with anticipation. 'I don't know why you're being difficult about this. I'd make sure we enjoyed ourselves. Don't you think we would have a good time together?'

Scarlett swallowed down the gross images that flitted through her mind at the thought of the two of them having a good time. She took a large gulp of her wine, even though she was determined to stay as sober as she could, in case she needed a clear head later. 'Maybe some other time,' she said vaguely, waving her hand in the air. Like in a parallel universe, when there is no air to breathe in.

'Okay. When?' he asked.

She glanced over toward the bar, hoping to catch Dylan's eye, but he turned away from her, his eyebrows drawing together, his lips set in a hard line. She had made a huge mistake. She'd humiliated Dylan, who thought she'd wanted to see him, and Todd thought she'd accepted his offer of dinner for the same reason. She needed to focus on Todd, though - after all, her diplomacy could be the difference between keeping her job, or not.

She managed to avoid answering his direct question, as Dylan took to the makeshift stage and started to strum his guitar. 'Hi there, all.' The room fell silent as he spoke, and he gave a little wave that made Scarlett's stomach flip with nerves on his behalf. She prayed he was as good as he seemed to think he was.

'If I'm too loud, or too annoying, just let me know, and I'll tone it down, or even, if you'd rather, I can shut up completely - I'm cool with that, too.' As he grinned at his audience, they all looked as if they were metaphorically egging him on, willing him to be fantastic.

After strumming a few chords, concentrating on his guitar, he raised his eyes and scanned the crowd, his gaze settling briefly on Scarlett who smiled encouragingly. He didn't acknowledge her but gave a rueful grin to the pub-goers, as if to say here I go, then. He started singing, melodic and soulful, his songs gentle and sweet.

Scarlett found herself both astonished and mesmerised. His guitar playing was brilliant, and so was his voice. She also noticed that he looked rather gorgeous in a pale blue linen shirt, unbuttoned just enough to show a smattering of curly chest hair. Okay, so the jeans had seen better days, but ripped knees were fashionable and at least they looked clean. How had she not spotted how hot he was sooner? Okay, she had clocked his long legs before and his wide smile, but suddenly the whole Dylan thing was as if she was seeing him for the first time.

He was relaxed and funny when he spoke in between songs, and when he finished his last song, he was greeted with thunderous applause. Some of the women even standing up to clap, and he beamed as he left the stage.

Feeling pride she hadn't earned, Scarlett wished Todd wasn't sitting opposite her, his prim mouth in a moue of disapproval.

Her heart stumbled a little, as Dylan, heading for the bar, caught her eye, but his smile died on his lips, his eyes sliding away from hers.

She felt cold at the thought that she had hurt him so thoughtlessly. 'Todd, I must congratulate Dylan, I won't be a minute.'

'Must you?' Todd snapped, his lips setting in a hard line, but Scarlett ignored him and walked over to Dylan.

She put her hand out to congratulate him, but he walked straight past her and behind the bar. 'You were brilliant, Dylan. Fantastic.' She sounded patronising, even to her own ears, but she smiled wider, hoping he'd forgive her for bringing Todd.

He looked brooding and angry, as he helped himself to another drink, pushing a small glass up to the dispenser, concentrating on the clear liquid splashing out. He raised the glass. 'Cheers.' He downed it in one and wiped his mouth with the back of his hand.

'Dylan?'

'Just don't, okay?' His voice was so low, he almost growled, his eyes flinty and hooded.

She didn't know what he meant, but she knew quiet anger when she saw it. 'Don't what?'

'Don't bother doing this artificial congratulatory thing, as if you care.'

'I do care.'

Dylan's smile twisted into something resembling a sneer. 'I think we're about done here, don't you?'

'What … What do you mean?' she stammered, as he glowered at her.

'You didn't need to ram it home, you know. I might not wear a city boy suit, or a posh uniform with stripes on my shoulders, but that doesn't mean I'm stupid.' He thrust his chin out in Todd's direction. 'Oh, I don't date, you know.' He mimicked her voice, falsetto.

'Oh, you mean …?' She glanced over at Todd, who was stabbing out a message on his mobile with his forefinger. 'No, he's a work colleague.'

'You let them all touch you in that way, do you?'

'No, and that's not fair.'

'I should have realised you were a flirt as soon as you said you were a stewardess.'

Scarlett felt her jaw drop. 'How dare you pigeon hole me like that? You know nothing about me.'

'And, Scarlett, the corporate air stewardess…' He pushed the glass up against the dispenser once more and scowled. 'I think it would be best if we leave it that way.'

His words hung in the air, as she took in his meaning, and she let out a breath. 'Fine by me!' Her mouth tightened as she glared at him. She wanted to stomp off, but couldn't seem to move, wondering how they'd managed to argue when they barely knew each other. 'You were the one who started this,' she threw at him, her own anger rising at the unfairness of his attitude. She didn't know what her point was, but she knew the anger she directed at him was misplaced.

'And I'm calling it in.' Dylan ran his fingers through his hair.

Their eyes locked, both firing a mixture of anger and regret.

'Is this chap bothering you?'

Scarlett raised her eyes, forced to break eye contact, as Todd placed himself between herself and Dylan.

'No, he isn't, and he won't bother her again.' Dylan's gaze raked over her face, the stark anger already replaced by sadness that belied his words.

'Let's go, then. I've paid the bill.' Todd put his hand on Scarlett's arm and threw Dylan a dirty look, while Dylan glanced at Scarlett as if to say Really? He's your sort of man?

Scarlett didn't want to leave with Todd, and she didn't want Dylan to think she did. She wanted Dylan to put his hand on her arm, staking a claim the way Todd did, but he didn't move. She threw him a pitying look, determined to hold the moral high ground. If that was how he behaved, then he didn't deserve her loyalty, anyway.

As Todd patted her hand, she groaned inwardly. What the hell was she doing?

She wanted to explain to Dylan how it was with Todd. The hold he had over her, manipulating her with his threats and sexual overtures. She was so confused, but really, she just wanted Dylan to like her again.

Except, that would mean she cared about Dylan and that wasn't how she felt, at all. Was it?

CHAPTER SIX

As Dylan turned up for his lunchtime shift at the pub, Mac, on spotting him, pushed the wooden cocktail stick he was chewing to one side of his mouth saying, 'Here, some poncy bloke's been looking for you.'

A new song Dylan had been composing coiled around and around in his head on a loop, its complexity and vibrancy occupying his thoughts, but he just about registered Mac's words. He placed his guitar carefully in the store cupboard, where it lived when he was at work, and gave it a little absent-minded pat before turning back to Mac. 'What did you say? What sort of poncy bloke?'

'The sort that has a flash Coutts card, sort. Fast sports car, sort. Stinks of aftershave and charm, sort.'

Dylan thought that last bit was a bit rich coming from Mac, who mostly smelled of eau de pub: a subtle blend of stale lager and cigarette smoke. He gave a casual nod, despite the alarm running through him. 'Really?'

Unsurprisingly, the song that was driving him mad took a back seat for a minute as he tried to think of someone - anyone, in fact - who might want to call on him, let alone a posh man in a flash car.

'He left his card somewhere - said to call him.'

'Really?' Dylan's vocabulary seemed to diminish as his interest increased.

Mac nodded and lifted up a crate of empties, staggering out of the back door like a drunk - which probably wasn't far from the truth.

Dylan waited until he returned and hovered around, mopping down the bar-top, but he offered nothing more. He knew Mac was waiting for him to crack. In all fairness, it didn't take long. 'And this business card would be where?' he asked impatiently.

'You want the card?'

'Yes, I want the damn card.'

'Well, you only had to ask. Now, where did I put it?' He patted his pockets and winked at Anya, who stood listening to their conversation with her arms folded.

'You are too cruel to the boy.' She snatched the embossed card out of Mac's top pocket and glanced at it. 'Oh, you are going to love this,' she said, passing it to Dylan.

'Oh, my God.' Dylan glanced at the front of the embossed card and ran his hand around his neck, as he read the scrawled message on the back of it. 'Oh, my God, oh, my God.'

'Is there a name for this new syndrome you've developed. Repetitive Repeating Yourself Syndrome, perhaps?' Mac had clearly read the business card earlier. 'I hope he takes you on. I'll be glad to see the back of you, that's for sure. Come to think of it, I'd also like to see the back of most of the regulars. They're all on benefits and nurse one pint all night. You're the worst, though. Spend most of your time muttering to yourself and undercharging the regulars.'

'I don't mutter, I'm composing.'

'Talk of the bloody devil,' Mac added, as Stanley

shuffled in wearing purple flares and a greasy looking porkpie hat, his latest fashion accessory that he said he'd found on a wall.

'Hey, Stan, what's up?' Dylan asked, not expecting a coherent answer.

'I thought I'd barred you,' Mac said cheerfully.

'What for?'

'I need a reason, do I? How about for being ugly and scruffy?'

'That's about right, I suppose,' Stanley replied. 'I'll have a pint of my usual.' He pulled up a barstool and clamped his long bony legs around each side of it.

'Stan, I've made it. An agent wants to see me.'

'Eh, what?' Stanley asked, as he pulled a grubby five pound note out of his pocket.

'Look.' Dylan flashed the small, embossed card at Stanley. 'Mr ...' Dylan squinted at the card. 'Mr Ridiculous Surname wants me to call him. Oh, wait, I haven't got a phone.' He bit his lip and looked hopefully at Mac.

'Hang on a minute. I'm sick of this, using all my stuff. I'm not your mother, you know.' Mac retreated through the door to the back, where most of the world's detritus seemed to reside, and returned minutes later, blowing dust off a large mobile phone. 'Take this, it was Tracey's.'

'What is it?'

'Well, it's not a bleeding Smith and Wesson, is it? Although, you'd wonder, the way you're looking at it.

I've written the number down. Here's the charger, and knowing Tracey, it'll still have money on the Sim card.'

Dylan stared at it. 'Mac, it's pink.'

'It is. Well spotted.'

Dylan grimaced and put his hands behind his back, refusing to take it.

'For God's sake, what's better, a pink phone, or no phone at all?'

'Err, no phone at all?' Dylan replied, but he took it gingerly from Mac, holding it between his finger and thumb as if it was a dead rat. He plugged the charger into the wall, watched as the phone lit up, squinted at it a bit and prodded it. 'Yeah, it works all right.' He dusted down his hands. 'Right, I'd better get on with my work.' He turned back toward the bar and plunged a pint glass into boiling water in the sink.

'You're not calling him? Nancy Boy?'

'It'll keep.'

'It won't bloody keep,' Mac roared. 'You ring him right now, or else I will.'

Dylan ran his hand around his neck again, clammy palms meeting clammy neck. 'What shall I say?'

'Dylan, you've spent the last year here, showing me what a smart arse you are. I think you can work out how a phone call goes. Hello, this is Dylan Willis, I believe you wanted to speak to me, might be a good starting point.'

Dylan ran his hand around his neck again. 'Right, right. Right.'

'He's at it again.' Mac rolled his eyes.

Dylan eyed the phone like it was Kryptonite. 'Okay, I will, then.'

'Bloody good.' Mac stared at Dylan, still rooted to the spot. 'Oh, for crying out loud, use the phone out the back, then we won't all have to listen to your painful conversation and forever remember what a complete dick you made of yourself.'

Dylan nodded. 'Thanks Mac.' He returned minutes later looking deflated. 'Answerphone.'

'I hope you left your number.'

'I'm not a total idiot.'

Mac rolled his eyes again, begging to differ.

Just then, the pink phone, plugged into the wall, started to sing a song about lollipops, and everyone turned to stare at it. Dylan inched over to it and peered at the number.

'Answer it, then, before they ring off,' Mac roared again. 'Otherwise, this saga could run longer than the bloody Mousetrap.'

Dylan picked up the phone, nodded a few times in response to the voice on the other end, and croaked out a few words before switching off his phone.

'Well?' Mac demanded.

'He wants me to send him a demo tape, and I'm meeting him for coffee and an informal chat next week at a hotel.'

'Brilliant. Sign here.' Mac thrust a piece of paper under Dylan's nose.

'What's this?'

'It's your contract for a six-month run at my pub every Sunday until further notice.'

'I can't sign this, Mac. I don't know where I'll be then.'

'You'll be right here, my boy, or else.'

'You couldn't wait to get rid of me a few minutes ago. You can't do this.'

'I can do what I want until you're famous enough to tell me to shove it. And when you are famous, don't forget, this is where it all started, sonny Jim. You never forget your roots.' He slapped him on the back, beaming.

'Mac, you didn't even know me a year ago.'

'Mere detail.' He waved a pen under his nose. 'Sign it.'

'I think it's good news Dylan,' Anya said, coming to the rescue. 'But it's early days yet. It will take some time to become famous. You are a good guitar player, no?'

'I'm a brilliant guitar player.'

'Then, you will make it.'

'Thanks. I appreciate that.' Dylan wished he shared Anya's confidence in himself, for all his bluster.

'Are you going to celebrate with your young lady?'

Dylan's stomach swooped in a familiar way that happened every time he thought about Scarlett: a mixture of shame and longing. 'I messed up big time, Anya.' He didn't think he would ever like himself again until he'd apologised to her.

'I know, but she seemed to like you very much. She hated the man she came in with.'

'How do you know?'

'I am a woman.' She waved a soggy cloth at him. 'Silly boy. Go and make the mends.'

'Amends?'

'Yes, you should.' She began to polish the tables, squirting her suffocating polish and giving him a knowing look.

She was right, of course, and he did want to celebrate, but not on his own. He looked at his watch as an idea took hold. 'Can I finish a bit early, Mac, seeing as it's not busy?'

'I suppose so, but, here, have a drink with me before you go, to celebrate your good news.' Mac, like most bartenders, found many excuses to have a nip of something special. He was already unscrewing a bottle of aged Malt he kept for such occasions.

Dylan groaned inwardly. He hadn't meant to conjure up the drinking fairy just by thinking about it - he'd fallen for Mac's lines before. Just a wee dram to see you on your way, or Have yourself a quick shot to warm you up. Next thing he knew, he'd be weaving his way home, apologising to every lamppost on the way, while devouring a dodgy kebab more likely to make him throw up than the booze.

Dylan didn't want to be churlish about Mac's offer, so he downed a whisky large enough to floor an elephant and convinced himself that he wasn't really going to phone Scarlett, even if her business card was practically phoning her number for him through wishful thinking. He'd checked that her home number was on the card, the minute she'd given it to him. A number he couldn't forget if he wanted to – it was etched into his brain.

He threw a glance at the pink thing plugged into the wall. It would be a lot harder to call her if he didn't have a phone, and that would probably be for the best. He picked up his guitar and headed for the door.

'Hey, don't forget your new phone. It'll go down well with your new gay friend.'

Dylan stopped. 'He wasn't gay, was he?'

'Well, he didn't exactly make me laugh, but you know where I'm coming from.'

'You're just jealous.'

'If you say so.' Mac snatched the phone and charger out of the wall and handed it to Dylan. 'What would you do without me, eh?'

'Cheers, Mac, I have no idea how I coped before I met you.'

Mac cuffed him around the head. 'See you tomorrow, Superstar.'

CHAPTER SEVEN

Dylan wanted to call Scarlett, he really did. The whisky had lent him a false bravado, and if he didn't do it right there and then, he probably never would.

Sliding into a doorway, he pulled out the pink mobile and called her. 'Hi, Scarlett, it's Dylan. The guitar player, Dylan,' he added, in case she knew lots of Dylan's, or couldn't remember the Dylan she did know. He jerked his thumb pointlessly over his shoulder, to where his guitar lay across his back, as if she could see it.

'Oh, hello.'

He sighed with relief that she didn't end the call, although she sounded decidedly cool towards him. Even so, he had to try. 'I'd really like to talk to you.'

'I thought you never wanted to see me again.'

'I'm sorry. I was jealous and a bit drunk. I'll admit it now and hope that will be enough for you to forgive my childish behaviour.'

Silence.

'I'd really like to see you.'

'It's ten o'clock at night.'

'I know, but I have some great news, and I need to tell someone. I need to tell you, in fact.' He held his breath, listening for an irritated sigh at Scarlett's end.

'What, I'm the only friend you have?'

At least she hadn't told him to piss off. 'I just want to apologise. Could we meet up for a drink?' Dylan uttered the bravest sentence in the world, waiting for her to comeback with the cruellest reply in the world. I'd love to, but I'm washing my hair.

Amazingly, what he heard was, 'Give me ten minutes, and I'll be in a fit state to talk.' There was a pause, before she added, 'Why don't you come over to mine. I've just changed into my comfy clothes and could really do without getting all tarted up again. I was given some Cristal today – it's chilling down in the fridge. We can celebrate with that, if it's really good news.'

'Okay, but I don't know if I like Cristal.'

'Then, you don't have to drink it.'

He definitely heard a note of irritation in her voice that time. Considering he'd drink sulphuric acid out of Stanley's trainers for her, if he had to, why was he being so picky? 'I'm sure I'll acquire a taste for it,' he added quickly.

'That's good to know.' She sounded amused, and he knew he'd be fine. She'd forgive him, so long as he kept his cool and didn't quiz her about the obnoxious pilot.

'Brilliant. What's your address?' He wrote it on his wrist, using the pen he always had to hand in case inspiration hit him, and promised to be there soon.

He beamed as he pushed the mobile deep into his pocket. He was going to visit Scarlett and drink Cristal with her, whatever that was. It sounded slightly druggy. He wouldn't have put her down as that sort, but who knew?

Who cared? Not him. He was on his way to seeing The Vision once more, in his new capacity of Rock Star, and nothing would stop him.

***

Scarlett tipped her head upside down, to tousle dry her hair. She had five minutes to go before Dylan showed up.

She wasn't sure why she'd been so ready with the invite. It wasn't as if she wanted the company. Although, she had thought about Dylan more than she should have, and she was upset that their tentative friendship had ended so badly. Even though there was no place for him in her life, he knew her sister and was kind to Elsa, so for that reason alone, she would try to accommodate him.

There was also a small spark of relief that he'd been in touch, but she ignored that. It was probably because she was ready to apologise herself for what had happened.

She clipped the foil off the champagne bottle and settled it into an ice bucket. It was only polite to offer her guest a drink, after all.

She buzzed Dylan in, when he pressed the intercom. She was unused to entertaining without smart clothes and makeup, but then she thought of Dylan's ripped jeans and casual tee-shirts and knew she was being silly.

She needn't have worried.

***

Reaching her open doorway, Dylan looked her up and down with a grin. 'Wow, you look amazing,' he said as he stepped inside the apartment and shrugged off his guitar.

'I do?' She looked down at the denim cut-offs and the

huge stripy sweatshirt she wore.

'Yeah, you don't look like you're an air stewardess, at all. No, that's good - I think,' he added, when Scarlett gave him a hard stare. 'You look like a softer version of yourself. I feel as if I've been allowed into your inner sanctum.'

'Okay, now you're spooking me. Maybe you better shut up, before I change my mind about this. Come in and bring your best friend.' She nodded towards his guitar.

'Sorry, I thought I might get bored, so I lugged this with me, in case I wanted to practice a bit. You know, relieve the monotony.' He strummed a chord, grinning again.

'Such a charmer,' she said, but she smiled, taking the edge off her words.

Dylan was so relieved he could have kissed her right there and then.

He followed her into her apartment. 'This is nice.' He stepped into the sitting room and gazed around the flat, taking in the softly polished walnut furniture, retro egg chair in brown leather and modern cream chaise longue, positioned underneath the window. It was so tidy and minimalistic he was momentarily afraid to move, but if he thought his scruffy presence might offend her, he'd cheerfully sit on the floor. Hell, he'd do the Tango on a bed of nails, if it made her happy.

From studying the apartment, he switched to absorbing the woman herself. Her creamy skin was dotted with freckles over her nose, and her full lips were so, so kissable. Baby soft hair fanned around her face, and he wanted to scoop it up and hold it to his nose, breathing her in. She was truly the most beautiful woman he'd ever seen, and he was totally besotted with her.

'Dylan?' She frowned at him.

He quickly rearranged the dopey expression on his face. 'Yes, please?'

She giggled. 'I didn't offer you anything. Sit down. I'll get you a drink.' She nodded over toward a pale grey sofa, and Dylan sat, as she lifted the chilled bottle from the fridge, picked two crystal flutes from a glass shelf, and poured the sparkling wine into them.

Dylan watched the bubbles escaping to the top, still not quite believing that he was drinking wine with the girl of his dreams. 'Is this the Cristal you mentioned?'

'Yes.' She placed her hands on her hips and her tone was aggressive, as if she was waiting for a putdown, or sarcastic comment.

'Do you always have champagne in your fridge?' he asked, wondering why she was so spiky.

She picked up the bottle and examined it as if looking for an answer. 'I suppose I do, but this particular one is from a passenger who couldn't be bothered to carry it into London. It was a promo gift, but she said it was too clunky to carry home. Champagne is probably as plentiful as water to her.' She raised her glass. 'Here's to rich passengers.'

Dylan toasted the unknown passenger and took a sip.

'Wow, that's pretty good.' He lifted his glass up to the light and examined the pale gold liquid, not that he was a connoisseur in any way, but it seemed the right thing to do.

Scarlett sipped her wine. 'It's about ten pounds a mouthful, so it should be good.'

Dylan raised his eyebrows and tried out another sip. 'Who was your passenger?'

'To be honest, I'm not supposed to talk about them. Someone once got the sack because they blabbed in the pub about taking the Prime Minister to Germany, but you won't have heard of her, anyway. She's a polite young model, mostly famous for sleeping with someone from the X Factor, and for falling out of her dress in public. She said her name was Coco, but whenever her phone rang, she answered with, Hiya, Stacey speaking, so the odds on her really being a Coco are pretty slim. She drank a bottle of water and ate some nuts, so I'm hardly a frazzled wreck, unlike some flights where I run up and down the cabin the whole time as if I'm some kind of sprinter on speed.' She raised her glass one more time. 'So, cheers to Coco-A.K.A. Stacey.'

They chinked glasses. 'This is perfect timing for my news,' Dylan said, taking the opportunity to share. 'News which, if not for you inviting me over, I'd be celebrating with Mac down at the Dog and Duck, getting trashed and learning more Scottish swear words.'

'Who's Mac?' she asked.

'The pub landlord.'

'Ah.' Her face softened, and she sank down on the egg chair and swung her legs up, holding her glass precariously as she tucked her feet neatly under her bottom. 'Okay, I'm ready to hear it. Go.'

Dylan stored all of her movements in his mind, noting the lithe way she moved, the tiny sips of wine she took, and the way she tilted her head as she threw her hair over her shoulder. He found it hard to concentrate on anything apart from Scarlett, but shook himself reluctantly, back to the reason he'd called her. 'Right, then, drum roll, I think.' He bashed out a syncopated rhythm on the arm of the chair. 'Get this. A music producer heard me play at Mac's, and he loves my music. He wants me to send him a demo tape, and I'm meeting him next week for coffee. I've checked the company out on Google and they look totally legitimate. How's that for news?' He picked up his guitar and twanged it for extra effect, before standing up and taking a bow.

Striding across the floor, he ran his hands through his hair. 'Oh, my God, I can't believe I just said that so casually. Do you know what this means?'

Scarlett inclined her head, 'That you're going to be a star?'

'Yes, I'm going to be a star.' Dylan tried to inject enthusiasm into his voice but he was slightly deflated by Scarlett's lukewarm response.

She held her glass out for a refill. 'I'm so comfy, would you mind?'

'No. Of course not.' She wasn't pleased for him, that

much was clear. He picked up the bottle and shook it, checking the level of wine left, deciding that a change of conversation was in order. 'That was quick. That's about fifty quid's worth gone already.' He glanced at the bottle again. 'I don't mean to be cheeky, but I'm famished, do you have any crisps to mop this up? I've already had whisky poured down my throat, despite my best efforts to escape from Mac.'

'Probably. I never have much fresh food in my flat, because I'm called out at short notice so often, but I'm sure I have something edible. I have another bottle of champagne in the fridge, too, if we fancy it. Although I'm not trying to get you drunk. Obviously.'

'Obviously. Though I could understand it, if you did, what with me being a famous rock star, and all. You probably can't wait to get me into bed.'

'Don't push it, Dylan.' Scarlett laughed, but he thought he spotted sadness in her eyes once more and wondered what had happened to put it there.

***

'I've met all sorts of stars, and believe me, it's not all it's cracked up to be.' Scarlett, sensing that Dylan didn't want to hear her thoughts on the downside of stardom, smiled to soften her words. 'I'll get some food and the bottle of boring old Moet, shall I?' She unfurled her legs and stood up.

'Yeah, Moet is cool, but just so you know, we stars prefer to spray it over the furniture, rather than drink it. That more than makes up for any deficiency on the taste front.'

'Fine, I'll mark you down for the Cava next time.' Scarlett threw him a mock look of disdain before heading for the kitchen.

She suppressed a shiver, as another old memory kicked in. She focused on Dylan, instead, as he plucked out a tune, flicking his hair out of his eyes as a stubborn curl flopped down.

She liked him, she decided, even though she'd tried not to. She liked his artlessness and lack of guile, and his enthusiasm for his music. He couldn't help but pick up his guitar at every opportunity, as if an invisible thread connected him to it. She sensed that, even when he was stationary, his mind was on the move, struggling to match the poetical words in his head to the chords on his guitar.

He certainly knew how to produce sweet music, and once a team of designers had finished with him, he'd look every inch the desirable star and would be breaking adoring fans' hearts in no time.

And that was the deal breaker. She really didn't need more trouble in her life, and Dylan was shaping up to be exactly that.

She bit her lip, wondering if she should ask him to leave before she started to like him too much. He would think her crazy. Being there with her was exactly what he wanted – he'd made that quite obvious.

She glanced at him again, as he quietly hummed a tune, stopping occasionally to gaze into space, only to start again seconds later. He was the first man to visit her flat since Sky, and she was surprised to find that she was enjoying herself.

A sudden, unwelcomed emotion welled up in her throat, making her want to cry, but she pushed it away. Dylan spending time with her was nothing like before. She would not allow her memories to taint the evening. He was guilt-free and a good person.

She took stock of the unlikely turn of events, marking it down as a milestone in her mind as she opened her fridge door. Smoked salmon and caviar sat inside, leftovers she'd brought home from the flight, along with the paraphernalia that went with it. The passenger hadn't wanted it, and neither had the ground staff, and she hated waste.

Suddenly deciding it might be a fun idea to serve it to Dylan, she smiled, and all thoughts of asking him to leave disappeared.

She popped the blinis in the toaster and found a packet of crostini and a jar of olives in her cupboard. There was also some feta cheese hanging around – quite a triumph in a fridge that was mostly awash with wine and devoid of food. She added the feta to her tray, upended ice cubes and smashed them up with a rolling pin, grabbed the fresh bottle of champagne, and returned to the sitting room.

'Are you beating the crisps into submission?' Dylan laid his guitar down on the carpet and grinned up at her.

Sliding off the sofa, he settled himself on the carpet, his long legs crossed in front of him.

When he patted the carpet next to him, it seemed like he was inviting her into a safe haven of comfort and trust, and her heart did a strange flutter. Sitting on the carpet seemed so much more intimate than the sofa, and she wasn't sure she wanted that.

Nevertheless, she eased herself down next to him. 'Just preparing some caviar.' She shrugged, as if it was something she offered all her guests.

Grimacing, he picked up his guitar once more. 'Great. So, where did you fly to today, then?' He twisted the pegs at the top of his guitar, his ear close to the frets.

He concentrated so completely on what he was doing, Scarlett wondered if it was worth answering. She also wondered when she'd been relegated to polite conversation: Dylan trying to keep her happy, whilst he occupied himself with a more worthwhile pastime.

'Listen, I don't mean to be rude, Dylan, but you phoned me, remember?'

He stopped tuning the guitar. 'Sorry, yes, of course. I just get carried away, sometimes.'

'That's okay. What were you playing earlier?'

'It's not finished, by any means.' He started strumming the strings again, as if he'd been given permission.

'Dylan?'

'Sorry, God, I'm so sorry. It's just, the last few lines are really bugging me.' He came out of his music-induced trance, placed the guitar firmly out of his reach, and sat down again.

'Do you know why you want to be a star, Dylan? I've met more screwed up people, whose heads have been turned by the fame thing, than I've met normal people.'

'Are you crazy? I can't wait to be one of those people, coked up out of my head, with cheap women falling at my feet, brushing my teeth with ...' He glanced at the label on the champagne bottle, 'Cristal, and being adored wherever I go. What's not to like?'

Scarlett set her glass on the table. 'Right. It was lovely to catch up, and I'm really pleased for you, but I think it's time you left. I'm quite tired.'

Dylan blinked and raised his hands. 'Wait, I was joking. God, what kind of a man do you think I am?'

'I have no idea, Dylan. I don't know you, at all.'

'Well, maybe you should stick around. Because I'm totally interesting.' His eyes twinkled.

She pursed her lips and picked up her drink.

'Okay, I'm seriously pissing you off, aren't I? I just don't feel I need a pep talk on how not to wreck my career before it's even started.'

'Okay, so, tell me about your life, then. When you're not singing, or filching drinks from Mac's bar, what do you do?'

Dylan threw a longing look at his guitar, but didn't reach for it. 'I suppose I'm a life in waiting. Without my music, I'm nothing.' He shook his head. He seemed sad as he stared toward the carpet. A heartbeat passed, before he said, 'Apart from being a pretentious prick, of course.'

She laughed in relief. 'You nearly had me there.' She wiped imaginary sweat from her forehead. 'Let me bring you some food, fit for the God you clearly are.' She headed for the kitchen and fetched out a small bowl of ice and two plates, followed by the caviar, smoked salmon and the warmed blinis, before returning to the kitchen for the crème fraiche.

After pouring the caviar into the little dish in the middle of the ice, she arranged the food on a low coffee table and slid to the floor next to Dylan once more, the flutter back in her heart.

'You like to do things properly, don't you?' Dylan watched with interest as she arranged napkins, knives and plates.

'It's part of my job, attention to detail, and all that.' She passed Dylan a small pearl spoon. 'Help yourself.'

He stared at the spoon looking confused and then eyed the caviar. 'Do I have to?'

'It would be rude of you to turn down a hostess's food.' Enjoying herself immensely, Scarlett led the way, placing smoked salmon on top of a blini, then a teaspoon of crème fraiche and a dribble of caviar. She didn't particularly like caviar herself, but she wouldn't let on to Dylan.

'Right oh.' He followed Scarlett's moves, and she smiled, noting that he set his glass close beside him, like he'd need it to swig from, if the caviar was too gross. He popped the loaded blini into his mouth, chewed a few times, and swallowed quickly. He nodded slowly. 'Hmm, not too bad.' He reached for another blini and plopped a wedge of feta on top of it. 'So, what was all that about, with that pilot, at my gig?'

She stared at him, surprised by his directness, and by the tempo of her beating heart as his blue eyes fixed unwaveringly on hers. 'I told you, he's a colleague.'

'And that's all?'

'No.'

Dylan sat up straight. 'What, then?'

'He's also my boss.'

'And that means?'

Scarlett sighed. She wasn't going to get away with fobbing him off. 'He wants more from me, I think.'

'And you don't? Want more, that is?'

'No! Never.'

Dylan let out a sigh. 'Good. That's good. So, why did you let him stroke your arm, the way he did?'

'He touched me, Dylan. It's hardly grounds for harassment.'

'There are ways of touching people, and you know the difference. Everyone knows the difference.' His eyes were still fixed on hers, unnerving her, demanding the truth.

She swallowed. How could she explain to Dylan how difficult it was to keep Todd at bay, while trying not to upset him, so he wouldn't make her life difficult? It made her sound pathetic. She shook her head, felt tears gathering. It was so hard. Just surviving was sometimes so hard. How could Dylan have an inkling of how she felt, when outwardly she had everything a woman could want?

She turned away, busying herself with plates and glasses on the coffee table. She jumped when Dylan placed his hand on her knee.

'Will you come out with me, Scarlett, on a date?' His voice was gentle and enticing.

She blinked at the change in conversation again, and her pulse rate quickened once more. That she wanted to accept, startled her. 'I truly don't date, at the moment. I'm sorry,' she said.

'Why not?' He removed his hand, picking up another blini, although he simply put it on his plate.

She stared down at her knee, still warm from Dylan's touch. She felt sad for him, for herself, too, that she found it impossible to move forward in her life. 'It always ends in failure. It's a boring story.'

'So, it's your situation stopping you, not the fact that I'm a handsome dude who is about to become a household name. Because if that's the reason, I have to tell you, your judgement is seriously flawed.' He waved his knife at her as if to emphasise the point.

'Thanks for clarifying that. I was obviously confused.' Her heart still thumped with something akin to excitement, and she touched her cheek, surprised to find it hot – she wasn't one of the world's natural blushers.

'And if your boring story is really boring, we'll have all evening to talk it through. We can then go on another date, and it won't be as boring as the first date, because we'll have got all the tedious stuff out of the way.'

She laughed. 'Are you always this charming?'

He leaned over and kissed her very briefly on the lips. 'I don't often try this hard, but for some reason ...' He shrugged. 'Please, say yes, I need an excuse to wash some clothes.'

'Yes, then, if it stops you from being antisocial. I'm away for a few days from tomorrow, but I have at least four days off after that.'

'I can wait.' He beamed at her, and she grinned back. He had no idea what a momentous occasion it was for her, and Scarlett wasn't about to enlighten him.

'I'll call you next week, then.' He drained his glass, stood up and slung his guitar over his shoulder. 'Can't promise champagne though, I'm afraid.'

'No worries, Cristal is so yesterday, anyway.' She walked towards the door, butterflies fluttering unexpectedly in her stomach, as he leaned towards her again and placed his hands on her waist. She liked the feel of his long fingers on her hips and instinctively put her hands over his, enjoying the warmth from his skin.

He smiled at her kindly, as if they shared a secret, but then his smile grew rueful, his eyes burning bright.

She cleared her throat.

'Sorry, am I outstaying my welcome?' he asked, blinking.

'Not at all. I'm just wondering if you are, actually, at some point of the evening, going to leave.'

Dylan raised his eyebrows. 'I guess I have to take that as a statement, not a question.'

She shook her head. 'Not an invitation,' she said firmly, although she guessed he was teasing.

He leaned towards her and kissed her, casually, as if it was the most natural thing to do, his hands still planted on her waist. She found herself reaching up to meet him halfway. His kiss was gentle, but his lips were firm, no hint of hesitation. It felt good, and she returned the kiss, alarmed by how her body reacted to his velvety lips.

'Until next week, then.'

She swallowed and nodded, surprised by the warm glow spreading throughout her body, and at how breathless she felt. Walking quickly into her kitchen to peer out of the window, she put her fingers up to her lips, reliving the sensation of Dylan's lips on hers. The orange glow of the streetlight lit up Dylan's guitar, making it look like an alien clinging to his back and she smiled softly. 'Until next week, Dylan, the almost-famous rock star.'

CHAPTER EIGHT

One week after his telephone conversation with Mr McLynstiver, Dylan found himself sitting on a blue velvet sofa, with gilt armrests, in the reception area of the Midhurst hotel. It was the most uncomfortable seat ever, and he hoped the delicate sofa was for sitting on and not just for show. He perched on the edge, trying to look nonchalant, while his stomach churned with nerves.

Gazing around the room, he took in the huge chandelier, polished wood tables and marble floor, and felt slightly out of his depth at the discreet grandeur of the hotel. Everyone spoke in hushed whispers, and his boots had sounded louder than a pistol cracking through the room, when he'd marched decisively over to a coffee machine he'd spied. He hadn't even wanted a coffee, but needed a prop of some sort to steady his hands.

After busying himself with the coffee machine, he dithered over whether he should speak to someone at reception and announce himself, or just wait for the man with the dodgy name to turn up. Deciding to lie low, he buried his head in a Financial Times, the only choice available on the side table next to the sofa. Maybe it would give him an air of intellect, and stop him feeling such a fraud.

He found an interesting article on the state of the tourist industry in Cornwall, and how they'd miss the European Union subsidy that had been propping up their ailing economy, so he barely glanced up when a tall man with steel grey hair, wearing a smart blue suit, came to rest by the sofa.

The man coughed, as his shadow cast its light over the newspaper Dylan was half-heartedly reading.

He drew his legs in, to let the man pass, then struggled to his feet, quickly realising the new arrival wasn't going anywhere. 'Hello.' His voice wavered as he jumped to attention.

'Dylan Willis? I'm Morgan McLynstiver.' The man held out his hand.

Dylan swiped his own hand down his jeans before shaking the man's hand and breaking into a smile. 'Oh, right. I didn't recognise you. Not that I knew you. I just expected someone a bit more …'

'Unconventional? I mostly save the ripped jeans and Black Sabbath tee-shirts for the weekends.' He winked, and Dylan swallowed down his nerves as he warmed to Morgan McLynstiver, despite the man's formidable exterior.

'Really pleased to meet you, because now the receptionist giving me evils will know I'm here for more than the free coffee.' Dylan waved a hand in the direction of the coffee machine in the corner.

'Oh, I was hoping it was free vodka day.' The man settled himself opposite Dylan, placing a conker-brown briefcase on the seat next to himself.

Dylan sprang to his feet again. 'I'll get you one. Double? With ice?'

'I'm joking, calm down. And anyway, I only drink decaf coffee these days, and I'm sure one of these hovering young ladies will oblige.' He waved in the direction of two immaculately-dressed young girls wearing starched white aprons and stiff smiles.

'Oh, okay,' Dylan said, a tiny bit disappointed at the respectable, forbidding man. He'd been hoping for a beer-toting, wild-haired individual sucking on a spliff until his eyes crossed, saying cool man at every opportunity.

'Let's go through some formalities while we wait for the main man to turn up. Assuming, of course, that you will be going forward with his record label.' Pausing, he focused on one of the pretty waitresses, who obligingly came running, notepad at the ready. 'A decaff espresso, please.' He turned back to Dylan, dismissively, before the waitress had time to respond.

Dylan privately thought that a decaff espresso was a bit of an oxymoron, but he was hardly about to argue the toss with the man who might hold his future in his hands. Knowing what it was like to be invisible to others, he threw the waitress a smile, before turning back to the man in front of him. 'Really, I'm in, am I?' He tried to contain his excitement as he inched forward on his seat, leaving his milky coffee to cool in front of him.

Morgan nodded tightly. 'I don't think Harrison would drag me over here, if he didn't think you had something worth listening to, but don't get too carried away, yet.' He glanced at his expensive looking watch and then over at the entrance to the hotel, as the throaty throttle of an engine broke through the piped music. 'Ah, talk of the devil.'

The noise generated by the new arrival interested a few guests enough for them to glance toward the window as a yellow Lamborghini pulled up outside the hotel.

Dylan leapt up in excitement, before he contained himself and sat down again. He didn't want to appear too enthusiastic, but … holy shit, a Lamborghini.

Mr McLynstiver sighed as the kerfuffle outside stretched out for many minutes. 'He does like to make an entrance, does our Harrison.'

Outside the window, a man climbed from the vehicle and handed keys to a valet, waving instructions before patting him on the cheek like a toddler. He tapped the car bonnet, shook the valet's hand, and, judging by the valet's beaming face, no doubt slid him a large tip.

He strode through the revolving doors.

Harrison Dominic had arrived.

'Now we're cooking,' Dylan said, recognising the style of a real Icon of Rock in Harrison Dominic.

The man stood well over six-foot tall, with broad shoulders, messy hair that'd probably taken hours to style, sunglasses jammed on top of his head, and a sharp jacket to counteract the – no doubt phenomenally expensive – tatty, designer jeans. A stunning girl on his arm finished off the showy ensemble, as he stormed through the lounge area with an air of purpose that said he was loaded and important, and anyone who disagreed wasn't worth a toss, anyway.

'Harrison Dominic is the man you want on your side,' Morgan said, as he began rising from his seat.

Dylan didn't doubt it. His mouth dried with nerves, and he immediately vowed allegiance to the approaching god who could be his route to stardom.

'Hey, you guys.' Harrison waved his hands for them to stay seated as he hunkered down, the shifting of his ripped jeans showing a sun-tanned knee and a flash of builder's bum. Not that his bottom was anything like a builder's, Dylan noted, trying not to gawp. 'This is Arabella,' he said, nodding to his companion, before casting her off with a, 'Go get yourself a drink, babes,' before turning to Dylan. 'Dylan, man, it's great to meet you. Are you cool with this? 'Cause I gotta tell you, we think you're gonna be really hot.'

'Gosh, yes, I mean, yeah, man, I'm cool with it.'

'I'm not wasting any time here, Dylan. Your shit was so hot. We want to hear what you've got, okay?'

'Yes, whatever you say. I mean, yeah, I'm cool with that, you know, my shit, an' all?' He frowned, knowing that hadn't come out right and unsure whether it was better to be hot, or cool. But if Harrison wanted him, he would happily sit at either end of the temperature spectrum.

Harrison grinned, showing perfectly white, veneered teeth, and Dylan had a flash of insight, imagining him when he was young and struggling, realising that he possibly wasn't born a god, but had worked hard to be where he was. He, no doubt, deserved his gorgeous girl, his Lamborghini, and his outrageous swagger.

Dylan did wonder, though, whether he was taking the piss out of him, with his old hippie talk, but decided it was just Harrison's way. 'Cool,' Dylan said. It seemed easiest.

'Right, then, mate, I'm pulling a gig together tonight in Camden, but we've had a bit of a disaster. Lead singer fell off the bloody stage – probably pissed again – so, I've got to go over there and sort it out. We could try you out, if you're up for it. Play a few low-key songs, while the hordes amass?' Harrison raised his eyebrows at Dylan, who gaped like a floundering fish.

Hordes amassing? Could he do hordes amassing? Sounded a bit like he'd be playing to Zulu warriors. He swallowed, his mouth suddenly very dry.

'Stage is all set up. It's just a bit of fun, so don't get all nervous on me.' He peered a bit closer to Dylan. 'Yeah?'

Dylan's palms and underarms immediately sprung a leak, but he quickly recovered and adjusted his face into a cool stare. He could do it. He would do anything for the opportunity, and a touch of intense sweating and amassing Zulu warriors wouldn't faze him. 'Sounds perfect.' He wiped his palms down his jeans and, aware of the wobble in his voice, coughed. 'Cool.' It was the only word he felt he could utter with confidence.

Harrison nodded slowly, still scrutinising Dylan's face, blue eyes on blue eyes. He must've liked what he saw, as he slapped his thigh with his palm. 'Great stuff. That's what I like to hear.' His grin grew wide, and Dylan followed suit as Harrison's confidence encouraged him.

Dylan knew a hurdle had been successfully climbed, and when Arabella returned, he grinned at her like he was part of the family. He immediately regretted it, as she appeared to take his grin as an invitation.

She was stunning, no doubt about it, all long brown legs and flashing cleavage, her floaty dress swirling around her lithe body like a rainbow coloured Will-o'-the-wisp. Her hair, a halo of auburn chic, framed her heart-shaped face, her eyes as large and doe-like as any Disney cartoon heroine.

She was the epitome of every man's fantasy, but Dylan only had eyes for Scarlett.

Fluttering her eyelashes at him, and glancing at the floor when he caught her looking, Arabella gave him a not so subtle come on. Unnerved, Dylan was almost embarrassed by her coquettish antics.

He inched further away, as she straddled the arm of the sofa, staring at him with a slightly spaced out, fixed stare. He wondered if she was on something more toxic than the lurid coloured drink she sipped daintily through a straw.

As if catching Dylan's nervous glances toward the woman, Harrison whispered, 'She bothering you?'

He leaned in close and whispered back, 'It's just the big, doe eyed thing. It's a bit disconcerting.'

‘Don’t worry. She does that whenever she’s let out near fresh meat. It’s not personal.’

As Dylan glanced toward the woman again, she tucked her chin into her slender throat like a swan and smiled a secret smile.

Harrison’s eyes lit up. ‘Do you have a girlfriend? Only, I can assign one to you. Arabella here appears to have taken a shine.’ He hoicked his thumb at the girl as she leaned closer to Dylan, silent and terrifying.

‘Assign a girl to me?’ Frowning, he ran his fingers through his hair. ‘No, I have a girlfriend, thanks.’

‘Great. You are a bit of a pretty boy. We don’t want anyone thinking you’re gay. Not yet, anyway. We can tap the pink pound later, if need be, but we’ll discuss all of that shit when you’re sorted out with a stylist.’ Harrison pursed his lips and looked Dylan up and down. ‘Hmm.’ He rubbed his chin.

Dylan instinctively wanted to stand up straight and clasp his hands behind his back, but then Harrison shrugged as if he was bored.

‘Let’s go get some lunch, and we’ll talk through this thing.’

Dylan was already anticipating telling everyone at the pub about his trip in a Lamborghini, where they’d almost taken to the skies as the rev counter hit the red. His mind went into overdrive as he imagined Harrison sliding into the passenger seat and asking him to take the wheel.

Sadly, Harrison simply led the way to the dining room in the hotel, which was, unfortunately, just a hotel dining room, with white tablecloths and plain wine glasses, rather than the Bacchanalian feast of his dreams, where wenches poured wine down his throat and covered themselves with honey for him to lick from their skin.

He sat down, trying not to look disappointed at the normality of it all.

For lunch, Harrison ate Caesar salad, shovelling it in, unselfconsciously, and swigging beer from the bottle, as Dylan picked at his salmon pasta, still the focus of Arabella, who continued to stare through her long eyelashes, ignoring the menu, but holding on to her drink for dear life.

'Were you at my gig, then, Dominic? I mean Harrison – or, hang on, is it Dominic?' He screwed up his eyes trying to remember the order of the man's name. 'Only, I don't recall seeing you there.' He didn't seem the sort of man to get lost in a crowd, and Dylan was sure he'd have spotted him.

Harrison shifted in his seat slightly. 'I believe you were seen by a scout who assures us that you are the real thing.'

Dylan deflated slightly, somewhat indignant that all Harrison's gushing came from second-hand information. 'Oh, so, you haven't actually seen me perform?'

Harrison looked at Morgan, who intervened neatly. 'I believe our scout videoed your act on his iPhone.'

Morgan peered sideways at Harrison, who nodded furiously, but Dylan felt they were blagging it, although he couldn't think why they would need to. He swallowed pasta mechanically, unsure why their interaction bothered him. It didn't change anything after all.

Harrison rubbed his hands together and scraped his chair back. 'Right, then, let's get off to Camden.' He turned to Morgan. 'Can we have a shuftie through our agency and see if there's anyone who might suit Dylan as a backing vocalist, and a bass guitarist? A drummer, too, eventually.' He turned toward Dylan, who suddenly knew what it must be like to be on a speeding train with no brakes.

He pushed his plate away and fought down queasiness at the thought of playing to a potentially critical audience. But there was something more immediate playing on his mind. 'Do I get a say in who I gig with, eventually? Not now, of course?'

Harrison quirked an eyebrow. 'Do you have someone in mind?'

'Maybe.' He was worried about what would happen to Beanie, if he wasn't there to prop him up anymore. He was hardly a class act on his own, even if he did show a modicum of thinking outside of the box. Dylan didn't think there was much call for triangle players in a modern-day band, and in reality, Beanie spent most of his time pulling on dubious roll-up's and feeding his dog leftover Big Macs.

At a push, Beanie could sing harmony, Dylan thought. His thin, reedy voice sounded quite soulful, when it didn't sound like a distant police siren. Dylan toyed with his napkin, thinking fast. 'Doesn't matter. It's not a big deal.' He didn't want to jeopardise his first chance to prove himself, and Beanie had survived without Dylan for most of his life.

Harrison shrugged. 'We never say never, but I think you're jumping the gun a bit here. Let's just concentrate on seeing what you do, shall we? Now, do you want to catch the tube, or ride with me?'

'In the Lamborghini?' Dylan impressed himself with how controlled his voice came out - not even a squeak of delight got through. Although, he did mentally punch a fist in the air. He was going to learn the art of cool through watching Harrison Dominic, and he was going to start right there and then. 'Okay. Sure.' The promise of a ride in a top-notch sports car was a wish come true he didn't know he had, but he paused as disappointment washed over him. 'Oh, I'll need my own guitar, though. I can't use anyone else's.' His guitar had accompanied him along the lonely road to stardom, and there was no way he would abandon it in his finest hour.

Harrison compressed his lips. 'Calling the shots already?'

'No, not at all. I just worry that I'll screw up if I have to use a different guitar. If it's a problem, I'll catch the tube.'

'I'm just kidding. We'll stop off at your pad. Give me directions, and I'll stick it in the Sat Nav.' The roar of the Lamborghini could be heard once more as the valet pulled up outside the hotel with impeccable timing. Harrison strode towards the door and Dylan watched in awe as the doors of the car opened upwards, like bright angel's wings, heading for heaven. Jumping to his feet, leaving Morgan to sort out the bill, he followed Harrison. No way was Harrison leaving without him.

'Baby, don't forget me.' Arabella's voice held a petulant whine, as she clumped to her feet in gravity-defying heels. She finally loosened her hold on her glass, slamming it on the wooden table, as she scrambled after Dylan.

Dylan took a swift look at Arabella, before zoning in on the bright yellow Lamborghini, not wanting to let it out of his sight. Oh, my God, he thought, I'm going to climb into a Lamborghini in front of all of these people, and then I'm going to climb out again in one of the scuzziest areas of London.

'There are only two seats.' Arabella's eyes levelled with Dylan's.

Dylan sighed, shooting a last glance at the car through the window of the hotel. He'd known, deep down, that it wouldn't happen. Just a wonderful dream that would always remain a dream. 'Go ahead, Arabella. I need to get my guitar, anyway.'

'I could sit on your lap?' She twisted a hank of her hair and stroked her top lip with the ends, before popping it into her mouth and sucking gently.

'I don't think that's legal, Arabella.' Dylan looked wildly around for some help. He was way out of his depth. 'Morgan. Great. Can you get me a cab, please?'

A doorman was summoned, but before he had a chance to dispatch Dylan, Harrison reappeared, striding decisively over to the small gathering. He counted off notes from a wad he pulled from his back pocket. 'Arabella, go buy yourself a pretty dress and follow us over to Camden later. Reception will call you a cab to take you to Harvey Nicks. Okay?'

Arabella scowled at Harrison, but she snatched the notes from his fingers and teetered back into the foyer.

Dylan grinned. That meant he was heading for the ride of his life. 'We'll likely get mugged when we get to my place, so keep the engine running and your windows closed,' he said cheerfully, as he climbed into the car.

He ran a hand reverently over the soft leather of the Lamborghini's interior before reaching into his jacket pocket for his shades.

He slid them on to his forehead. Him and Harrison: peas in a pod.

***

They pulled up outside his run-down house. Never the most fastidious of people, Dylan took in the sight of the overflowing garbage from the kicked-over bin, the broken gate, and the tiny garden full of weeds and the twisted bike frame that had just been dumped one night. It made him realise how badly he wanted to be away from it all. Although he knew he could go home to open green fields and get high on ozone from the sea air, he only wanted to do that when it was by choice.

Please, God, give me this chance to make it work, he begged.

Opening the front door, he breathed in the foul smell of stale food and overused trainers. He ran his gaze over the dirty dishes on the coffee table and past books, piled high, as if the owner was trying to win a book-style Jenga contest. He managed to resist kicking them, but then lashed out at the parade of empty beer cans lined up on the draining board, instead, enjoying the clatter they made as they tumbled on to the floor.

It was time to move on, that was for sure, especially since he'd seen Scarlett's beautiful flat. He knew he'd have to up the ante, if he wanted her to take him seriously.

Afraid that Harrison might knock on the door, if he took too long, he glanced towards the window, grabbed his guitar from its stand and headed out of the front door, only really drawing breath as he left.

As he fell into the seat of the car, he inhaled the smell of leather and wealth. This was the life he envisaged, driving a sports car with his girl beside him - and if he held on to his dreams and didn't bugger it up, it would come true. He was finally getting his big chance. He'd worked hard for it, and no way would he blow it.

He thought of Scarlett, who he'd already handpicked to be the beautiful girl by his side, and wondered if it was too late to invite her to Camden. After all, he intended for her to be there for the rest of his career, so she should be there for its inception.

He drummed his fingers on his leg, wondering what to do for the best.

'Problem?'

'What? Oh, no. It's just this girl – my girlfriend,' he amended, for Harrison's benefit. 'I'd really like her to be here tonight, but she's probably busy.'

'You'll have so many girls, you won't know which way to turn, or which way to turn them.' Harrison laughed, the sound hollow. His teeth flashed as he grinned at Dylan.

'I don't want anyone else,' Dylan said quickly, and realised it was true, no matter what was on offer.

Harrison gave him a sidelong glance. 'I do like that touch of innocence you have about you. It would be good to keep that. So, what does she have that's so special?'

'She's beautiful.'

'Hey, beauty I can get you by the shedload.'

He smiled. 'I'm sure you can, but you're in a position to order it up. I have to earn my girlfriends, and this one isn't making it easy. She's a keeper, though, whatever happens.' And I'm blagging it more than usual, he thought.

His fingers itched to take out his phone and text Scarlett, but he still had the pink phone Mac had given him, and he didn't want Harrison to think the Pink Pound brigade would be earning him money sooner than he thought. Besides which, Scarlett was most likely 35,000 feet in the air. She could've been flying over any one of the seven continents, as far as he knew.

He was starting to realise why she didn't do relationships easily.

Withdrawing his hand from his pocket, he made a note to buy a new phone as soon as he had a few quid in his pocket.

Harrison turned up the music and sang along to a tune Dylan had never heard, so he sat back and enjoyed the ride while running through the songs he thought would go down well in Camden.

CHAPTER NINE

They arrived at the venue, and Dylan saw it all come together in a matter of hours, his eyes widening at the machinations of a professional team pulling together. He wandered around for a while and chatted to a few people, mostly feeling a bit like a spare part, as Harrison was off doing Important Things.

'I can tell what you're thinking, but it's all down to money.' Once again by his side, Harrison ate a sausage roll out of a paper bag as he surveyed the action. 'It's easy when you know how. Pay enough people enough money, and you can do anything you want.' He shoved another paper bag at Dylan. 'Eat. This might be your last chance 'til it's over.'

Dylan peered into the bag at his own sausage roll. The contrast between a humble Greggs sausage roll, and a man who could conjure up a gig out of nowhere and drive a flash Lamborghini, was not lost on him. He was happy to be the Greggs customer for the moment, but he'd have killed to be the Lamborghini guy, too. One day, he thought. One day.

'There's beer, too.' Harrison popped the ring-pulls off two beers and passed one to Dylan, and they chinked cans. 'Cheers.'

'Cheers. Such service, I could get used to this,' Dylan said, as he bit into his sausage roll. A simple thing had never tasted so good.

'Impressed, huh?' He chuckled, throatily. 'If you're as talented as I believe you are, one day you'll have someone to do everything for you. And I mean everything.' He lifted his eyebrows suggestively.

Arabella appeared from nowhere and slipped her arm around Dylan's waist. 'What would be your ultimate dream, to prove you'd made it?'

He resisted the urge to remove her arm as he thought for a moment. 'Someone blowing ...' Pausing, he grinned, before continuing, '... on my eyes to cool them down when I have hay fever.'

'Hey, reach for the stars, man?' Harrison's lip curled, but his eyes twinkled.

'Yep, that's my Utopian dream. But I'd have to pay them. I don't want them to do it for love. That would defeat the whole point.'

'I'm good at blowing on things – to cool you down, or to heat you up.' Arabella breathed the words into his ear, her voice loaded with meaning.

Dylan shivered involuntarily, trying not to imagine the scene she was setting.

'Do you want a quick warmup in half an hour?' one of the roadies called across to Dylan.

Saved from having to answer Arabella, who almost had her tongue in his ear, he pulled away. 'Yes, brilliant.' Thank God.

'You're not on until about ten o'clock, by which time they'll all be nicely oiled, and you'll go down a storm,' the roadie added.

Dylan gave him the thumbs-up, despite being pretty sure he hadn't paid him a compliment, but he took it in good humour. As soon as there was a lull in the frenetic activity, he took the opportunity to take a breather outside.

Arabella joined him within minutes. 'Smoke?'

'No thanks, it's not good for the voice. Or anything else, come to that.' Dylan knew he sounded like his mother, but it was true. He inched away from her and her threat of passive smoking.

She lit up a rolled cigarette, and as she blew out, a familiar aroma filled the air. Ahh, so it was that sort of cigarette.

'Here, this'll help your nerves.' She passed him a bottle of something without a label.

He shook his head, but then thought, what the hell. If it got her off his back. He took a large swig. 'Shit, that has a bit of a kick.' He coughed and passed it back to her, quickly realising he'd lasted about an hour in his role of rock star before taking some kind of stimulant.

He returned inside to the relative safety of Harrison, before Arabella could try tempting him with more recreational vices. As they stood together, companionably quiet, people buzzed around them, like worker bees keeping their queen happy.

'While we're here, man, is there anything we need to know about your past? Best to get it out of the way now, so we're prepared. No need to be shy.'

'Oh, umm.' Dylan frantically tried to dredge up something that might be noteworthy, but it seemed his life was blemish free. Damn it.

Harrison stared. 'No? Let's move on, then, while we have a few minutes to spare. I am assuming you're straight, as you say you have a girlfriend. I think it's fair to say you're a decent kind of chap, and I think you'll appeal to all age groups, which'll be a good selling point.'

Dylan wasn't sure that was how he wanted to be portrayed, but had to concede that Harrison was more or less right. His mother was a schoolteacher, and he loved her too much to let her down in the close environment where he grew up. What chance did he have to be a bad boy?

'Our stylist only lives minutes away, luckily, so she's popping over to take a look at you, to see what can be done.'

Dylan was puzzled. 'What can be done? What do you mean?' He looked down at his Timberlands, his almost-clean jeans, and his, admittedly ancient, tee-shirt that bore a logo so cryptic even he couldn't work out why he'd bought it all those years ago. All in all, he was good to go, as far as he could tell. Though, when he thought about it, how cool would it be to have a stylist of his very own?

He grinned again, re-thinking the idea. Scarlett would be the girlfriend of a designer-clad dude before she knew what'd hit her, and she'd be the one trying to keep up with him. He couldn't wait to see what the stylist would come up with.

'Stand by your beds, here she is.' Harrison waved a hand in greeting.

Lost in his Scarlett dream, Dylan thought Harrison meant that Scarlett was heading his way, but soon realised the woman striding toward them and waving at Harrison was the stylist. She looked nothing like a stylist – not that he'd ever seen one, as far as he knew.

'Hi.' She looked Dylan up and down as if he was an inanimate object she was thinking of buying, but had changed her mind about.

He returned the look, his disappointment palpable. He'd expected a chewing-gum-toting platinum blonde, quizzing him on his holidays and saying innit a lot, but she was an immaculately-suited, thirty-something, pointy-nosed lady, as thin as a stick of rhubarb and just as sour, going by the sucking a lemon look she gave him.

She dug deep into a noisy, plastic bag and popped pumpkin seeds into her mouth with annoying repetition. 'Yep, I can do something with him.'

She took a step closer, peering at his face, and he peered back, thinking there was something of the Wicked Witch of the West about her. He'd have bet his last pound she'd melt in water. The thought made him smile.

'Lovely smile,' she said.

He instantly felt guilty and allowed her to take another step towards him, but was still on the lookout for a green tinge to her skin. Her lips turned down as she peered at his hair, taking a strand of it between her fingers. She ruffled the top of it, tugging it from one side to the other while peering closely, until Dylan wondered if she was looking for nits.

'He'll do,' she said and winked at Dylan, surprising him all over again. 'Book us a date, and I'll get on it.'

Harrison grinned, before kissing her full on the lips. 'Atta girl,' he said, slapping her bottom.

She kissed him back and threw Dylan a mischievous grin as if challenging him to comment. Dylan's eyebrows shot up to his hairline, but he was too surprised to say a word.

'She's my proper girlfriend,' Harrison said as she sauntered away. 'Saved my life, metaphorically and literally, more times than I can remember, and I love her to bits.' He stared after her retreating form. 'But don't tell anyone. It'd totally destroy my street cred.' He sighed, almost sorrowfully, as she disappeared through a door.

Dylan watched her go, too, but rather than sharing Harrison's affection towards her, a sense of dread and an urge to buy new underpants washed over him. He knew he'd have nightmares that she'd turn up out of the blue, wielding a tape measure and expecting him to strip off and put on a pair of paper pants. Or was he confusing that with a beauty parlour?

Just when he thought the focus on himself was almost over, the sound engineer decided he should sing a few preliminary lines, which seemed to give Harrison more ideas, as he climbed onto the stage, beckoning Dylan over. 'Give it your best shot, eh?'

Dylan picked up his guitar and shrugged, happy to play for as long as they wanted. He felt like part of the gang already, and his nerves had all but disappeared. It was only Harrison, after all. They'd shared sausage rolls, straight out of a paper bag. You couldn't get much closer than that.

He tuned his guitar and sang Please Believe You're Beautiful, the song he'd been perfecting for months and had thought was faultless, until the comments started pouring in. It seemed that even the lighting guy had something to say about the lyrics, and Dylan deflated under the weight of the criticism.

Harrison nodded his approval, although he motioned for the song to be bigger, louder, better. Dylan sang it again, with feeling, and again with a slightly different intro. And once more with a different tempo, until he was sick to death of hearing his own voice, and hoarse from trying to hit the high notes that he normally sang an octave lower without anyone noticing.

The time flew by, until Dylan realized that the song he held close, like a precious jewel, had become Harrison's property. It had been taken out of his hands, picked apart and polished to within an inch of its life, and repackaged. So much for a spontaneous gig, he thought, as more people became involved. The whole experience was exhausting. They all took it so seriously.

It had also slowly dawned on him that his music was

only a small part of the package, and that he had a lot to learn if he wanted to make it big time. Almost instantly, he had turned into an investment to promote and protect, and he wasn't sure if it was comforting, or terrifying.

Glancing at his watch, he saw he'd been singing for three hours and had yet to see an audience. Exhausted, he longed to creep home and return to the normality of the Dog and Duck for a beer, or two.

In the end, he only sang three songs to an audience of mostly indifferent student types, who seemed more concerned about where their next drink was coming from than Dylan's talented debut. At least his songs were well received by Harrison. At the end of the night, he'd slapped him on the back and finally sent him on his way, scrawling his personal phone number on the back of his business card.

By which time, Dylan had grown pretty fed up with the day and was glad to be heading home – until Arabella offered to join him, an image that scared him witless as she made no bones about her capabilities in bed.

He quickly shut down the inner demon in his head that suggested he ought to find out if she was telling the truth, and after brushing her off by telling her that he still lived with his parents, he slid into a shop doorway to phone Scarlett, shielding the pink phone from view.

He knew it was indecently late to call her, but he needed reassurance that she hadn't changed her mind about going on a date with him. He secretly hoped she'd invite him over to hers again, and wistfully dreamed of a rerun of the chaste kiss they shared, while he waited for the ringtone to kick in – or more, if he was being honest with himself. He also wanted to share the surreal experience he'd just been a party to, in case he woke up and found it was all a dream.

Luckily for him, she answered the call immediately, and he launched into his spiel. 'Hi, Scarlett, I wanted to invite you to my first ever professional gig, but I didn't get a chance, and now it's too late.' He hesitated, wondering how far he could push it. 'I wondered if I could see you?'

'Sure, that'd be great. Skype me.'

'Sorry?'

'Either that, or catch the overnighter from Heathrow, then I can meet you for lunch tomorrow.'

'What?'

'I'm in Rome, Dylan.'

Not so lucky, then, he thought, as disappointment punctured his bubble of anticipation. 'Oh, I thought the line sounded odd.'

He studied his pink phone as if a Skype app might jump out and smack him in the eyes, even though it was one of the earliest Nokia's ever made and barely had digits, let alone Apps. 'Skype is a distant dream for my phone, so it'll have to be a personal visit, but it might take me some time to get to you. I don't even have my passport on me.'

'Dylan, I'm joking. I don't expect you to come and find me, lovely as that would be.'

'Oh.' It took a minute to take in her words, and he wasn't sure whether to be relieved, or not. But she had said it would be good to see him – he definitely heard her say that. 'I know this probably isn't protocol, but I've missed you, you know.'

'Aww, that's nice to hear. I'll see you when I get back. I won't be gone long – maybe meet up on Wednesday?'

'Sure. That'd be cool, man,' he replied.

The line went quiet, and he could hear her talking to someone: a male, judging by the deep voice. He tried to listen in to the conversation, jealousy spiking him in his gut.

'I have to go, Dylan,' she said, coming back on the line. 'Oh, and don't practice your rock star talk on me. I'm far too jaded.'

'It's the way I'm gonna rock and roll from now on, babes.' He smiled down the phone, wondering what she would make of the pet name.

'Yeah? You just keep rolling … babes. I'll see you soon.'

'Cool. Night.' The line went dead, and he looked at the phone, unsure whether he'd run out of credit, or if she'd cut him off. 'Missing you already,' he said regretfully. But he was happy. He'd spoken to his almost-girlfriend, and she definitely wanted to see him again. He slipped the phone back into his pocket. 'Cool, man,' he said.

He returned to his house so wired he was sure he'd never sleep again. He was going to see Scarlett very soon, Harrison had given him his personal phone number and was going to call him about a magazine interview, and he had his very own scary stylist to magic him into a rock star dude.

He lay on his bed, suddenly too exhausted to undress, but his mind raced as the turn of events played over. He finally drifted off to sleep as daylight broke, trying to think of a word that wasn't harlot, to rhyme with Scarlett, so he could write the song he'd promised her. It would be the best song ever written and would guarantee that she would fall in love with him.

All was good.

CHAPTER TEN

As she disembarked from the aircraft, Scarlett spotted a familiar sight. She was used to seeing huge camera lenses at the airfield perimeter, as journalists discovered, by whatever furtive means, that someone famous was on board her aircraft, but she had learned to dread the sight of this particular journalist, distinctive by his chequered red cap. The long lens attached to his camera was aimed at the aircraft, and it took only an instant for her to realise there wasn't a famous starlet about to launch herself out of her aircraft door, posing for all she was worth. No boy band members hid inside the aircraft either, their spiky hair sprayed to death so the wind wouldn't touch it, as they positioned themselves like matching piano keys on the aircraft steps.

In fact, her two passengers, who were something big in Microsoft, had already left the aircraft in an understated Mercedes. Which left only one person as the focus of the journalist's attention – and Scarlett had a really bad feeling that one person was herself.

The flash of his camera confirmed it as she walked down the steps. She missed her footing as she glared at him, stumbling down the rest of the stairs. Thankfully, one of the engineers caught her and saved her from hitting the tarmac, and though it shook her up, she was more upset about being photographed than almost breaking her neck on the steps.

As the journalist disappeared into the distance, she watched him anxiously, knowing she could do nothing about him. She was totally on her own this time.

The engineer stared at where, only seconds before, the journalist had been snapping away for all he was worth. 'What's that all about, then?'

'No idea,' she lied, shielding her face in case more stray photographers lurked around.

She made it into the office without any more incidents, but her heart hammered, as George looked up from his computer, with interest in his eyes.

'Someone's been checking up on you, Scarlett. Errant boyfriend, I'm thinking? Tried to be clever and cagey, but he didn't bank on my deflective skills. I'm guessing he doesn't realise we tell more fibs in aid of our clients than Billy Liar.'

'What did he want to know?'

'If you were seeing anyone, mostly, even though he tried to couch it as something else.'

Letting out a sigh, she checked the date on her phone and cursed. She should have known something would happen once Axel, Sky's brother, was let out of jail. She bit her lip, thinking fast. Damn it. 'George, text me if you need to get hold of me. I might not be answering my phone for a few days.'

George stared at the computer screen, already losing interest in their conversation. 'Sure thing.'

She quickly filed the paperwork from the flight and said goodbye. After climbing into her car, she slid on her sunglasses and pulled the sun visor down for extra camouflage, unsure of her next move.

She decided to risk going home, but as she drew level with her apartment, she spotted a man hovering around the grassy area in front of it. As soon as he turned toward her approaching vehicle, she knew he'd be a journalist. They all had that same shifty look about them.

Putting her foot down, she swept past him down the road. She knew just the place to go. Somewhere they wouldn't find her.

***

Dylan wasn't busking, as she'd hoped, but luckily, she spotted Beanie attached to his dog by a long piece of string, loitering outside the sports shop in the high street.

He smiled as she approached him. 'Looking for Dylan?' he asked.

She nodded, praying that he could be found. Even her sister's house was out of bounds, right then, and her heart began knocking against her ribs as panic set in. She had no idea where she'd go if she couldn't get hold of Dylan. She just knew she couldn't go through the same scenario as last time: journalists jostling her as they threw questions at her, wanting every intimate detail of her relationship with Sky, their camera lights flashing in her face and making her feel like a criminal.

Fortunately, Beanie was happy to oblige with Dylan's address, and Scarlett passed him a ten-pound note as she thanked him, having no idea if it was vagrant etiquette, or whether he'd be insulted. 'Food for your dog,' she added hastily, just in case.

'Cheers. He'll have pie and chips with me at the chippie later.' Beanie palmed the money and gave her a cheery smile, before pulling on the dog's length of string and disappearing.

Reaching Dylan's place, she tried the bell, but it didn't seem to work, so she banged her fist on his door. A couple of guys on tiny jump bikes, their hoods up over their heads, rode close, and as she stood there, trying to ignore the way they seemed to be circling her; she felt both overdressed and vulnerable.

She knew Dylan hadn't much money, but the road where he lived had to be one of the worst she'd ever seen. She'd passed houses with cardboard pushed up against the window-frames in place of glass, cars without wheels, and debris flowing out of battered bins that looked as if foxes or rats had been at it. Handbag held tight to her chest, she tried not to judge Dylan because of where he lived, as she waited.

Dylan opened the door, wearing his usual faded jeans and tee-shirt. 'Hey, Scarlett, what brings you here?' His threadbare top declared: 'Frankie's Gone to Hollywood', to complete his dishevelled look.

Even so, he looked gorgeous, and Scarlett couldn't help the smile that spread across her face as she tried to convince herself that she was just relieved he was in. 'You like Frankie Goes to Hollywood?' she asked.

'Don't be daft. I'm wearing it ironically.'

'Of course you are.'

'Come in.' A small grimace passed over his face as he added, 'If you're feeling brave.'

She pushed past a bike, its tyres thick with mud, and climbed over a crate stacked high with empty bottles, almost falling into the sitting room. She took in the piles of books, clusters of beer cans and random detritus, and blanched. 'Wow, have you been burgled?'

'What? No, it's always like this. I've given up trying to tidy it – waste of time when my housemates seem intent on destroying the place.'

He took in her face, registering shock. She knew she was pale and her eyes wild, and was already regretting the loose ponytail, knowing tendrils would have escaped. She wasn't used to showing herself in a less than perfect get-up even though Dylan was always casually dressed.

He put a hand out to her cheek and she leaned into it, immediately knowing she'd made the right decision in finding him. 'Are you okay? What's happened – why are you here?' He sounded almost panicked on her behalf and she realised that it must be a surprise to find her standing on his doorstep.

She waved a hand in front of her face. 'Bit of trouble. Sorry,' she added as her eyes filled with tears. 'I'm in a bit of a state and not sure what to do for the best, apart from drink myself under the table.'

'I'd love to see that. No … I mean …. Sit down.' He hoisted a pile of books off a chair and onto a table cluttered with used mugs, newspapers and, strangely, a flowering hyacinth in a pot. 'Let me get you a cup of tea.'

'No!' She didn't mean to sound as panicked as she did. 'Sorry, but the bacteria in this house could keep a scientist in work for years.'

'It's dire, I know. And you with that OCD thing going on. This can't be easy for you?'

'I do not have OCD. I just like things to be in their proper place. Or at least clean.'

'Sorry. Shall we get out of here?'

'That'd be great.' She nodded enthusiastically. 'I thought we could grab a drink somewhere, as I don't think I'm going to get much else done today. My mind is too pre-occupied.'

'Sure,' he replied. 'It's so lovely to see you, by the way. I've been waiting for you to come home. You didn't forget you had a date with me, did you?'

'I'm here, aren't I?'

'But this doesn't count as the date, does it?' he stressed. 'This is just an added bonus, right?' He treated her to a flash of his sincere eyes, pools of dark blue, insistent and caring.

'Dylan, I have far more important things on my mind, right now.'

'Oh, so, I haven't been on your mind, then?'

She rolled her eyes, ignoring his question, not in the mood to pander to his neediness. 'Can I leave my car outside your house?'

'Depends if you ever want to drive it again.'

'Really? It's that bad?'

'We can park it in Mac's car park, if you like. He won't mind, and we can go somewhere else afterwards. We don't have to spend the evening watching Stanley slop beer over himself and having Mac spit chewed peanuts at us.'

'Okay. That would be great.'

Dylan frowned. 'You okay?'

'No, not really.'

'Let's go, then. You look like you could use a drink.'

'Yeah, I believe vodka is popular to counteract floating bacteria.' She picked her bag up and dusted it down.

'That's very rude, if I may say so.' Dylan laughed and slapped his arm. 'Damn airborne microbes. Look at that one, Legionnaires disease, if I'm not mistaken.' He raised his palm to show her the imagined dead germ and turned eyes full of amusement in her direction.

She smiled and touched his hand. 'Thanks for this.'

His expression softened. 'Anytime. Seriously.' He caught her fingers in his, held them fast. 'I'm sorry about this, but I just have to do something.' He cupped her cheeks in his hands, lifted her face up to meet his, and lowered his lips to hers.

His lips were soft, his caress tender, and she surrendered to the sensations that she'd forgotten existed. He pulled away before she did, leaving her breathless with the heat that washed over her.

'And you did that, because?'

'I knew that, once we reached the pub, I'd spend the whole time wanting to kiss you, so I thought I'd get it out of the way.'

'I'm supposed to be flattered at such a gesture, am I?'

'You are, I can tell.' He grinned and kissed the tip of her nose. 'Mustn't forget this.' He picked up his guitar, stuffed it in its case, and slung it over his back.

Scarlett rolled her eyes once more. 'Dylan!'

'Love me, love my guitar, I'm afraid.'

She sighed. 'Go on then, stick it in the boot.'

After Dylan slammed the door on his messy house, they walked down the road to where her car was parked. 'Here we are.'

Dylan whistled low when he saw the sleek Audi sports car.

'And before you say anything, I paid for it with my own money.'

'What else would you do, steal it?'

'No, but some people think I couldn't possibly earn enough to fund a car like this, so assume I must have a Sugar Daddy.'

'I hope you don't, or else I'm in serious danger of getting beaten up.' He ran his hand down the sleek bonnet and nodded appreciatively. 'Not quite a Lamborghini, but not bad.'

'You do not have a Lamborghini, that much I do know.'

'Not yet,' he said simply, as Scarlett opened the doors with a click of her key fob. 'But I will.'

***

As they pulled up outside the Dog and Duck, Scarlett felt herself growing more panicky by the moment, until Dylan took her hand.

His eyes burned with determination as he turned them on her. 'I don't know what's going on, Scarlett, but I can see you're nervous about something. I'm here for you. I think you should know that.'

'Thanks. That's good to know.' She entwined her fingers through his, noticing how right it felt. She briefly imagined his fingertips tracing the contours of her body and realised she'd missed the physical contact of a man more than she'd thought. No, she couldn't think like that. It wouldn't be right. 'I might want to leave, if … if ….'

'It's fine, we can do whatever you want.' He smiled reassuringly and they climbed out of the car.

'Ready?' he asked as he pushed the pub door open.

She gave him a small smile and straightened her back along with her resolve as she entered the pub.

As Mac spotted Scarlett, he winked and raised his eyebrows at Dylan who tried out a discreet thumbs up.

'I saw that,' Scarlett said, smiling, despite her turmoil.

'He just wants me to be happy. What can I say?' Dylan said as he gently steered Scarlett towards the bar. He nodded to what Scarlett assumed were the regulars. 'Meet Stanley, he's … well, he's just Stanley.'

Stanley was folded around his favourite bar seat like he'd never been banned. 'Hey there, love. Have you changed your hair colour?' he asked Scarlett, lifting a grubby finger up to her hair.

She flinched and stepped out of his reach. 'No, and it's not a colour, it's natural.' An unlikely twinge of jealousy stopped her in her tracks, as she wondered who Stanley thought she was, and her mouth twisted as she remembered the old days of feeling constantly pushed into the background.

Dylan could end up being a rerun of those days, if she wasn't careful, but right then, he was the only person she wanted to see, and if that was a bad thing, she'd deal with it later. She pulled her thoughts back to Stanley as Dylan introduced her to his friend.

'Stanley, this is Scarlett. She's an air stewardess.' He nudged Stanley in the ribs. 'She's very posh, so be polite.'

Stanley stood up, and she thought he was going to shake her hand, but he waved his arms in the air, skimming her nose. 'The exits are here and here.' He flicked greasy, grey locks over one shoulder, pouting and giggling before sitting down again, deadpan, as if his outburst hadn't happened.

'Good one, Stanley.' Dylan grinned, until he caught Scarlett's glance and re-arranged his face into irritation. 'I'll bet you get that a lot, don't you?'

'If I had a pound.' But she nodded a greeting towards Stanley. 'As long as he doesn't call me a Trolley Dolly.'

'So, is this the one you keep going on about?' Stanley waved his pint in her direction. 'What do they call 'em,

Trolley Dolly's, isn't it?' Stanley swallowed a mouthful of beer, looking pleased with himself.

'Stanley, don't.' Dylan stood in front of him, trying to block him from her view.

Scarlett shrugged. 'Don't worry. I've had them all. The Captain's groundsheet was the worst insult, but it doesn't get to me anymore.'

'Ooh, nasty.'

'Thing is, the woman who fired the insult works in the local Spar shop and has never even flown on an aeroplane, so she was hardly qualified to judge me.'

'Should have asked her if she had a nice pair,' Stanley interrupted again. 'You know pear. Food. Spar shop?' He outlined the fruit with his hands while also miming weighing a pair of boobs.

'Yeah, good one .... Or not.' Dylan countered on seeing Scarlett's face.

'Do you think we could go somewhere else?' Scarlett asked Dylan with a grimace.

'We're already gone. Come on.' He took her drink out of her hands. 'Do you want to go back to yours?'

'That's the thing. I can't.'

He turned to face her. 'There is a Sugar Daddy?'

She hoped he was joking. 'No, but there are ... people outside my flat.' She swallowed, reliving the past, hating that it was happening again.

Dylan's expression changed from understanding to incomprehension. 'Right.' His forehead wrinkled. 'Okay. You don't like people?'

'Not these sort.'

'Whatever you say, Scarlett, I'm on it.' Questions hung in the air, but he didn't ask any, and for that, she was grateful. 'Do you have your flight bag with you?'

'Yes. My very upmarket, Mulberry bag is in the boot, being bullied by your working-class guitar case.'

'Then we have all we need. Come on.'

'Where are we going?'

'My house.' He took hold of her arm and led the way outside.

'I can't spend the night there, Dylan.'

'No, not that house. My real house, where I grew up. I'll drive.'

'You drive?' She tried to keep the surprise from her voice but failed. 'Are you insured?'

'Yes, of course. I am a grownup.' He grinned as he held out a hand for her car keys. 'You're rubbish at hiding your surprise, by the way.'

'You're good at surprising me.'

'Stick around. It can only get better.' He winked at her. 'Hand them over.'

She didn't want to go to his house, wherever it was, but she knew she couldn't go back to her flat, and she certainly couldn't spend one minute more than necessary in the tip he called home. So, she handed over her keys and stayed silent as Dylan settled himself in to the driver's seat.

He manoeuvred out of The Dog and Duck car park and set the Sat Nav. Scarlett raised her eyebrows, questioning their destination, but he kept quiet as he sped through the streets, a slow smile spreading on his face. 'This is really neat.' The slow smile turned into a full-on grin, and he nodded. 'Yep, I could get used to this.'

'You sure you have a licence? Only you look a bit like a kid with a new bike.'

'Yeah, 'course I do. I also drive an ancient VW Beetle that thinks thirty miles an hour is living on the edge.'

'Ah, so the fact that you are kidnapping me under the guise of rescuing me, and stealing my car, to boot, is making you a bit cocky.'

He patted her knee. 'Now you're getting it.'

The radio soothed her, as Dylan drove them through brightly-lit streets packed with cars, then onto quiet, twisting roads. The pale blue sky turned grey as the day wore on, and the presence of Dylan, strong and capable, calmed her, while the warmth in the car made her eyes grow heavy - until they finally closed, and she escaped from the world that'd caused her such pain, for a few blissful hours.

CHAPTER ELEVEN

The change in speed pulled Scarlett groggily from sleep, disorientated and perplexed at seeing Dylan at the steering wheel of her car. She pushed herself upright and squinted through the misty window, the gloom of early evening clouding her view.

'I'm just nipping in here to get some food.' Dylan climbed from the car and slammed the door closed, as Scarlett took in her surroundings.

She was no wiser, though, apart from the familiar Spar shop logo looming large in front of her, so she waited patiently until Dylan returned.

He dumped two carrier bags in the boot before re-joining her inside.

'Are we here, then?' she asked.

'Two minutes.' He gunned the engine to life again. 'This is the high street. We're on top of the hill, just about … here.'

He pulled up outside a large white house, with shutters at the windows and a trellised garden. It overlooked a large green on one side, and the sea on the other. People sprawled out on the communal grassy area, clutching drinks from the pub just yards away. Children ran around like whirlwinds and Dylan watched them, an amused smile on his lips. 'It is, unfortunately, situated in one of the most popular tourist haunts but we've learned to live with it.'

Scarlett peered up at the house and across to the wide

bay, where the fading rays of sun twinkled on the waves as they slapped against the groynes and retreated smoothly. 'It's beautiful Dylan. I had no idea you lived in a place like this. I'm starting to think you're a bit of a dark horse.'

'Not really. We just don't seem to have talked about my life very much. I can bore you with the details later, if you like, once we've eaten.'

As he unloaded the bags and headed for the front door, Scarlett followed, taking it all in, almost stupefied at this new unlikely Dylan she had been confronted with.

'Where are we, though?'

'Southwold. Suffolk. Born and bred here.'

'But that's miles away, isn't it?'

'Relatively speaking, it's quite close, if you compared it to, say … Inverness, or Cornwall. You did say you had four days off, didn't you?'

'Yes.' She closed her eyes against the situation she'd found herself in, trying to blot out London.

'Consider it a mini holiday, then. And you're doubly in luck, because my parents are away, and my brother, who normally shares the converted basement with me, is on a gap year in some godforsaken country, living on rice and peas and saving the planet from drowning in carrier bags, or something like that. So, we'll be on our own. Lucky you, eh?' His eyes twinkled.

'If you say so.' She twisted her fingers around one another, unable to stop thinking about her predicament.

He laced his own fingers in between hers, forcing her

to quit the nervous action. 'Scarlett, you need to chill out, and when, or if you want to talk about what's going on, trust me, I won't let you down.'

'Thank you, Dylan.' She smiled weakly, as he picked up her flight bag and passed her a carrier bag full of shopping. He slung his guitar across his shoulder, and they headed along the path towards the house.

The old leaded lights in the front door flashed diamond jewels of red and blue across the hallway, as Scarlett followed him into the house and took everything in.

The place smelled of polish and woodwork, with an underlying odour of dog. Walking boots littered the polished parquet floor, and Barbour's and fleeces hung on wall pegs. Like a proper family home, Scarlett thought and felt a pang of longing for something she'd never had. She trailed Dylan through to the kitchen and dumped the carrier bag on a large, scrubbed-pine table, but before she could absorb the room, Dylan grabbed her hand and propelled her towards the stairs.

'Let's go upstairs. I want to show you the view before it gets dark.'

Scarlett laughed, putting her hands on her hips. 'Yeah, I've heard that line before.'

'I'm serious!' He took her hand again, pulling her along.

Steep stairs, a landing, then another set of twisting stairs were navigated, until they came to a ladder with a door at the top.

‘Careful how you go here. I can’t tell you how many times me and my mates have fallen down this ladder, not realising quite how pissed we were, until we ended up in a heap at the bottom. We never even noticed the bruises until we’d sobered up.’

He guided Scarlett up behind him and pushed the door open theatrically. A rush of cool, salty air greeted them, and Scarlett gasped at the sight.

A huge canopy, like a stripy yacht sail, hung above rattan seats that’d been laid out on the rooftop. A blue and white hammock creaked in the breeze, and a giant palm waved in front of an incongruous, large, American-style fridge in the corner.

Scarlett could have been in the desert seeing a mirage. It was a perfect piece of paradise, and that was before she’d even looked across the rooftops to the sea. The oblong squares of the beach huts sprouted far below, their bright summer colours fading a little in the dusk, and beyond those, ant-sized people strolled up and down the pier.

‘Dylan, what on earth are you doing living in a poky little hole in London, when you have all this at your fingertips?’

‘I wanted to see if the streets were paved with gold. Apparently, they’re just littered with deadly germs.’ He flashed her a smile and swept a hand across the cushions on the rattan sofa. ‘Sit down, and I’ll get us some nibbles. Would you like some wine? I can almost guarantee there’ll be something chilled in the fridge. My mother is a great one for impromptu parties, and would never be caught short for the ladies who lunch.'

He opened the fridge door and peered inside, before pulling out a bottle of sparkling wine. He popped the cork and grabbed two glasses, which were suspended between metal grooves by the barbeque in the corner. He poured the wine until it was almost brimming over and raised his glass as he passed the other one to Scarlett. 'May every new dream turn into reality, and may all of your dreams include me.' As he spoke, a cloud ate into the last of the sun, obscuring its orange glow and coinciding with a gentle clap of rumbling thunder. He raised an eyebrow. 'Hmm, I could have timed that better. Hope you're not superstitious.'

'No, I'm not. Now, stop threatening me with nightmares and come over here.'

'Certainly.' Dylan sat down beside her and put his arm around her, grinning. 'That's more like it.'

'I only wanted you to block out the wind,' she laughed.

'That's nice.' He pulled a sad clown face as he removed his arm. 'I'll put the heater on, if you're cold.' His eyes were quizzical, unsure, as if he was eager to please her.

'That'd be great. I could sit here all night.'

As she snuggled into the squashy cushions, tucking her legs in tightly, she wondered how she and Dylan appeared to have moved forward in their relationship so quickly, without her even acknowledging it. She liked

Dylan more than she'd expected to, and was truly grateful for his concern for her welfare.

Realising he was staring at her, she gave him her attention, taking in his anxious eyes and his uncertain smile. Her gaze fixed on his lips, and she relived the soft sensation of them touching hers, admitting to herself, for the first time, that she would like a repeat performance.

Dylan reached out for a wayward tendril of her hair and wound it around his finger. 'Scarlett?'

'Yes?'

'Do you want to tell me what's going on in your head?'

She swallowed, hoping that he hadn't guessed. 'I'm not really sure, but I think it might include you.' She bit the side of her cheek, wanting the reassurance of having someone on her side, but scared of the Pandora's box she might inadvertently open.

He gave her a measured look over the rim of his glass as he sipped his wine. 'Just answer me one question, and I promise I won't demand to know anything else.'

'What do you want to know?'

'Is there a significant other in your life? Is that what this is all about? Are you somehow tied up with another man?'

Scarlett pursed her lips as she pondered the question. 'I guess the answer is no, although it's complicated.'

Dylan ran his fingers through his already tousled hair and shook his head. 'How did I know the answer wouldn't be straightforward?'

She pleaded, silently, that he'd understand, as he

inched closer.

'So, if I did this.' He leaned forward and kissed her, gently. 'Would that be wrong?' He touched her hand as he kissed her, his thumb smoothing across the inside of her wrist. A strangely tender gesture that made Scarlett tailspin into a cloud of confusion and longing.

'No, that would be very right.' Her voice came out smaller than she expected, as heat from Dylan's touch warmed her body.

He nodded, his eyes piercing hers for the truth. Seemingly satisfied, he heaved out a sigh. 'Good.'

He traced the outline of his top lip slowly, as if deciding on his next move, then he pulled her to her feet. 'Come on, before I get carried away. Let's go skim some stones on the sea, and I'll show you the sights.'

Scarlett took a moment to process the change in direction, before quickly brightening at his suggestion. 'Perfect! But I haven't got a coat. I'll freeze.'

'I'll get something of mum's. You'll look cute in one of her fleeces. There's a pink one downstairs, and there are only about a million dog hairs stuck to it. You're not allergic, are you?'

'Not to dogs, but I might be allergic to a large pink fleece,' she said, wrinkling her nose.

'It's okay. I'll be able to see past the outer layers into the inner you.' He looked at her askance. 'And I promise not to tell my mum what you said about her clothes.'

'Hey, don't. You know what I mean.' She slapped him playfully, and he caught her hand and held it tight.

Another look passed between them, sending her heart into a freefall and setting her skin tingling. As a small breath escaped her, she knew for certain that she was falling for Dylan. She didn't know precisely when it had happened, but there was no denying that her body had betrayed her resolve, whether she liked it, or not.

Recovering quickly, she tried not to give herself away, but Dylan's eyes were evaluating, questioning. He nodded to himself, as if satisfied by what he saw, and squeezed her hand as if they'd made a promise to each other.

They wound their way back down the stairs and into the kitchen, where Scarlett pulled Dylan's mother's fleece over her head, spluttering as she suffocated under the voluminous material. Her gaze caught on a photo on the wall, as she emerged from under it: of Dylan, wearing a mortar board and gown, his smile wide, framed by white against the sage green wall. She stared at it in disbelief. 'This is you? You have a degree?'

'Yes.'

'But you never said. I didn't have a clue.'

'Does it make a difference?' He gave her a stern look. 'It shouldn't, you know.'

'No, but ....' She felt silly that she'd imagined him to be just another friendly, singing bum who deserved a chance to be lucky. In fact, she felt cheated, almost as if she'd been duped.

Her mind mulled over the image Dylan had presented of himself, aware that it was nothing like the man who stood in front of her. Not too many hours ago, she felt they'd finally connected, believing in the Dylan who had diligently and persistently pursued her. She tried to re-label him in his new capacity of someone educated from a decidedly middleclass background, but Dylan, the street busker, was too firmly set in her mind. She couldn't but wonder what else there was to discover about him.

Or maybe she was about to find out, she thought, as she peeked through an open door into a vast room housing a white, baby grand piano, piled high with sheet music. Next to it, three guitars took up stands - one bass guitar in glossy black, and two acoustics, similar to the one Dylan dragged around with him like a tatty shadow. A dark silhouette took up the bay window, as if an overly-large man had tried to hide there, and she identified it as the outline of a double bass standing tall in a recess.

She tugged on Dylan's arm, preventing him from moving, as she stepped inside. 'I don't believe this. Why am I getting the feeling that you're not just a street singer, but are actually a bona fide musician?'

He raised his arms in surrender. 'Maybe I might know just a little bit more about music than you imagined, but I've never lied about my talents.' He attempted a cheeky grin, but it died on his lips when Scarlett didn't return it. He sighed. 'Okay, my dad is actually in a symphony orchestra, when he's not messing around with antique clocks. And my brother Angus is really talented - he wants to be a conductor eventually, if all goes well.'

'And not on a bus, I assume,' she said dryly. 'And your mother?'

'Oh, she's just a music teacher. My parents met at the church choir. Both have lovely voices, incidentally.'

'You don't say.' She raised her eyebrows. 'And when were you thinking of mentioning all of this?'

'Why? Does it matter? Surely, it's the person inside who counts?'

'I don't know. It's as if you made out you were some down-and-out who just happened to be good at music.'

'Not really. You just assumed it. And it doesn't make me a different person. I'm still the same cute, loveable guy you always knew. Maybe just a bit more talented.'

'And modest,' Scarlett added.

'Yes, modest could go in there with the rest of my attributes, I guess.' He smiled innocently. 'You don't know how lucky you are to have me.'

Scarlett sighed, thinking that maybe it was time for them to talk properly and establish what part of him she did 'have', or he thought she had. He appeared to be taking their relationship status for granted, just from a few chaste kisses, and although she was leaning toward his way of thinking, there was still a long way to go before it could be considered a done deal.

Before she had chance to reply, though, he pulled her towards the front door. 'Come on, let's go to the beach, before it's too dark.'

CHAPTER TWELVE

They strolled along the seafront and Dylan took her hand leading her down to the beach. It seemed a natural progression, although in London, they'd been much more distant.

He pushed at some stones on the sand with his foot, before bending down and picking a few up, hefting them in the palm of his hand. 'I'm guessing you've skimmed stones before, but I have to tell you I'm a bit of a pro. My misspent youth mostly consisted of building dens, chucking stones into the sea, and sinking in homemade rafts with my brother.'

Scarlett pictured the scenes in her mind, wistfully imagining the young Dylan she never knew. Reluctantly, she had to admit that she didn't know how to skim stones. 'My parents were too busy arguing to take us anywhere, so my sister and me used to mostly play happy families with our dolls in the bedroom we shared.'

'Oh.' Dylan looked genuinely surprised as if he couldn't imagine anyone having a less than idyllic childhood, by right. His gaze softened, and he took a step towards her.

She stepped backwards warily, wanting to deflect him. She didn't want to tread that particular, well-worn path with him. Her memories were hard enough to bear at the best of times, and dredging them up for Dylan, especially when the recent past was proving hard to deal with, was not the way to cement their relationship.

Dylan inclined his head, but instead of pushing her for an explanation, he held out the pebbles he'd collected. 'Okay, then, first lesson coming up. Choose your stone carefully.'

She picked up a thin, grey one, as smooth and round as a well-worn penny, glancing up at him for approval.

'Great choice. Now, hold it between your thumb and finger and crouch down as low as you can, aiming to keep the pebble horizontal.' He hunkered down, a pebble at the ready, and Scarlett followed suit.

'The trick to a good skim is to spin it as you throw it. One, two, three.' He swung his arm back and his stone bounced across the waves at least four times, before disappearing in a plume of sea foam. He automatically raised his arms and did a victory dance. 'Yay!'

Scarlett straightened, scowling at her pathetic attempt as Dylan turned puzzled eyes on her.

'What?' he frowned. 'Didn't you throw yours?'

'Yes,' she said, pouting. 'I think it sank.'

'Aww, don't worry. We'll have another go, together.' He picked up a large pebble, checking its edges for smoothness and suitability. Standing behind her, he took her hand, manipulating her fingers in to the right position.

Behind her, his thigh, solid and steady, pressed against her leg as the warmth of his fingers seeped into her own. As his breath breezed over her neck, she almost twisted around to kiss him. Suddenly she really wanted to kiss him.

'Ready?' He swung her arm backwards, level with his. On their forward flick, the stone flew across the water and bounced a couple of times before disappearing. 'Yes!' He held on to her hand, pumping her arm in the air as he danced her around in a circle.

'I did it.' She joined in with Dylan's happy dance, jumping up and down until they were both breathless.

Dylan slung his arm around her. 'Welcome to the Southwold initiation. You've passed part one with flying colours.'

Scarlett allowed herself to snuggle into the warmth of his chest. 'How do I become a full member?'

'You'll find out when we get to the pier. There's a rabid dog waiting for you.' He winked, and she knew she didn't need to worry about a rabid dog, or possibly anything at all, so long as Dylan was by her side. It was a comforting thought.

The sky darkened as they walked, and a sudden jazz of lightening illuminated the dark clouds, right before a smattering of fierce rain fell.

They made a run for the shelter of the beach huts, ducking under the canopy of one named Lady Luck.

In the shadows, Dylan turned Scarlett into his chest and held her close, and as she watched the rain bouncing off the sand, the same uprising of emotions surfaced again. With a sigh, she finally admitted to herself that it wasn't just his warmth she was enjoying. She liked the sensations that washed over her whenever she was with him. Comfort. Safety. And, surprisingly, a bit of lust had crept in without her noticing.

He dropped a kiss on the top of her head, and she groaned. Whatever was happening between them was moving fast.

Dylan drew her away from him. 'What is it?' He peered into her eyes, the intensity of his stare pitched at the usual one hundred percent wattage, something she was beginning to get used to. 'Scarlett, you really confuse me. One minute, you appear to like me, and the next, you act like you're suffering my presence under the sentence of death.' He didn't look upset, just puzzled.

'I don't know. I didn't expect you to come into my life.' She sighed and grasped a strand of her wayward hair, pulling it across one shoulder. It immediately took flight again, and Dylan caught it, winding it around his fingers, drawing her closer.

'What's wrong with allowing me into your life?'

'Nothing, really. I wonder if I've just become used to thinking that I'm not allowed to ....' She shrugged. 'It's difficult.'

'So you said,' Dylan agreed, exasperation clear in his voice. He released her from his arms and closed his eyes briefly, his lips compressed. 'So, once again, can I assume that it's not me, but outside influences stopping us from doing whatever it is we want to do together?' He raised his hands then let them drop to his sides. 'Oh, crap. Why am I talking in riddles? For God's sake, Scarlett, I want us to have a good time here. Together. I want us to walk along the beach like we're joined at the hip. To be silly together. Feed each other food. Kiss. Make out together – do what lovers do. If that's too much for you, then you need to tell me now, because ....' He leaned in closer again, his voice lowering as he said, 'Because, I'm seriously falling for you.' His eyes, when he finally looked at her, seemed troubled and full of pain.

Scarlett's stomach twisted at his words, and she closed her eyes as the past rushed at her, once more. She was sick of the past. She wanted to let go of her own pain. She wanted to try and regain happiness. God, she was tired of constantly feeling weighed down.

Reaching out to Dylan, she let her fingers brush his arm. It was time. She could take the leap. Dylan would be worth the risk. It had been a long and hard road, and she was ready, finally, to take a different path.

As her lips twisted in the effort to speak without crying, sudden tears clogged her throat, but Dylan seemed to sense her emotions and curled an arm around her shoulder. 'Come on. I'll show you the wee-wee men.'

'The wee-wee men?' Swiping her tears away, she peered up at him.

'That's what Angus used to call them, and the name stuck, but don't worry, they're statues, not real men.'

'Pleased to hear it.' She breathed freely again, relieved that they were back on a normal footing. She'd been so close to telling him everything. She shivered as she recalled his words. He wanted her – that much had sunk in. Was she ready for such a commitment, though? She knew he wouldn't push it, but she would have to make a decision eventually. It wasn't fair of her to think of her own salvation at Dylan's expense.

***

The rain stopped as quickly as it'd started, and Scarlett and Dylan jumped down from the wall, back onto the sand. Squinting in the gathering darkness, Scarlett read out some of the names of the beach huts as they passed them. 'Moon Coin. What a lovely name.'

'One day, I'm going to own one of these.' Dylan swept his arm grandly towards the huts. 'I'm going to paint it bright red and call it Scarlett.'

Scarlett lifted her face to the sky, trying to work out what to say to such a statement. She needed to deflect his intensity away from her; he didn't seem to pause for breath in relaying his emotions and it was a little bit scary. Yes, she really liked him, but she didn't think she could take much more of his unfounded worship. She didn't like being put on a pedestal, especially as she had so spectacularly fallen off the last one she'd ventured to climb. But in the end, she didn't need to say anything, as the relentless waves, pounding the beach with a noisy determination, made talking impossible.

Surf sprayed over their feet, when they ventured too close to the edge and a particularly strong wave broke over their legs. Scarlett squealed and ran behind Dylan, who put his arm protectively around her shoulder. Even though the gesture was slightly proprietorial, she liked the way that he always looked out for her. Maybe a bit of adoration would be a good thing, she decided as she nestled her head into his shoulder.

As they stood gazing out over the stormy sea, a zigzag of lightening crackled overhead, highlighting the frenetic waves and a distant crack of thunder promised an inland storm.

'This is wonderful, Dylan,' Scarlett said, watching the show. She couldn't remember the last time she'd felt so relaxed, so calm. 'How can you ever want to leave such a place?'

'I don't really, but when you live your whole life somewhere like this, you do start to wonder if there's a bigger picture out there.'

'And do you think you've found the bigger picture?'

'Well, yeah, of course. I've almost landed a recording contract. You can't get much better than that, can you?'

Scarlett sucked in her cheeks. There were many, many things that were better than landing a recording contract, but Dylan would need to find that out for himself.

He glanced at her, as if waiting for her opinion. When she didn't offer one, he said, 'I've just thought, the pier will be closed by now. We'll have to do it tomorrow. It's worth it, though. We can read some of the dedications on the railings – they're wonderful and heart-breaking at the same time.'

'What dedications?'

'When part of the pier was rebuilt, visitors and locals were invited to dedicate a plaque to their loved ones, stating things like how much they loved to stroll around Southwold, and stuff like that. Some of them are really touching tributes to people who've died.'

Scarlett's eyes filled at the thought of so many messages. So much declared love within a few simple words. She tried stifling her emotions when Dylan peered down at her, but not quickly enough.

'Don't cry, Scarlett. Why are you crying?' He framed her face in his hands and turned her toward him, his eyes sad and troubled. 'I really need to understand the bigger picture here. What's holding you back from living and loving? I can tell it's all connected somehow.'

Scarlett had no answer for him, though. Not then. Not yet. She just shook her head dumbly as she tried to stop her tears.

'Okay, we'll leave it for now. The last thing I want is to upset you.' He pulled her tightly into his chest and hugged her.

She buried her face into his shirt, while he rubbed her back, whispering soothing words as she softly cried. Eventually, she sniffed and smiled up at him.

'Shall we go back?' he asked, keeping a firm grip on her shoulders.

'Yes. Thank you for this. I'm sorry if I'm all over the place, but I am trying to get sorted out, and I ...' She dashed a final tear away, blinking. 'Sorry.'

'Don't apologise. It's fine. It's why we're here, right?' Tightening his arm across her shoulders, he walked her back along the beach, with the rolling black sky above and wild sweeping waves ahead.

When his mobile rang, he answered it, excusing

himself. After speaking briefly to whoever was on the line, he returned to Scarlett. 'I'm having a bit of a jam session with my old mates at the pub tomorrow lunchtime. I texted one of them to say I was back for a few days. Are you okay with that? We've been jamming for most of our lives. I think we were about fifteen when we started gigging there. We thought we were the best thing that had ever happened to Southwold.'

'Brilliant. Can't wait.' Scarlett gave him a watery but determined smile.

'Great.' Dylan beamed in return. 'We must have looked a right bunch of buffoons back then, but they're wonderful guys, and I'm looking forward to seeing them.'

'I'd like to meet them all.' She meant it, too - she wanted to meet Dylan's friends and be part of his life. She'd finally made a decision: The past was gone, and hopefully her future would include Dylan. 'Come on, we can watch the storm from the roof, can't we?'

Dylan's smile told her how good an idea he thought it was, and they walked slowly back to the house and climbed the stairs once more.

Scarlett found herself sitting back on the huge rattan sofa, looking out to sea, while Dylan fussed, bringing blankets and positioning the canopy so that the wind wouldn't bother them.

Above, the sky had pitched into blackness, and only

white pinpoints of light danced across the waterline: boats heading homewards, or anchoring up for the night. She tried to imagine what it would be like to be out on one of those bobbing vessels. Were the occupants having a good time enjoying the wildness of the sea with someone they loved, or were they just chugging along as quickly as they could, dreaming of a hot meal and a soft bed?

Thinking about it, she was grateful that she wasn't one of them. She much preferred getting comfy with Dylan, her worries sealed into a box she didn't need to open for three more days.

Turning towards him, she watched with a growing fondness, as he flapped blankets in the wind after firing up the heater. 'This was a wonderful idea, you know. It can't get much better than this, looking up at the stars and listening to the waves below.'

Dylan stopped, his hands full of blankets. 'I'm glad you think so.' He dumped the blankets at the end of the sofa and gave her one of his broad smiles. 'The night is yet young, which means it can only get better.' He winked, and she giggled, surprising herself.

His smile was infectious, though, and her own lips widened, the muscles on her face creaking to life after a long time of polite air stewardess smiles, hiding her unhappiness. Dylan Willis and his positive spin on life was decidedly good for her, and if she was going to start living again, there was no better person to help her do it.

CHAPTER THIRTEEN

Scarlett had never looked so beautiful to Dylan, her silky hair lifting in the gentle breeze, the glow of the heater highlighting her cheekbones and throwing the rest of her face into interesting shadows. Lavender smudges under her eyes made her look vulnerable and lost, and he wanted to fold her into his arms until the anguish that marred her face disappeared.

No, that wasn't quite accurate. He wanted to make beautiful love to her, tenderly and completely, before folding her into his arms and holding her while she slept. But that particular ball was totally in her court.

He closed his eyes, but quickly opened them to stop the images in his mind from becoming too graphic. He wanted to sleep with her, he really did, but he wanted her for keeps, not just for kicks, and that meant he needed to put a stop to his wayward thoughts. He might be a gentleman, but he was still human.

'Best to knock it on the head for tonight, do you think?' He pushed to his feet. 'I can sort out Angus's bed for you, if you want?'

'I don't want to go inside.'

'Okay.' In truth, he didn't want to, either, although a sudden image of her asleep in his single bed like a glamorous Goldilocks presented itself fully formed.

To drive away the lustful thoughts, he tried to imagine her in his brother's bed, out of harm's way, but he shook away that image, too. It wasn't right. She needed to be with him, wherever he was.

He shook his head clear. Enough with his single-mindedness – before he got way out of line. 'I think I'll sleep out here tonight.' He'd had no plans to do that – he'd probably freeze to death if he did, but he wasn't sure how strong his resolve would be, if they cocooned together in his bedroom.

'Really?' She inclined her head. 'Then, I'd like to stay here, too. We can drink this lovely wine, watch the sky showing off, and I can fall asleep in your arms.' She patted the sofa. 'If that's okay with you. Come on, it'll be cool. We can watch the sun rise in the early hours.'

He inwardly groaned, wanting desperately to lie on the big sofa with her, but thinking that maybe a cold shower first might be required. 'Okay. Your call,' he said nonchalantly, as if he often fell asleep with a beautiful girl in his arms on his parents' roof.

He picked out a couple more blankets from the chest and shook them in the wind before folding them around Scarlett. He sat down next to her, and her big eyes fixed on his, full of an invitation he wasn't sure what to do with.

Her lips trembled, with cold or desire, he didn't know, but he didn't need to find out. Just being next to her was good enough, for then.

Rain began to pitter-patter around them, but they were safe in their cocoon, sheltered by the canopy and cosy within their blankets. Dylan stared into the distance for several minutes, before turning to Scarlett with a frown.

'What's wrong?'

'You sitting here with me, drinking wine. It's a dream come true, and I'm worried that it's too perfect. I'm waiting for the thunderclap that will take it all away.'

'Dylan, don't put me on a pedestal. I'm just normal. Look at you – you might be a household name before you know it.'

'I guess.' He smiled. 'You should make the most of this, before I disappear in a mosh pit of middle-aged women, all trying to get a piece of me.' He quirked an eyebrow and pushed out his chest in exaggeration.

'Don't flatter yourself.' But she laughed and lifted a corner of her blanket. 'Come and join me, and I'll try and work out what, exactly, making the most of you entails.' She put her wine glass down, her smile inviting.

He slid over to her, and she folded the blanket around them both. When she didn't make another move, Dylan wasn't sure what she had in mind. He twiddled his thumbs, exaggerating the action as the silence grew. 'Still thinking about it?'

'Hmm, I'm done thinking.' She scraped her hair away from her face, lifted her lips up to him, closed her eyes and pouted.

Dylan laughed. 'Really?'

Scarlett opened her eyes. They widened as she took in his expression, and she giggled and fell sideways. 'I don't know why I did that. Just kiss me, will you, Dylan, before we both go off the idea?'

'I won't, ever.' He took her hand, pulling her upright once more and gathering her against his chest. 'Believe me.'

She let her hair fall and it framed her face in whispers of golden thread dancing around her cheeks and neck. Dylan gathered it up, threading it through his fingers. She was his dream come true, but since the dream had come true, the fantasy took on a sharper edge. He wanted more. He wanted her to fall in love with him, as he intended to love her in return.

Letting her hair slide through his fingers, he gazed into her eyes, cupping her cheeks in his palms, before lowering his lips to hers, unable to hold back a second longer.

His need hitched up a notch as her breasts pressed against his chest and her breath audibly caught in her throat. She wrapped her arms around his neck and pulled him down to the softness of the blankets, meeting him halfway. The tip of her tongue touched his lips, and a small sigh escaped her mouth as her fingers trailed from his throat to his chest.

Dylan groaned – he couldn't help it. He explored her lips, trying to keep it low level and languid, but she pressed her hips into his and a hit of adrenalin and desire throbbed through his veins. He allowed his fingers to skim very briefly over her breast, as he dropped his hand to her waist, finding bare skin under her top. The silkiness of her warm body set his adrenalin soaring again, kicking slow and languid out of the window, and the low burn of his kiss heated into a fiery longing, as he crushed her lips with his own, deepening the kiss, his tongue gently probing.

Scarlett threw her head backwards, even as she clutched at his shirt, her breath erratic. 'Oh, God.' Her voice sounded full of indecision.

'What?'

'I don't know.'

'Do you want to stop?' He searched her face for a sign of hesitancy, or anxiety, but could only see smouldering eyes, flushed cheeks, and divine, pink lips, parted and waiting to be kissed.

'I don't think so. No.'

'Good.' He kissed her again, trailing his lips down the side of her neck. Her moan of desire amped up his need a notch more, as his fingers roamed higher, touching warm responsive skin slowly, very slowly, giving her ample opportunity to ask him to stop. He found her breast again, and he moaned as he pushed aside lace and found her nipple, pert and responsive. He caressed it, gently exploring the contours, until he needed more. He slid his hand away and reached for the top button of her shirt, taking it slow as he unbuttoned it, their eyes locking as she signalled her permission.

He pushed aside her shirt, his lips already kissing her shoulder, tasting heaven on her skin. 'Do you think we should take this to my bedroom?' he asked.

'No, I want to stay here.'

Dylan didn't argue. They were hidden from prying

eyes on the rooftop, and he was far too busy planting kisses on his way down to her breast to want to stop.

She gasped when his tongue slid over her nipple. As he took it fully into his mouth, she wriggled completely out of her top, and Dylan undid her bra, his hands around her back. 'God, you have no idea how much I want you,' he said, his words muffled against her throat.

'I'm starting to get the vibes, I really am.' Her breath was long and indrawn with a desire that was impossible to miss.

Dylan forced himself to pull away from her slightly, steadying his own breath – measured and calm.

'What's wrong?' Scarlett's eyes clouded with confusion.

'I want you to know, I will never do anything to jeopardise what we have.'

She smiled, raising her eyebrows. 'Do we have something special?

'Yes, we really do. Trust me.'

'Show me,' she told him.

He moved in for another kiss, and Scarlett sank back on the sofa, her breasts standing to attention in the cold wind.

'Give me half a chance, and I will,' he said, his voice roughened by desire.

She curled her arms around his neck and pulled him close. Her taut nipples pressed into his chest, and he longed to be naked next to her. He unbuttoned his shirt and Scarlett pushed it over his shoulders, clutching him to her chest once more.

He groaned as her fingers skimmed his crotch. 'Jesus, don't touch me there – no, do. Do.'

She giggled, and when she slid her hand inside the waistband of his jeans, he groaned again. 'Sorry, that isn't enough. Scarlett, I'm in pain here.'

'Don't give me that old line,' she said, but didn't argue as he unbuckled his belt, making a show of it. Scarlett took over, unzipping his jeans, teasingly slowly.

He shucked out of his jeans as the intensity of his erection did indeed become painful. 'Oh, Scarlett, you send me to places ...'

'That's not a line from a song, is it?'

'No, but now you mention it – let me just fetch my notepad.' He grinned and reached out to his rucksack, sitting on the floor.

'Don't you dare. I need you.'

'I so wanted to hear that.'

They peeled off the rest of their clothes in a frenzy, until they lay naked with each other, legs tangling, lips clashing, touching and tasting skin. It took moments for them to slow it down, kissing deep and sensually until they could barely contain their desperation.

'Umm, do you have any … you know, condoms? Only, I haven't been taking precautions since ...'

Dylan pushed down his jealousy, even as he wanted to ask her to finish her sentence. Since what, or, more likely, who? 'Yes, I do,' he said, pushing his questions aside. 'And they all have your name on them – forever.'

'That's good to know.'

Dylan slid his fingers down to touch Scarlett, and she sighed, crying out as she guided him into her, finally, arching her back as she called out his name.

Dylan thrust into Scarlett, never wanting it to end, yet desperate to climax. Waiting to hear if Scarlett was ready, he prayed she was as ecstatic as he was about the turn of events. As her muscles tightened around him, he climaxed on a drawn-out gasp before collapsing on top of her, taking his own weight on his arms. 'Scarlett, Scarlett.' He kissed her eyes, her cheeks, her lips, any part he could find. 'Don't let this ever end.'

'I think it just did.' She gasped once, then breathed in deeply, her head thrown back. 'Jesus, Dylan.'

'I know, I know.' He lay down next to her, drawing her legs around his, entwining them together once more. He stroked her arms while kissing her hair, and he pulled her close, never wanting to let her go. 'I knew it, Scarlett, I knew we were going to be great together.'

'Mmm.'

Dylan hoisted himself up on to his elbows. 'Are you saying we weren't?'

'No, I'm saying it was fantastic, and I'd just like to lie here awhile, in a glow of post coital-thingy.'

'Oh. Well, as long as I know.'

'Yes, it was amazing. Goodnight.'

He grinned and buried his nose into her hair once more. 'I guess that's okay, then. If you're sure you don't want an extra time replay?'

She smiled up at him sleepily. 'It's been a very lovely, but long, day and I'm really tired, but happy. Truly, I am.'

'Cool.' He snuggled into her back, throwing the blankets over them both. He tucked them tightly around Scarlett before entwining his legs around hers and scooping her small frame against his own.

As he listened, her breathing steadied out, and he rested his head close to hers, content and at peace with the world. Glancing out across the night sky, he thanked God for the simple pleasures of life, and in that moment, he made a promise he intended to keep: that he would never, ever take Scarlett for granted, vowing to cherish her until the day he died.

CHAPTER FOURTEEN

Dylan woke up in the early hours of the morning, his back and his legs numb with cold. The blankets he'd shared with Scarlett had slipped off him and into a heap on top of her.

After pulling his shirt on, he retrieved a share of the blankets and checked on Scarlett. She was fast asleep, her breath steady and regular. He touched her cold cheek, tenderness replacing desire as he coiled his body around hers for warmth. Even there, though, the wind snuck into every unwrapped part of his skin, biting and raw, and he knew the blankets wouldn't be enough to keep them both warm until the morning.

They needed to move.

'Scarlett, come on, wake up. We need to go inside, or else we'll freeze.'

She muttered something indecipherable, tucking the blanket under her chin, and snuggled down.

'Scarlett, get up.' He shook her arm and tried to lift her up to a sitting position.

'No. Leave me alone. Oh.' She sat up, blinking as she took in her surroundings. 'Christ, it's cold.' She pulled a blanket around her shoulders and snuggled down once more.

'We need to move, come on.' He rubbed at her arm.

She sat up again with a groan and grabbed her shirt with her free hand. Pulling the blanket with her, she trailed it along the floor as Dylan frog-marched her zombie-like form down the stairs and through the house until he reached his old room. He took in the single bed, wondering if he should sleep in Angus's room, but quickly decided against it. He wanted to spend the night with Scarlett. He didn't want to waste a minute of their time together.

After manoeuvring her into the wall side of his single bed, he slipped in next to her, pulling her soft body into his. He breathed in the smell of her, brushed his cheek against her hair, and tried to damp down his threatening erection.

'This is a cool room,' Scarlett mumbled into the ancient Superman wallpaper. Turning into him, she snuggled into his neck, asleep again in seconds.

He smoothed her hair absent-mindedly. It felt so right that she was finally next to him. Dylan didn't think he'd ever felt so content. He hoped she knew, too, how great they were together. His life was heading in the direction he wanted it, and Scarlett was going to be a part of it.

The urge to wake her and check that she felt the same way was overwhelming, but he knew if he woke her, he'd want to have sex with her again, and it seemed a bit unfair when she was sleeping so soundly. So he did neither, just sighed and dozed on-and-off as he held Scarlett tight, watching the flicker of dawn turn to daylight through the blinds.

As the sun pushed through the window and on to his eyelids, he finally crept out of bed. Spaced out from lack of sleep, he was desperate for coffee, but unsure whether to leave Scarlett on her own to wake up in a strange bed. She was still out for the count, though, so he snuck out of bed after giving her one last, lingering look.

He headed for the bathroom first and took a reviving shower, before throwing on a clean set of clothes, then feeding the coffee machine little silver capsules. Waiting for the hit of caffeine only good coffee could offer, he realized how much he'd missed it since moving to his seedy house.

He whirled around at a discreet cough behind him. Scarlett.

Smudges of makeup under her eyes made her look vulnerable and frail, a stark contrast to her sexiness from the night before, but she was still the best sight in the world. She looked waiflike in his oversized shirt, her bare legs sending a frisson of desire through him.

'Thank God it's you. I thought, for a minute, Mum had come back.' He felt strangely awkward in the starkness of the morning light.

Her mobile rang, and she frowned down at it, before looking brightly up at Dylan. 'Yes, that might have been awkward.' Her light reply only highlighted the fact that she pointedly ignored whoever was phoning her, and Dylan knew her smile well enough to know the one she threw him was her fake air stewardess smile.

'Aren't you going to deal with that?' he asked, when her phone beeped for a second time. It had vibrated in her bag at least eight times since he'd woken up, and he'd steadfastly resisted the compulsion to see who it was.

She didn't answer – him, or the phone.

He took a step forward; his arms open to embrace her – he could never get enough of her. 'Hi. Again.' He couldn't keep the grin from his face.

When she took a step backwards, his smile wavered.

Her mobile rang again. She deleted the call without looking at it.

'Would you like some breakfast?' he asked.

She shook her head.

'Okay.' He groaned on the inside. Please don't let this be as awkward as it's shaping up to be. 'Would you like a shower, maybe?' Christ, he sounded like her butler. He could see why people legged it after a one-night stand. Their exchange was becoming excruciating – how could she behave like a stranger after the glorious intimacy of last night?

'Yes, please, that would be great. I'll just follow the wet footprints, shall I?' Her smile was small and lost, and it hurt Dylan to see it. She didn't want to be at his home, with him, it was clear.

He'd imagined spending their day laughing and teasing each other, snatching kisses and wandering down to the beach café to read the newspapers and enjoy the fresh air.

Something had obviously gone very wrong since he'd conjured up those thoughts.

Scarlett moved to the bathroom without speaking, and Dylan sat on the kitchen stool and stared out of the window. The ancient plum tree in the garden had started to look forlorn with its drooping leaves. A few late straggly plums, half dead on the bough, just about clung on to life, and Dylan wondered idly what outrageous recipes his mother had conjured up for the year's batch to make sure they weren't wasted.

His old swing, tied to the top branch, lifted in the breeze, as if a younger Dylan still sat on it. Up on the shed roof, the deflated football his brother had kicked up there one summer was still there, fading and shrinking as each season passed.

He glanced over at the stairs, waiting for Scarlett to appear once more, feeling as if he was waiting for a guilty or innocent verdict. Despite being in his own home, he felt lost, and completely baffled as to what had caused the change in Scarlett since she'd woken up. Probably to do with the constant buzz of her mobile, he figured – or maybe she just wasn't a morning person.

He padded through to the music room and picked up one of his guitars, tuning it and smoothing away a light smattering of dust with his arm. As he tested out a song he'd recently written, he considered whether it was polished enough to play at the pub later. He pulled off a capo from one of the other guitars and tried the tune in a different pitch, then picked up the bass guitar and tried it out in a blues and jazzy rhythm.

Better. Not what he'd had in mind when he had written it, but it was good.

As he lifted his head, he caught sight of Scarlett leaning against the doorframe, looking more like the air stewardess she was, and much less like the girlfriend Dylan wanted her to be. He stopped playing, his mouth drying as he watched her watching him, her eyes large, and her sensational mouth glossy and dewy.

'Don't stop, it's lovely. I haven't heard you play for a while.'

'I'm pleased with it.' He gave her a wry grin and placed the guitar back on the stand, before following her out to the kitchen.

'So, Lara Croft duvet cover, eh? Do you want to talk about it?' she asked, her expression dead-pan as she filled the kettle and switched it on.

Catching the corner of her mouth lifting, Dylan grinned, thanking God they were back on a level footing. 'It was just a phase. I went off her when she didn't reply to the fan letter I sent her.'

'Even though she's a fictitious person?'

'Mere detail.' He waved a hand airily.

'It's one up from my Brittney Spears lamp and lightshade set, I guess. That was my pop phase.' She fiddled with her hair, twisting it up in to a loose chignon.

'Let's skim quickly over this conversation. Shall we take a stroll to the pier, being as I didn't get a chance to introduce you to its delights last night?'

Scarlett smiled tightly. 'I'm not sure. I think I should make my way back to London after I've had a cup of tea.'

Dylan swallowed. He couldn't bring himself to respond to her plans, his disappointment was so acute. 'Was last night so –'

Her phone beeped again.

'For God's sake, why don't you just speak to them, whoever they are?'

'I don't want to.' She sighed. 'But I think I might have to.'

'Of course you do.' Deflated, he turned off the coffee machine, put a tea bag in a mug, and faced her. 'I know, it's okay.'

'You know?'

'I know you don't want to stay. You have your reasons, so that's cool.'

'No, Dylan, it's not cool. And I do want to stay. It's just that something needs sorting out, back home.' She frowned again as she peered down at her phone, letting it ring out once more.

'Will you stay to meet my friends?' It wasn't the question he wanted to ask. He wanted to ask who the bloody hell kept calling her, and why didn't she want to speak to him – assuming it was a him.

'Yes, of course, I'd love to meet your friends.' Her mobile rang again. 'Oh, for heaven's sake.' She pressed the off button and slammed the phone on the table. 'Can you get out to the garden from here?'

'Yes, through there.'

She picked up a pair of boots by the door and pushed her feet into them. After grabbing her mug, she disappeared from his view.

Her phone vibrated once more. Dylan hesitated before picking it up and answering the call.

'John Small, Daily Mercury. Come on, Scarlett, just a one-line quote about you and Axel will do. You owe me.'

'She owes you nothing.' Dylan dropped the phone back to the worktop. What the hell?

He headed out to the garden, his mind racing, and found Scarlett pushing herself through the air on his swing, her hair flying behind her.

She didn't look as if she had a care in the world, but Dylan knew better, and it was time he found out what was going on.

Before he had a chance to ask her, his own phone rang, and he turned it on to speaker, deliberating on how to confess to Scarlett that he knew a journalist wanted to speak to her. 'Yeah, I'll be there in a half an hour,' he said, although his mind was anywhere but on the matter in hand. He shoved his phone into his back pocket and took a steadying breath, and crossed to the swing. Grabbing the ropes, he held them, steadying Scarlett as he brought her to a standstill. 'Scarlett, I need to go to the pub to practice. If you want to go back to London, or if you want this to be goodbye, can you tell me now, please? I'm a big boy, I can handle it.'

She blinked. 'Sorry? I'm coming with you, aren't I? I said I would.'

He raked his fingers down his face. 'Look, I hate to do a heavy scene here, and I'm aware how uncool it is, but I am strictly a one-woman man, and I expect the same kind of dedication in return.' He pushed his curls away from his forehead. 'Fuck, I'm so rubbish with this whole dating thing.'

'Dylan, it's okay.' Her smile was gentle as she took his hand, folding her fingers around his. Her eyes levelled with his. 'Really. I need to speak with someone, but it can wait. I want to stay here.'

He watched her silently, as she bit her lip and slid her gaze away from his, noting how even she didn't look convinced by her own words. 'If you say so.' He'd thought, for a second, that she might open up to him, but he let it drop. She was staying. For now, anyway - and that had to be enough.

'Push me on the swing, please. I haven't done this in, like, forever.' She pushed her legs out straight and up high, and threw her head back, like an excited little girl.

'You win-again,' he muttered. As he positioned himself behind the swing, his thoughts focused on what the phone call he'd intercepted could mean. His own imminent rise to stardom certainly wasn't important enough for a newspaper to be interested in him, and she had information on someone called Axel, apparently. It made no sense, at all. She was an air stewardess - so, what kind of information would she have to make a national newspaper pester her?

He tried to push the negative thoughts away, as he watched her swing her legs back and forth, her hair escaping from its loose fastenings.

He should try to be laid back, like the dude he was supposed to be, but who the hell was Axel? He wanted to take her in his arms and kiss her - to take things back to the way they were, before her damned phone started buzzing – but he couldn't help the frustration and annoyance that bubbled in his chest. Besides, he knew he wouldn't act on it. She didn't have to tell him anything she didn't want to. He just wished she liked him enough to confide in him and trust him.

Snagging her around the waist, he stopped the swing once more. 'Come on, let's go to the pub. You can watch me make a fool of myself.' His smile was wan and his enthusiasm for the day had faded, and if he didn't get outside his own head for a while, he'd drive himself nuts.

Scarlett bounced off the swing and landed on the grass, her eyes sparkling. She laughed up at Dylan and threw her arms around his neck, kissing him hard. 'That was fun. Cheer up.' She grabbed his hand. 'Let's go.'

He nodded from within his cloud of confusion. She was killing him with her mysteries and mood changes.

CHAPTER FIFTEEN

Dylan opened the pub door, to the twang of guitars and general din and was greeted like a returning hero. 'Hey, Dylan, man, how've you been?'

Hands slapped his back, as he high-fived someone wearing denim from top to toe. 'Still going with the double denim look, eh?'

'Can't all be as cool as you,' Double Denim replied.

'Hey, Curly Ginger, how you doing?'

'Dylan. Wow, what's with the hair, man?' He was a tall guy with a thatch of curly ginger hair, and a broad, square jaw.

Dylan narrowed his eyes. 'You're asking me?' He laughed, giving his friend's hair a ruffle. 'Surprisingly, it's grown since I last saw you - over a year ago.' He pressed down his corkscrew hair, trying to tame it, but it just sprang up again.

'Ooh, hello, who's this, then?' A round man, wearing an oversized hounds-tooth jacket and a bow tie, gave Scarlett the once-over.

'Hugo.' He pumped Hugo's hand, a grin spreading wide. 'Still on your way to making a million from renting out those decrepit boats, are you?' Turning to Scarlett, Dylan took her arm, about to introduce her, when another man pushed his way through the throng.

'Gollum, hello.' Dylan shifted an inch or two closer to Scarlett, as the man peered at her through bottle-end glasses, his eyes widening with interest. 'Err, yes. Hello.

Scarlett, this is Marcus, more commonly known as Gollum.' Dylan sent Scarlett a nod of reassurance. 'He doesn't get out much,' he said by way of an apology as Marcus's nose almost touched hers. 'Earth to Gollum. This is Scarlett. She's a friend from London.'

Marcus continued to stare at Scarlett as if he wasn't sure what he was viewing.

Dylan snapped his fingers in front of his face with little effect. 'Ignore him,' he told Scarlett. 'He's a little strange. He still thinks body popping is cool.'

'The Angel brothers. It is you, isn't it?'

Dylan frowned hard. 'Scarlett, Gollum. Her name is Scarlett.'

'I'd recognise you anywhere. I was a huge fan.'

Dylan made a smoking motion and twirled his finger in the air. 'Wacky Baccy finally got to him, I think. Come on, let me introduce you to the others. Are you okay, you've turned a little pale?'

He placed his hand under Scarlett's elbow and pulled her across the room. 'Sorry, if it's all a bit much. I should've warned you – they can get a bit rowdy. I'll introduce you properly later.' He settled her into a chair beside a large table littered with used glasses, and introduced the two women already seated there. 'Hannah and Emily, meet Scarlett.' He waved a hand towards Scarlett. 'Be kind to her. She looks like she might do a runner, given half a chance.' He winked at the women, who immediately turned toward Scarlett to include her in their circle.

And breathe, he thought.

He turned back to the band and surveyed the large room. Tourists and locals passing a contented couple of hours with good food and beer, considered him with interest, but they soon turned back to their drinks and conversation as the novelty of listening to a band for free wore off.

They set up the stage and tuned in their instruments, and Dylan settled back into the groove with his old singing buddies.

Guitars started up, and Hugo began to sing. Dylan and Curly Ginger harmonized until finally they were all joining in.

Curly Ginger tapped his foot and called out, 'One, two, three,' and they were off.

***

The band put paid to Scarlett's tentative conversation with Hannah and she was soon engrossed in their music. Their style was more toe-tapping pop than Dylan's contemporary-yet-soulful style of music, but Dylan joined in, as if it were only yesterday that he'd been part of their band.

Dylan kept looking over at her and grinning, and she found herself feeling proud to be with him. More than that, she had a sudden revelation that she would be very happy to be his girl.

Her pulse quickened and her heart did a little loop-the-loop, as his eyes fastened on to hers. For a moment, it was as if they were connected by their thoughts, as if he knew everything had changed for Scarlett. It was a huge relief that she was moving on, but instead of wanting to run wild and tell everyone she was finally free, a tear slid from the corner of her eye.

So, not completely free, she thought, angrily swiping at the dampness on her cheek.

A sudden increase in the noise level made her turn, to see a gaggle of young women entering the pub, clapping and calling out the band members names.

'Here come the girls,' Hannah sang.

The gang of newcomers were louder than the music and Scarlett balked, hoping they weren't going to sit at their table.

'The groupies,' Hannah explained. 'They turn up every time Daft Donuts play. Hardened followers. Oh, no.' Her eyes widened, and she nudged Emily with her elbow and inclined her head towards a pretty woman, whose dark hair was a mass of dancing curls. 'Kate must have heard Dylan was home,' she said in a loud stage whisper.

A sudden tension in the air made Scarlett fasten her eyes on the new girl, who gazed up at Dylan with large kohl-rimmed eyes as she inched closer to the makeshift stage.

Dylan turned toward his admirer, and for a moment, he faltered, shock creeping over his face before he smiled down at her.

She waved up at him, crimping her fingers like a little girl, and Scarlett's stomach clenched with foreboding.

Dylan seemed distracted from that moment on, flunking his lines, his eyes flickering over the heads of the crowd across at Kate, then back to Scarlett. The warm cocoon that had shrouded her from harm evaporated, leaving her once more feeling vulnerable and hating that one person, once again, had the power to hurt her.

She focused on Kate, as the girl swung her hips to the music while quaffing something Ribena-coloured from a pint glass. She appeared totally at ease and was probably a regular at the pub, so it was perfectly possible that she was no more than an old friend, but instinct said otherwise. Scarlett found she couldn't drag her gaze away, as Kate's eyes remained resolutely fixed on Dylan.

Kate's friend elbowed her in the ribs every time Dylan glanced her way, and Scarlett accepted with a calm certainty that there was history between them.

A cold fear settled in her stomach, replacing the warm fuzziness that had nestled there only a short while ago. She really shouldn't have got in so deep, so soon with Dylan, but it was too late. Or was it? Worry gnawing at her belly, she rested her chin on her hands and waited for Dylan to finish.

As soon as the gig ended, the large table in front of Scarlett was cleared of glasses, and a platter of sandwiches and sausage rolls set down in their place. The band members joined the women and settled into seats around the table, ribbing each other as they downed pints and ate with the speed of starving men.

Scarlett tried hard to join in and feel part of the crowd,

until Kate sauntered over. She could spot a losing battle when she saw one and knew she was about to be beaten by the old friend's hand.

'Don't tell me, it's Marmite and cucumber all over again.' Kate sniffed the sandwich tray like a hound.

'Yup. In Dylan's honour,' Curly Ginger said, picking out a sandwich and passing it to Dylan.

Dylan held it up triumphantly and took a bite. 'And just as wonderful as it always was,' he said, through a mouthful of bread, closing his eyes in exaggerated ecstasy.

'It was all Dylan would eat for school lunches, every single day, until he left school. His poor mum,' Hannah said, directing her comment to Scarlett. 'And no one wanted to sit next to him.'

'Apart from me.' Kate pulled up a stool and plonked herself down next to where Dylan sat opposite Scarlett.

'And it wasn't his Marmite she was after,' Hugo bellowed, guffawing while beaming at everyone, as if waiting for them to appreciate his joke.

An uncomfortable silence followed as Kate glanced over at Dylan, but he was staring toward Scarlett, as she studied Kate.

'This is Scarlett, Kate, she's a friend of mine.' Dylan looked as if he'd just remembered Scarlett was there and was having trouble remembering her name.

Scarlett narrowed her eyes. A friend?

'Pleased to meet you.' Kate swivelled her head toward Scarlett, and her eyes widened – she looked anything but pleased. 'How long have you known Dylan?' she asked, visibly put out.

Scarlett resisted the urge to tell Kate that they'd been in bed together only hours ago – that was how friendly they were. 'Oh, a couple of months.' She hoped Kate wouldn't ask uncomfortable questions. She didn't want to have that conversation, and certainly didn't want to be surrounded by people who knew Dylan far better than she did, sharing old stories. Nor did she wish to discuss her and Dylan's relationship with his ex-girlfriend, if that was what Kate was.

She looked over at Dylan for help but he was preoccupied, discussing a piece of sheet music one of the guys was working on. He took out a pen and started scribbling notes on it.

Scarlett felt totally alone. In fact, returning to London seemed a far better option at that moment, rather than waiting for the backstory of Kate and Dylan to play out, which it surely would, if the drinks kept flowing.

Dylan and Kate were among old friends, whereas it appeared that not even Dylan had time for Scarlett right then. She knew it wouldn't take much for her to crack, and she didn't intend for her fragile state of mind to end up laid wide open for all to see.

She reached down into her bag to check she had her keys. If she left now, she'd be home in three hours and could visit Axel to hear his take on what to say to the journalists. And if she waited until dark to do so, maybe the eager photographers wouldn't be so virulent in their stalking.

'If you'll excuse me, I ought to be getting along,' she said to Kate, hoping to make a clean getaway.

'Oh, that's a shame. Nice to meet you, though.' Delight was written all over her face. She may as well have shooed Scarlett out of the door.

Dylan glanced up briefly, as Scarlett waved generically at the gathering, trying not to draw attention to herself as she slid along the bench. In her estimation, the odds on her being missed were as slight as the odds on Kate not trying to pick up where she and Dylan had left off, the minute Scarlett left the pub.

CHAPTER SIXTEEN

Scarlett was half way down the hill, when she heard someone running behind her. She stopped, unsure whether to be glad, or mad, that Dylan had finally realised she'd gone.

'Scarlett, wait, I'm sorry. I get so single-minded when I'm doing music things. Please don't leave.'

'It's okay, I'm not upset, or anything. It's your time here. I'm just an intrusion. You stay and spend time with your friends, I'll be fine.'

'I thought you'd gone to the bathroom. It wasn't until you'd been gone a while that Kate said you'd left. Why did you leave?'

Scarlett's resolve crumbled. She put her hand up to her head as if it might help clarify her fuzzy and uncoordinated thoughts. It was so hard to work through her emotions when she'd been so resolutely convinced she'd never get involved with a man again. 'Maybe it's best.'

'No, I don't want to hear about what's best. You don't want that, either. Stay, and we'll talk about it – about us.' He scooped up her hand, his eyes pleading. 'Let's go home.' He smacked his head, as if an idea had just occurred to him. 'Was it because of Kate?'

Scarlett sighed. 'She didn't help, admittedly, but then neither did you, when you introduced me as a friend.' Scarlett swallowed back the wobble in her voice, aware that she'd been the one avoiding commitment. 'I'm a bit weary. It makes me emotional, you know?'

'I know. We didn't get much sleep last night.' He peered into her face, trying out a gentle smile to jolly her along. 'Kate is ancient history, but I don't want to hurt her. She still carries a bit of a torch for me, I think.'

'You don't say.' She peered back up the road toward the pub, almost expecting Kate to come bounding after Dylan, her large breasts bouncing as she ran. Suddenly, it seemed silly to have been offended. She sighed, her earlier decisiveness scattering again and regrouping into something more tangible and pleasant. 'Oh, Dylan, I'm sorry, too.' She shook her head. 'I really have no idea why you're putting up with me. I'm a total lost cause.'

'I don't know, either. I've always been a supporter of the underdog, I guess,' he teased. Turning her towards him, he tilted her face upwards with a finger beneath her chin, kissing her briefly. 'Truce?'

'Absolutely.' Her smile was watery at best. 'Let's walk along the beach to the pier, like we said we would.'

Dylan didn't need a second invitation, and he grabbed her hand and led the way, all tension gone. 'I think you should know that this is no ordinary pier. It's the best pier in the country, and I'll show you why, after we've had a coffee.'

They dawdled over their drinks, at peace once more, as they gazed out to where the blustery wind whipped up the waves and sent them crash-landing against the rocks. Intrigued by Dylan's comments, Scarlett craned her neck trying to see along the pier to what was so special about it, but she couldn't see anything out of the ordinary.

Eventually, Dylan drained his coffee cup. 'Right, if you've finished, we have the second part of the Southwold inauguration coming up, with the wonderful Under the Pier show. It's totally silly, but fun.' He stood and took hold of her hand, turning her fingers over. 'You have to push this pretty little hand through some bars and hold it there, while a rabid dog tries to eat it. You okay with that?'

'Totally. Why wouldn't I be?' She blinked big, innocent eyes at him, as he ushered her towards a booth, where a large metal dog's head, its jaws wide open, was positioned inside a cage.

She frowned. 'It's not real, is it, so why wouldn't I manage it?'

Dylan popped two twenty pence pieces in the machine, grinning. 'Go on, then.'

She gave him a patronising look. She could so do it. She stuck her hand in the cage, but winced as warm drool dripped on her fingers.

The dog started shaking as it worked up to a frenzy of snapping and panting, the movement vibrating through her hand.

Wavering, she sent a nervous glance toward Dylan. 'I really don't like it.'

Dylan smirked as she determinedly held her hand steady, while the huge fangs started closing in. The drool increased, turning into a steady stream.

'Yuck, it's horrible,' she wailed. The urge to pull her hand away grew more appealing.

'Thirty seconds to go.' Dylan grinned, making a show of timing her, as her hand trembled.

The dog drooled some more and the panting grew louder as it growled and prepared to bite. Scarlett screamed and whipped her hand away. 'Argghh.' She shook the drool off, laughing. 'I can't believe I flunked it.' She wiped her hand playfully on Dylan's jeans.

'Hey, these are my best.' He twisted away from her, slapping at her hand.

'You have best jeans?' she asked, rubbing the back of her hand on her own jeans. 'God, that was horrible.'

'My turn.' Dylan slid another coin into the machine and kept his hand in for the whole time, as dog drool smeared his fingers and dripped down his elbow.

'You're bound to have mastered it. You've had years of practice.' Scarlett laughed when he tried wiping his hand on her. 'Go away.' She shoved him off, but he caught her around the waist.

'You failed the inauguration, so now you have to bow to my superiority,' he whispered as he nuzzled her ear. 'You can make up for your failings later, though.' He pulled her around to face him and backed her against the wall, drawing her into their private world as he kissed her slowly, until she felt weak with desire and heat pooled in her groin.

'Better stop this, Dylan. We are in public.'

'You're right, but you are so delicious.' He pulled away, whispering, 'Later though,' in her ear. He sighed and straightened. 'Right then, back to business. The next task, should you choose to accept it, is to come face to face with Crankenstein's anger.'

Scarlett, once more, thought it would probably be a breeze. 'This is one nutcase invention, but I can handle it.' Her lips set in determination, as Dylan bought Crankenstein to life and instructed her to turn the handle. A scary metal convict, with stripy uniform and huge eyes, rattled his cage as she turned the large handle at the bottom of the metal bars.

She cranked it harder as Dylan shouted, 'Go faster.'

She glanced over at him. 'What's supposed to happen, it's just a bit of cage rattling? Shit!' She jumped backwards, as Crankenstein roared at her, baring huge teeth, his face popping through the bars. Scarlett put her hand to her chest as her heart raced in fright, panting as the convict slid back to his chair. 'Jeez, nearly gave me a heart attack. It's not funny!' she said, fanning her face.

Dylan slapped his thigh, wheezing with laughter. 'Priceless. We can save the Under the Sea treat for another day.' He threw his arms around her again, hugging her. 'Just the wee-wee men now, and then we can go home.'

The wee-wee men in the water tower sculpture proved to be just as entertaining, as, right on time, the metal statues dropped their trousers and peed on the flowers, while a gathering crowd laughed and tossed coins into the pool of water.

Leaving the bustle of the crowd behind, Dylan and Scarlett strolled to the end of the pier, braving the wind that whipped their clothes flat against their bodies and blew their hair across their eyes.

'These are the plaques I was telling you about,' Dylan said, indicating small brass plaques that lined the wooden balustrade. He rubbed a sleeve across one that was clouded with sea spray.

'Some of these messages are heart rending, aren't they?' Scarlett said, as she ran her fingers over the plaques that would preserve someone's memory forever.

'Yeah, but most are uplifting, and it's a charming way to remember your loved ones.'

'You're just an old romantic at heart.'

'Stick around, you'll be pleasantly surprised.' He kissed her again, lingering and deep, hooking her fleece in his fingers to pull her closer.

'Dylan. Save it for later.' Scarlett pulled away reluctantly, wishing they were warm and cosy in Dylan's bed once again.

'I just can't help it. I want later to be right now.' He kissed her fingers before letting go of her hand. He turned toward where a fisherman sat at the end of the pier. 'How's it going?'

The man pointed to the sea, then up at the sky, and said something Scarlett didn't catch. Dylan laughed, though, and watching him, Scarlett felt her heart twist in a familiar way – the way she thought love might feel, if she had to place a name on the sensation.

Dylan was a good man, and she didn't mind that she was falling in love with him. Indeed, she couldn't help it, even though it scared the hell out of her. As far as she could see, she had two choices: she could stay, or she could go.

She didn't even need to consider which way to jump.

She returned Dylan's usual sunny smile, as he rubbed his hands together and threw a glance over at the sea. 'We could go fishing? I haven't been for years.'

'Um, I've never been fishing, at all. It's a bit blowy, isn't it?' Scarlett shivered and pushed her hands into her pockets.

'Yeah, I guess so. We'd be better off indoors. Will you stay with me tonight?'

She smiled ruefully. 'Yes, please. I'm sorry about my wobble back in the pub. All in all, this has been a great day, Dylan, thank you.'

The sun dipped behind a cloud, as Dylan wrapped his arm around her shoulder and pulled her close, jiggling his eyebrows. 'Wait until tonight, darling, you ain't seen nothing yet.'

She bumped him with her hip. 'You're not supposed to mention such things. It's not gentlemanly.'

'Why not? We are an item now, I take it, since … well since last night. You know?' Once more, he directed intense, querying eyes towards her, his smile gentle but confused.

He certainly was a one-woman man, Scarlett thought, and although she loved the way he assumed their relationship was solid after what they'd shared, she wished she felt as confident. It had moved from a tentative start to full-blown relationship in no time at all, and she'd barely had time to think.

'When we get back to London, I'm going to move house. I can't have my girlfriend staying over in that place,' he continued, his voice indistinct as the wind snatched it away.

Scarlett's eyes widened as she glanced at him. She had never met a man more determined, or so open about wanting her. It was daunting, but actually quite lovely, too.

He caught the look. 'What? You know what I'm like. I saw you, and knew I would make you mine. I also decided to be a singing sensation, and look at me now. I've already been gigging in Camden with my new best friend, Harrison.' He preened and flicked his hair, mocking himself.

Scarlett smiled, although she wished he hadn't mentioned London. She wanted to live in her fantasy bubble a bit longer.

As if sensing this slip in her happiness, Dylan swung her around to face him once more. 'You know, the great Harrison Dominic offered to assign a girl to me. That's the kind of world we live in now.'

'He didn't, did he?' Her sigh was audible that time. 'I hate all of that. And the fakery that surrounds stardom.'

She bunched her hands into fists, stuffing them into her pockets.

'Why do you say it like that?'

'What?'

'Stardom. Like it's a dirty word.'

She let out a shuddering breath, preparing to tell him something that haunted her, even now, although it happened a few years ago. 'I did a tour with a young female pop star a while back. It makes sense for them to hire a private aircraft, so they can sleep properly and no one bothers them for autographs, and stuff. They tend to keep the same crew, so I was a good few months on the road with her, so to speak. I got to know her really well, and I discovered she was mostly friendless and depressed and drank to excess to numb her loneliness, since her meteoric rise to stardom.

'Anyway, she used to beg me for vodka, to steady her nerves, as she put it. Once, I caught her asking the ground staff to nip across to another aircraft and ask them if they had any spare miniatures, because our catering hadn't yet arrived. It got so bad that we were told by her management to offload every drop of booze from the aircraft before she was allowed to board. I can still see her beseeching eyes, and her restless fingers plucking at her clothes, as she became more agitated. She was as pitiful as a thirsty toddler. It was heart-breaking.' Scarlett shook her head as she recalled the memory.

'Poor kid.' Dylan kicked at a stone, chasing it with his toe until he lost interest.

'Yeah, but the worst bit is that, as soon as the concert ended, two heavies would bring vodka and champagne to her hotel room, or onto the aircraft if we were flying back to someplace. Cue a few hours of solid drinking with various hangers-on downing whatever they could, until my cute little star could barely stand.'

'That's terrible. I guess she was an adult, though. You can't blame the management.'

'No, but my point is, they didn't care about her. They just wanted her to remain sober enough to perform on stage, so they made their money. She's in and out of the Priory every other month now and can barely sing a note.'

Dylan looked at the ground as he walked, his hands deep in his pockets. 'I shan't be like that. I don't like vodka.'

Scarlett laughed bleakly. 'That's okay, then. I'm sure you'll be immune to the other hazards of the job.'

'Are you sure you weren't a school teacher in another life? I swear you sound just like my mother.' Dylan swung his arm around her shoulder, pulling her into his side and kissing the top of her head.

'Sorry, I'll shut up now.'

'No, it's fine. I won't be lonely like she was, because I'll have you, and you will no doubt slap my wrists if I step out of line.'

Scarlett really wished he hadn't said that. If only he knew how useless she'd been the one time she was really needed. She bit her lip. It was definitely the right moment to tell him why she'd found it so difficult to start a new relationship, but she was almost sure she'd become emotional, and might even upset Dylan with her revelation.

Regardless, she took a deep breath. 'When we get back to yours, I'd like to talk through something with you,' she told him.

He glanced sidelong at her. 'Is it a good something, or a bad something?'

'Erm, it's just me offloading, really.'

'Cool. I want to know all your thoughts and dreams, and …'

'Yes, I know. I get the idea.' She widened her eyes. 'You want my body and soul, don't you?'

'Yup.' He kissed her forehead. 'So long as you know.'

She smiled as she tucked her head into his shoulder. Dylan would be a good man to have on her side, she was sure of it. She would tell him everything - well, almost everything. And once it was all out in the open, maybe they could move on. Together.

CHAPTER SEVENTEEN

Dylan brought Scarlett to a stop outside the small Spar shop. 'I'll just nip in here for some more wine. We can get a takeaway tonight, if you'd rather stay in?'

'Sounds great,' she assured him.

His hand hovered by the shop door. 'Do you drink red?'

She nodded. 'Red's good.'

'Perfect. 'He pushed open the door and Scarlett waited outside, gazing at the sun as it slipped behind the blue sea. Above it, lumpy grey clouds gathered once more, in the distance.

She glanced through the shop doorway, where she could see Dylan picking up a newspaper, and couldn't help appreciating his long legs in his ripped jeans, and his languid, fluid movements. The friendly smile he gave to the shopkeeper was both sexy and cute, and she found herself lingering over delicious thoughts of what the night held for them both.

Catching her staring, he sent her a very secret-looking smile. Returning the gesture, she realised she was happy that she'd decided to become his one-woman girl, happier still that her life might finally take a new direction.

Coming back from her thoughts, she wondered what was taking Dylan so long and glanced through the doorway of the shop once more. He'd picked up a newspaper, which he'd lifted closer to his eyes to enable him to read it in the dim lighting. He glanced over at the door and caught her eye, but quickly looked away, as once again his gaze was drawn towards the newspaper. Frowning, he raised his head again, and his shock was evident as his troubled eyes locked on to hers.

Immediately, Scarlett knew the story - or non-story, as she saw it - had made the nationals. Closing her eyes for a moment, she wished to God she'd explained her situation earlier, and a clammy, creeping dread crawled over her skin as she thought about what the article would've told him.

He strode out of the shop, the newspaper flapping in the wind as he thrust it towards her. She took a step back, trying to prepare herself for the onslaught as a myriad of emotions closed in on her, her mind darkening with memories she hoped never to have to air again.

'Is this you?' He sounded incredulous. 'It is, isn't it?'

'Yes, Dylan.'

'But you're kissing ... who the hell is this?' His eyes flickered down the page. Again, he waved it in front of her nose. 'What the fuck? And who is this?' He stabbed at another image of Scarlett talking on her phone beside a Range Rover, while a dark-haired man blew her a kiss through the open window. He turned the page, his jaw dropping as he studied the photographs and read the caption. 'The Angel Brothers?' He pushed his hair out of his eyes. 'You knew the Angel Brothers?'

She glanced down at the newspaper. Shit. They'd put in the topless one of her on the beach in Barbados again.

Probably did it out of spite, because she'd refused to talk to the journalist - John, or whatever his name was. She still didn't know where the hell that photo had come from in the first place. A friend who obviously wasn't a friend, she supposed.

She tore the page from Dylan's clenched fingers and glanced quickly through the images. They had certainly gone to town this time.

An image of her stumbling down the aircraft stairs, taken by the journalist a few short days previous, took up a quarter of the page. The headline: Has Sky's ex fallen for Axel? was in bold capitals, with a picture of Sky's brother, Axel, embracing her outside the jail.

She shook her head in disgust at how low the newspaper would sink. 'Put it back, Dylan.' She shoved the crumpled newspaper into his chest.

He almost let it drop to the ground, but grabbed at it and screwed it up into his fist at the last moment.

She took in his horrified face, his hurt eyes and his hunched shoulders. His knuckles whitened as he hugged the newspaper to his chest. 'Put it back, and I'll tell you the full story. The truth.'

His face contorted with anguish. 'No, I can't. I have to read it for myself.' Stepping back into the store, he tossed some money on the counter.

After flattening out the paper's pages and shoving it under his arm, he marched on ahead of her, his strides long and purposeful.

Struggling to keep up with him, Scarlett eventually fell behind, as his fury appeared to give him Olympian strength in his legs.

He stormed up the path, and she followed him meekly. He looked as if he wanted to slam the front door in her face, and for a minute, she hoped he would. It would be so much easier to run away from the confrontation she knew was coming, than to confess that she was a hopeless girlfriend who didn't deserve anyone's love.

Swallowing hard to dispel the lump in her throat, she wondered how ready she was to talk about Sky, although it had been two years since he'd died. Two whole years of grief and regret, the desperation of missing him almost defeating her. He wasn't coming back - ever, no matter how many vivid dreams she had, from which she awoke with a smile on her face, only to have the terrible truth overwhelm her once more.

Dreams where Sky caught her around the waist, whispering words of love, where he celebrated his latest chart success, watching her laugh as he poured champagne into a slim flute until it overflowed. Dreams where he punched the air, as his latest song was broadcast live on television to a screaming audience. The illusion that Sky was still alive was always just under the surface of her waking moments, but she knew it would be too surreal for Dylan to understand. No one could understand it, unless they had stood in her shoes.

She'd hoped the lump of stone that had become her heart might've thawed, the weight of her guilt and sorrow that had dragged her down every single day eradicated by Dylan's love and sincerity. Her grieving days were almost done, but her chance for happiness was slipping away before she'd even told Dylan that she wanted to be his one and only.

Dylan slammed through the rooms, depositing the wine on to the table, the newspaper and his keys following with a thwack. He whirled around to face her his eyes flinty. 'I don't fucking believe this. You were screwing Axel Angel, until he got sent down. That's what your big mystery is. Were you just biding your time until he came out of jail? Was that why you were so coy, playing the poor me, I'm not sure I'm ready for this angle, making me think you were virtuous?' He paced the floor, running his fingers through his hair as he turned towards her, eyes blazing. 'And me, stupid dummy that I am, trying to play it straight, trying to make sure I wasn't pushing you too soon, or too hard. Not only that, but it seems half the world knows about you and him, and I'm the only idiot who doesn't. Even sodding Marcus knows, and he's away with the fairy's half the time.'

He unscrewed the lid from the wine bottle and tipped the wine into two huge glasses. The liquid glugged too quickly from the bottle's almost vertical position, spilling wine over the table, but he didn't seem to notice.

He took a slug and worried at his forehead with the tips of his fingers before running a hand across the back of his neck. 'I asked you if there was someone else. I asked you, twice.' His anger seemed to suddenly deflate, and he slumped into a wooden chair by the kitchen table. 'Oh, Scarlett. Why?' It seemed like the whole gamut of emotion was in that one word.

She'd asked herself the same question so many times. 'It was Sky, not Axel. My boyfriend. Just to put you straight.'

Dylan looked up at her through anguished eyes, as he dragged his fingers down his face. 'But this photo was taken last week, it says so here.'

'That one is a photo of Axel, Sky's younger brother who's just been released from jail. We were hugging. It was totally innocent. You can see how similar they are in looks.' She sank into a chair by the table and gulped at her own wine. 'As you probably know, Sky is dead. It's a dreadful story, Dylan, and I'm afraid I'm still coming to terms with it.'

Dylan's demeanour softened as he took in her words and her obvious distress, but he didn't reach out for her, or speak, just gripped his wine glass as if his life depended on it.

Lips pressed together, she summoned up her composure, waiting until she could control the quiver in her voice before taking a deep breath to begin. 'Sky and his band used our aircraft on a summer tour of America. I went to every show and hovered around backstage, because there was little else to do. The pilots did their own thing after each flight, so I was basically on my own.

There are only so many galleries and shopping malls a person can visit before they run out of things to do. Anyway, I got close to him – to Sky. I ran around for him and cheered him on, and eventually we became lovers.

'But we had to be secret lovers. Because I'd have been sacked, as having a relationship with a client is strictly forbidden, and Sky wanted to be seen as a bit of a player for his adoring fans.' She swigged back another mouthful of wine and glanced at Dylan, who sat immobile opposite her.

'Sky was photographed with beautiful woman all over America, while I smiled in the background, hurting and feeling slightly ridiculous.' She blinked hard to allay the burn of tears that gathered behind her eyes. 'That auspicious start to our relationship was the way it played out the whole time. For four years, I faded into the background, pretending I didn't mind seeing his hand on some other woman's bottom as he kissed her – strictly for the camera, of course.

'We were an item to everyone who knew us, but outside our circle of friends, I was cited as his PA. My airline was okay about it, once the tour was over, until the drug abuse stories started circulating. That was when they suggested that I either disassociated myself with him, or find alternative employment.' Her cheeks burned with embarrassment as she thought back to the humiliating conversation she'd had with the human resources department. She patted her scalding cheeks with the back of her hand in an effort to cool them down.

As she glanced at Dylan to see how he was taking her revelation, he seemed unable to even look at her. Instead, he focussed on the dregs of his wine, swirling it around in the bottom of his glass as he bit his lower lip.

Despite his evident struggle, his decency won through within moments, and he placed a hand over her own. 'I'm so sorry – for everything,' he said.

She shouldn't really have expected Dylan's initial reaction to have been any different than it was. As far as he was concerned, he'd seen the evidence of her betrayal right in front of him, but still it hurt that he hadn't given her the benefit of the doubt.

She shook her head. 'Don't be. The whole relationship was a mess by the end, but I didn't want him to die.' As she said the words, the usual twist of desolation and grief hit her, as it did whenever she remembered that dreadful day. She drained her glass, and as Dylan refilled it with a steadier hand than minutes before, she stood up to gaze out of the bay window, not wanting to look at him as she divulged the sad story of Sky's addiction.

'Short version?' she said quietly. 'Sky started using heroin. And Axel, being the doting younger brother that he was, sorted out a constant supply. Sky became a total junkie. He was abusive, incoherent, devious, and, finally, unbearable. Before we destroyed each other, he destroyed himself.' She choked back the last few words, determined not to let Dylan see how much they hurt. 'Axel was jailed for supplying. I think he was maxed out of his head, too.' She shrugged. 'I was there for him, that was all. He was just a kid who adored his brother. Seems a bit stupid to jail someone for loving a person so much they'd do anything for them, even if they killed them with what they thought was their kindness.'

'And the newspaper wanted to dig some dirt because Axel was let out of jail last week?' Dylan asked.

'Pretty much, I guess. He was let out early, and he called me, because he still hasn't made peace with his mother. The press found out and, I think, looking at the photographs, were trying to insinuate that we were having a relationship.' Silently, she begged for him not to question if the allegation held any truth. For that, she wouldn't have been able to forgive him.

'It was a journalist hanging around outside your flat?' he asked quietly.

She breathed out in relief that he was no longer on the defensive. 'And a couple of photographers. Two-faced bastards, the lot of them, trying to make out they were on my side. Last time, they even managed to find a photo of me with the young alcoholic popstar I mentioned to you earlier, as if I was somehow responsible for her condition.' Exhaling, she turned away from the window. She was bone weary and just wanted to go home, but she owed Dylan enough to at least explain herself. 'They probably hoped that Axel would come back to mine. That would give them a great story, right? You know how big the Angel Brothers were – there are still people who would find a story like that interesting.'

Dylan drained his own glass and sloshed more wine into it, before he raised it to his lips and swallowed half of it in one go. A blip of time passed as he stared out of the window. He closed his eyes as if struggling with what he wanted to say next. 'I'm sorry for your loss, and for my reaction. I should have trusted you.'

Scarlett blinked back tears. 'They tried every way they could to incriminate me, and I don't even know why. They seemed to hate me.'

'What happened afterwards?'

'I was questioned by the police. They assumed that I had to be implicated for the sheer fact that I flew to foreign countries. Bit of an arse over tit way of thinking, if you ask me. You can get drugs outside the local Co-op, if you want to stand there long enough for the hoodies to turn up.'

'And how did you end up at StarJet?'

'The usual. Who you know, not what you know. A friend of a friend. Hence why I'm always careful not to upset Todd, I suppose. I have form.' She smiled, but it felt lopsided.

Dylan nodded. 'And Axel?'

Scarlett didn't like the way he said his name, but she didn't rise to the bait. 'He'll always be welcome in my life, Dylan. I can't do otherwise. He loved Sky, and I loved Sky.'

Dylan's mouth twisted. 'Have you arranged to see him again?'

'I have his mobile number, and yes, is the answer to that. I won't turn him away if he needs me.' She thrust her chin out, daring him to argue, but Dylan's shoulders slumped, the fight seeming to drain out of him.

He dropped to his knees by Scarlett's feet. 'Do you still miss Sky?'

'It was the worst time of my life, watching him destroy himself and the love we used to share, and being totally helpless to stop it. It was as if a demon was living inside him and wouldn't let him go until he was finished.' The words were whispered as her tears finally spilled over her eyelashes. She put her hand over her mouth as choking sobs, unladylike and raw, made her double over.

Sniffing, she wiped her sleeve across her face, smearing tears and mascara over her cheeks. 'I'm sorry. I think I'm all better, and then wham - it hits me again, as if it just happened.'

She glanced towards the big window. Beyond it, the huge expanse of sky and sea called to her like freedom, although she knew she could never escape her own mind, no matter how far she travelled.

From below, Dylan watched her, his face both honest and trusting. She knew she would have to leave him before he became embroiled in the mess that was her life.

'You're just starting out, Dylan. You don't need to be drawn into the legacy that Sky left, and you surely will, if you stick around with me.' Her words set her off crying again. It was too unfair that Sky could stop her from loving again, even from the grave.

'No way. I'm not letting you cop out so easily.' Standing, Dylan gathered her into his chest and pulled her onto his lap, as her sobs and gulps filled the air.

She buried her face in his shirt, while he smoothed her hair and whispered into her neck.

'Shh, shush, it's all going to be okay. You have me now.'

She raised her head. 'You say that now, but how long until the temptations of your new life rear their heads? The all-night parties where you'll get totally off your face, and you'll tell me you're really sorry you slept with whoever, but you were drunk, so that's okay.'

Dylan sighed. 'We're not back to that again, are we?' His eyes bore into hers. 'Scarlett, please listen to me. I'm not Sky, okay? I feel as if I've been sentenced and immediately found guilty. I don't even have a contract, and already I'm a condemned man.'

Scarlett swallowed and swiped at her eyes with the heel of her hand. 'I've seen it happen too many times.' She shook her head. 'I'm not sure I can cope with it all again, Dylan. I'm not as strong as I was.'

'I'll be strong for both of us. Trust me.' He rested his chin on the top of her head and tightened his arms around her shoulders. 'I should've realised there was a reason you disliked my guitar. I saw you giving it evils the day I first spoke to you in the café. Yeah, I'm not as dumb as I seem.'

She appreciated his attempt at humour and raised her head, smiling wanly.

'That's better. You know what, I think this day has been a bit much for you. Why don't I run you a bath? I know mum has some outrageously expensive bath oil she won't mind sharing. I'll rustle up some food and find another bottle of wine. Yes?'

'Sounds perfect.'

'We can get past this, Scarlett. Do you trust me?'

She nodded with a sniff and snuggled closer to Dylan, who stroked her arms and crooned reassuring words into her ear. She stayed cocooned in his cotton wool embrace, until the tears had slowed and she was ready to leave the safe haven of his arms.

'Better?' He peered into her eyes, and she blinked away the last of the tears.

'Yes, thank you.'

'Good.' He tipped her gently off his lap. 'I'll run you that bath.'

He disappeared into the bathroom, and she undressed, wanting only to lose herself in the heat and warmth of deep water and later, Dylan's love. She padded into the bathroom after wrapping a towel around her body, oddly coy about showing her naked self to Dylan.

Dylan turned off the taps and sloshed bath oil into the water, giving her a shy smile as he left. 'Take as long as you want.'

She waited until he'd left before submerging herself in the warm water, the delicious scent of freesia wafting up through the steam. She hoped Dylan's mother would forgive him for using so much of her Jo Malone bath oil as she relaxed, feeling the tension in her shoulders and the knots in her stomach unravel.

Eventually she was roused by Dylan knocking on the door. 'Scarlett, are you okay?' he called.

She hauled herself out of the water. 'Yes, just getting out.'

'No chance of an invitation to join you, then?'

Scarlett folded a huge towel around her body and opened the door. 'No chance, cheeky.' She flicked the corner of her towel at him and headed for the bedroom, doing a double-take, as Dylan followed her across the hallway. She gave him a dirty look, but he ignored it. 'Can I help you with something?'

Dylan grinned. 'I know I should leave you in peace. I really do know that, but I don't seem able to.'

'You think I'm going to dress while you watch?'

'A man can dream.' He took a step towards her. 'I personally think the best plan is to do away with the whole getting dressed thing and cut to the chase. I could pick you up, all macho-like, take you to bed, and kiss you all better.'

'Erm ... well ... that sounds interesting.'

He fixed her with a look so full of tenderness and longing that she couldn't have turned him down any more than she could have turned down a stray dog looking for a home.

He ran his fingers lightly down her arm, angling his head, lips so close to her ear that she shivered when he whispered, 'It is a good idea, isn't it?'

His breath on her neck made her quiver, and she leaned into him, the perfect antidote for her melancholy. 'I think it's one of your better ideas, yes,' she whispered into his shoulder. If she could lose herself in the wonders of Dylan's body until the only emotion that bombarded her was love, or lust - preferably both - then all would be well with the world once more.

'That's good to hear.' He scooped her up and carried her to the bedroom, kissing her as he walked, laughing as he tried to manoeuvre the steps without tipping her out of his arms.

He set her down in his bedroom, drew the curtains, and as he switched on a sidelight, an image of Batman lit up across the wall.

Scarlett had to laugh. 'This is your idea of a seduction?'

'Damn that Batman light. I'd forgotten all about it. I've had it since I was ten. We don't want him to watch, do we?' He pulled his tee-shirt over his head and aimed it at the light, dowsing the image.

They faced each other, and Dylan brushed her hair from her face as he gazed into her eyes. His eyes had never been clearer, telling her that she could trust him. That he was there for her.

With her gaze locked on his, Scarlett slowly undid the knot that kept her towel in place and let it drop to the floor. Dylan's eyes swept the length of her naked body, and he swallowed. His eyes softened as his body reacted.

He took a hesitating step towards her, pushing his fingers through her hair as he drew her close. 'God, you are so beautiful,' he whispered, grazing her ear with his lips.

She shivered at his breath, light and teasing. His kisses sparked over her neck and blazed down her throat, as he ran his hands across her arms and over her still damp breasts, cupping them gently as if he was scared he might break her. He smoothed his hands lower to her waist, around her back, and down to her bottom, his touch firm and determined, as if he needed to reassure himself that everything was in the right place.

Her legs quivered as heat gathered inside her, and she placed the flat of her hands against his chest to remain stable. His chest was firm and muscular, something she'd barely had time to notice the night before in the intensity of the moment.

He caught her hands in his, holding them close to his chest for what seemed like an age, as if they were making a silent pact. Slowly, he released her, and his fingers started to explore her curves once more, starting at the column of her throat and trailing down to her breast, tracing the areola before moving across to her nipple like a will o' the wisp, not quite landing anywhere, but leaving a memory of a feather light touch and burning heat.

He trailed his fingers past her stomach and down lower, tracing the contours of her figure. Scarlett breathed in sharply as he explored the intimate folds of her body, all the while locking her with his eyes. Heat engulfed her, and she just about managed to stay upright as an exquisite explosion pulsed through her whole body, Dylan's fingers teasing out an unstoppable orgasm. She gasped and threw her head back, her breasts pressing against his chest as he held her tight and kissed her.

Her nerve ends tingled, and her stomach flipped so many times it was like being on a rollercoaster. She was vulnerable in her nakedness, but she felt desired, loved, and it made her tremble with a longing to feel Dylan inside her body.

Dylan dipped his head to her nipple, pulling and teasing it with his lips, tasting with his tongue, one hand firmly pressed into her back as the other caressed her breast, and she inhaled a sharp breath. Finally, he gathered her up and laid her on the bed, and a long shiver escaped her as she gave herself up to Dylan.

'I told you this would be a night to remember, didn't I?' he whispered, his breath fanning her throat that was slicked with sweat.

'You're not doing too badly, so far,' she whispered.

Her heart beat so hard from his touch, she could hear it pulsing in her ears. She reached out for him in the quiet darkness, as he lay down next to her, her fingers rippling lightly over his skin. She inhaled his scent, scared for a fleeting moment that she might have to commit it to memory, before she remembered he was going nowhere. He was not Sky, and she was going to trust him with her heart and her body.

Dylan's eyes met hers in the dusky night, as a faded, yellow Batman shimmered against the wall, lighting their contours as they began another slow adoration of each other's bodies, their eyes scouring each other, until Dylan's lips trailed past her throat to taste all of her, once more. They moved in unison, touching, tasting and treasuring each other, until finally they both shuddered and stilled, satiated and complete, in each other's arms.

Cocooned together in the single bed, Dylan pulled her ever closer into his chest, whispering endearments and stroking her stomach, sounding sleepier with every uttered word, until his voice drifted away on a half-finished sentence.

Scarlett didn't think she'd ever felt so at peace as she lay in his arms, but she found it hard to sleep, as she fought off expected, but unasked for, images of Sky, an almost nightly occurrence since he'd died.

Sky, still alive in her head, gorgeously ruffled, dark and dangerous, casual with her offered love, taking it when he felt like it, and towards the end, cruelly taunting her when he didn't. She bit her lip as the darkness surrounding them deepened into blackness, Dylan's breath already steadying in slumber.

She should have been able to exorcise Sky's memory by now, surely. As steady tears trickled on to her pillow, she swallowed down any attempt to sob, desperate not to make a murmur to wake Dylan. What had happened with Sky had passed two long years ago, and so long as Scarlett held any kind of control, history wouldn't repeat itself. She'd make sure of that.

CHAPTER EIGHTEEN

By the time Scarlett stirred, she was alone, but the distant sound of footsteps padding around upstairs gave her a vague idea of Dylan's whereabouts. As the memory of last night hit her instantly, she burrowed into the duvet, content to do no more than think about Dylan. That she was falling in love with him would be scary, if it wasn't for the fact that he was Dylan.

She stretched languidly. Being loved again was good for the soul, that was for sure.

The smell of coffee and warm bread finally roused her from his bed, and she made her way into the kitchen, where Dylan was already eating toast and reading at the table.

'Good morning.' He bestowed a smile upon her and indicated the coffee machine. 'Help yourself. There's fresh bread by the toaster.'

'Hi.' She was a bit put out that he didn't jump up to kiss her or offer to make her breakfast, but she swallowed it down and headed for the coffee machine. 'What on earth is on that toast? It smells gross.'

'Peanut butter and banana. Good for energy.' His gaze didn't leave the newspaper.

Scarlett frowned at his pre-occupation as he read last night's newspaper. 'Dylan, please don't read that article again.'

'Oh, I wasn't. I was just reading the sports page, but then something caught my eye.' He folded up the newspaper in a way that made one article stand out. 'Look. He called me a few minutes ago, wants me to appear on a national television show that's well loved by housewives of a certain age. Not exactly the audience I had in mind when I started this thing, but anyway.' He stabbed at the newspaper. 'What a coincidence.'

Scarlett reluctantly peered at the article he pointed to, wishing she'd had the forethought to throw the newspaper in the bin, or even set fire to it, to make sure it had gone forever.

On the page, a small picture of Harrison Dominic, sitting in a flash car, had been positioned incongruously next to a grim picture of Sky's body being removed from the ambulance. She hated that the paper had seen fit to republish that, regardless of how insensitive it might be. Underneath the picture of Harrison was a brief one-liner. Sky was one of the good guys; it's a terrible tragedy, but he has left us the great legacy of his music.

Scarlett closed her eyes, wondering how she'd managed to miss that article yesterday. She fervently wished Dylan had missed it, too.

'It's weird that he's also my manager, isn't it?' He flicked at the page. 'It occurred to me that you must have known him - could even call him up, if you needed a favour, perhaps?'

Belatedly, she realised that his smile was steely, false, and edged with anger. She swallowed down the bitter taste rising up in her mouth. 'Yes, how strange,' she managed weakly, as she picked up a mug from the draining board and poured out fresh, hot coffee, the delicious aroma filling the air.

Dylan pushed his chair back and remained staring at her, a comic rictus of a smile on his face. He blinked. 'Well?'

'Well, what?' She poured milk into her coffee and busied herself with the toaster, hiding her face from Dylan.

'Well, what? Is that all you have to say?'

She rounded on him. 'Don't talk to me as if I'm a kid who needs chastising.'

'And don't you try to instigate some kind of self-righteous anger to deflect the bloody obvious.' The smile had disappeared, replaced by a raw anger that she couldn't really fathom.

She shrugged. 'I was trying to help you.'

'So, you let me call on you, late at night, to bounce around your flat like Tigger, telling you my news, when you knew all along? Let me show off to my friends, believing that my raw talent was enough to snag a top manager. Me, bigging it up in the pub, and Mac, silly sod that he is, actually being proud of me, thinking I'd managed it through merit alone. You must have been laughing your socks off behind my back.'

'No, Dylan, never.' She raised her mug to her lips, holding it tight with her trembling fingers to stop from sloshing coffee onto the floor. His calm fury was worse than his anger, and she felt ill equipped to deal with it, especially when she hadn't been expecting it.

'Now I think of it, how naive of me to think it would all pull together so easily. I meet a famous producer, and within weeks, I've got gigs booked up, and I'm calling him on the phone as if he's my best mate and …' He gave a small laugh. 'And eating sausage rolls straight out of the paper bag with him.' He stared at her bleakly. 'You know him well?'

She nodded.

'And you never said a bloody word.' He drawled out the sentence, his disdain clear. 'I could have done this thing on my own, eventually. I didn't need your help, you know.' He pushed to his feet, his eyes flinty.

'No, you couldn't.' She flashed anger straight back at him. 'Have you any idea how hard it is to break in to the music industry without an in by someone in the know? Grow up. You would have been playing on the streets for years, if I hadn't helped you out.'

'So, because you slept with a superstar, you'd know all about these things, would you?'

She stared at him in horror, before slumping. They hadn't even had breakfast together, before the spectre of Sky raised his ghostly head. 'How dare you bring that up?' She slammed her cup down on the table and pulled her shirt tight across her breasts. She'd carelessly thrown it on, not even fastening the buttons, half hoping that she would tempt Dylan back to bed.

How quickly things change, she thought.

She drew herself up to her full height. 'I didn't want to go out with you, remember? You were the one who chased me. I barely knew you when I spoke to Harrison. I was just doing a favour for the friendly busker boy whose feelings I'd hurt by turning him down. I thought it was the least I could do – and I did it because I wanted to help, no other reason.' Her mouth twisted as she tried to maintain her stance, but it was hard to sustain.

'And there was not one minute, in the time we've been together, when you thought it might be a good idea to tell me this?' He threw the folded newspaper on the table. 'I thought we trusted each other.'

Anger flared from deep within her. 'Trust? Hah!' He had no idea how hard it had been for her to put her trust in another man. 'You know what I should have trusted? I should have trusted my instincts and kept right away from you. This thing –' She stabbed her finger at the newspaper '– and this man I loved, will always come between us, because you can't handle it.'

'It's not about him, at all. It's about truth and honesty.'

'Bollocks, is it. It's about you using such qualities as a weapon to keep me in line, demanding fealty to the Mighty Lord who expects absolute devotion. You can't bear the thought of me having had a relationship before you.' Her anger choked her – she didn't even know where the words had come from. She'd thought herself in love with him only minutes before.

'How much more is there to tell me, Scarlett? What else are you hiding?' His voice dripped icy anger and contempt, as if he hadn't heard her words, but just wanted to twist the knife he'd already plunged into her heart.

Scarlett sighed, her own emotions shifting to calm acceptance as the inevitable outcome of their argument took shape.

Dylan must have sensed the change, because his own anger seemed to dissipate, and a pleading tone crept in as he repeated, 'I thought you trusted me.'

She tried to hide her desolation that, once again, she'd failed. 'I thought I trusted you, too.'

Dylan took a half step toward her, but she didn't want to know if he intended to placate her or rant at her. She didn't care. She wanted out.

As tears threatened, she stormed out of the room and down the stairs. She pulled on the rest of her clothes, casting a last, sad look at the crumpled bed where she had spent the most magical night of her life. It was too much.

After pushing the bedroom door shut to keep Dylan out, she threw the few things she'd unpacked into her bag. She checked her face in the mirror determined not to let Dylan see how much he'd hurt her. Dragging her fingers through the mess of her hair, she pasted on a smile and pulled the door open.

Dylan, clearly agitated, paced at the top of the stairs and lunged towards her as she emerged from his room. 'I'm sorry, Scarlett, I don't know what I was thinking.'

She shook her head in sorrow. 'For a couple who were supposed to be falling in love, we appear to have argued more than is traditional, don't you think? That's not right, is it?'

'I was pissed off. Am I not allowed to be?'

'Yes, of course you are. It's just that ...' She shook her head again as words failed her. She put her hand to her forehead, sweeping her fringe out of the way. 'I don't think any of this was a good idea. But it's okay.'

'It is?' His relief was palpable as he moved to take her overnight bag out of her hand.

She waved him away. 'No, I won't stay. Probably stayed too long, as it is. I need to ...' She jerked her thumb towards the hallway, her mouth twisting in pain. 'It's best,' she added.

Dylan's smile of gratitude faded. 'No, it's not best, for either of us. Don't leave, please. We can sort this out.'

'We really can't. It's plain to see how this will end, and I don't think my heart could bear to go through it again. You were my first since … since, you know.' She inclined her head towards the table where the newspaper had been ripped and scrunched up. 'If this was no more than an exercise to see how I would fare, let loose on the circuit, as it were, it would be deemed a success. I've proved I'm not up to the task.'

'No, it's my fault, Scarlett – all mine.'

She shook her head sadly. 'And I wouldn't relish being left on the side-lines again, being needy and pathetic because my boyfriend is famous and every other woman wants a piece of him. At least I know one thing for sure, Dylan, Harrison was happy to help, but he wouldn't waste time with you, if you didn't have what it takes. I just gave you a leg up.' She pushed herself up on her toes and kissed him on the cheek. 'For which, it appears, I am supposed to be sorry.' Despite it feeling as though her heart was bleeding out, she fixed on a wan smile. 'Good luck, although I don't think you'll need it.'

She headed down the hallway, opened the front door, and pressed her key fob. The Audi lights flashed as the car came to life, and for a moment she faltered, suddenly hoping that Dylan would find a way back for them both, wishing she could turn the clock back.

Dylan followed her down the hallway, and she turned to him in panic, but he just pushed his hands into his pockets and stared bleakly at the Audi, refusing to meet her eyes. 'This was all a game to you, wasn't it? The bit you never intended to happen was for us to be together.'

'Believe that, if it makes you happy.' She drew herself up, thrust out her chin, and marched down the pathway. 'Stupid bastard,' she muttered, as she snatched open the car door. Once she'd thrown her bag on the passenger seat, she settled herself into the car, hoping that her blurred vision would clear before she set off on the long haul home.

Her tears showed no sign of abating, though, and waiting until she'd rounded the corner, where she was sure Dylan couldn't see her, she fumbled for the tissues in the glove box. She grabbed the whole box. Something told her she'd need them all before she reached the sterile safety of her home once more.

CHAPTER NINETEEN

Dylan arrived at Liverpool Street station three weeks later, never being less pleased to see London in his life. He normally took on board the buzz that was his chosen city, the minute he arrived, but this time it just looked dirty and noisy.

When he hauled himself back to the hovel he called home, he saw that, too, with fresh eyes. It was a disgrace that grown adults lived there, and he would stay true to his word and move out as soon as he could, even though Scarlett was no longer part of his life.

He was fed up with being miserable, and with missing Scarlett, and refused to believe that what they had together wasn't worth saving. He'd decided to win her back, but he was stumped as to how to go about it. He was also due in the television studio, to be figuratively mauled by a scary television presenter at the weekend, but he'd been toying with calling it a day and getting a sensible teaching job, as his mother had advocated. Except, he couldn't even be bothered to think about a different career option, couldn't summon up enthusiasm for anything much, apart from pining the loss of Scarlett. He was becoming exceptionally good at that, he noted.

He hauled his rucksack up on his shoulder and hoisted his guitar across his back, steeling himself for the next part of his journey. He glanced at his phone, wondering whether it was worth pretending to Scarlett that he hadn't noticed she was ignoring his calls.

Hi Scarlett, guess who's back in town?

He texted, ending the message with a smiley face. He stared at it for a moment, then deleted it with a sigh. No way would she fall for that.

Leaving the flat, he re-acquainted himself with the London he used to love, dazed by the teeming throngs of people jostling and talking loudly. He really wasn't sure what to do next, as getting Scarlett to speak to him was as likely as his fellow lodgers finding jobs. He had few choices, none of them particularly appealing, and he narrowed them quickly down: getting trashed in the pub, or hovering around his old patch to see if Beanie turned up with Scrappy-doo. At least he'd make Beanie laugh by telling him about his new role as Housewife's Favourite, rather than Pinup God to beautiful young women, and he would always have a friend in Scrappy-doo so long as he had biscuits in his pocket.

It seemed like a lifetime ago that his days had consisted of singing on the streets and pulling pints, he thought, as he stared at the empty space where he used to play, conjuring up an image of Beanie tinging his ridiculous triangle. He could also picture Scarlett, as she'd passed by on that fateful day, toying with her hair as she chatted on her mobile. The very moment he had fallen for her.

He swallowed the lump in his throat, and the knife edge of pain that was permanently lodged in his breastbone twisted savagely. 'Decision made. The pub, it is,' he said to the empty air, before the hopelessness of his mission overwhelmed him once more.

He pushed on the door to the Dog and Duck, painting on a smile even though his heart was heavy.

'Hey, if it isn't the Superstar himself. How's it hanging?'

'Mac, no one says that in real life.' He gazed around the almost empty bar. 'Looks like you missed me.'

'Sod off, did we. Where've you been?'

'Ha, so you did miss me.' Dylan leapfrogged onto one of the barstools, momentarily pleased that at least someone wanted his company.

'Only because we ran out of things to talk about. What's new?'

'I don't have much to tell, sadly.'

"But you are still on the way - you know, stardom, and all that?'

'Yeah, I guess.'

'Beats me what they see in you.' Mac's eyes glittered with the prospect of taking the piss out of Dylan.

'Yeah, you're rubbish,' Stanley joined in, poking Dylan in the ribs and grinning. He laughed into Dylan's face, his mouth like a black cave with a few resident stalactites glinting dully in the darkness.

He knew they were joking, or at least he hoped they were, but it really wasn't what he wanted to hear right at that moment, knowing what a fraud he was. 'A pint and a whisky chaser, please, Mac.'

Mac pulled a face, but obliged, shaking his head when Dylan produced some coins. 'This one is on the house, Superstar, as I'm getting these vibes that all is not as well as it should be in the Dylan camp.'

'You could say that, Mac. Cheers.' It seemed ironic that his friends had decided on such a nickname for him. If only they knew. He took a slug of the whisky, hoping the fierce burn would eradicate his pain. It looked as if it might, as he drank steadily, watching the minute hand tick by on the clock over the bar. He became more morose as he drank, even though he finished off two packets of crisps and a bag of nuts in the vain hope that they'd stave off the after-effects of five whiskies and three pints of lager.

By the time he rose unsteadily from his stool, he was pretty drunk and glad of it. It certainly took the pain away, and it occurred to him that whisky might just become his new best friend.

Deciding not to go home to little more than an overflowing bin of rubbish and a television that spent most of its life hidden behind the sofa, in case the TV licence man came to call, he took a left turn out of the pub, then a right, until the advert hoardings and double decker buses fell away, and he was left with a warren of thin roads, lined with depressing-looking shops. He was completely lost, he realised, and very, very tired.

He passed a tramp in the doorway of a dress agency shop, mingling in with the faded browns of the late autumn leaves gathering around him - a barely noticeable person, incongruously drab, next to a window filled with bright, gaudy clothes. Dylan was quite comfortable with down-and-outs – they made up half of the clientele in the Snug at Mac's pub, after all – but he could imagine what the shopkeeper would think if she knew what her doorway was used for, once they'd shut up shop.

A thatch of wild, white hair tumbled around the ruddy, wind-weathered cheeks of the tramp. His lips, dry and chapped, were just about visible under a wiry, grubby beard, but his eyes twinkled, as if he still had a story or two left in him. Dylan felt the pull of his gaze drawing him into the doorway, like the Ancient Mariner fixing him with his glittering eye.

The tramp rattled his tin towards Dylan, who flopped down wearily onto the hard step. 'I've got nothing for you, mate. Or me, either, come to that,' Dylan muttered, deep in his own thoughts. 'I could keep you company for a while, though, and maybe we could have a bit of a chat to cheer ourselves up.'

'And you'd be more than welcome,' the old man said, bundling his greasy-looking sleeping bag on to his knees to make way for Dylan. 'Fergal is my name, and I'm very pleased to meet you.' He thrust out a hoary hand, and Dylan wrapped it in his. A cushion and a blanket appeared out of the depths of a heap of rags. 'Here, put this over you, and you'll stay nice and warm.'

Dylan looked at the blanket dubiously. He was all for sharing, but could do without fleas to add to his misery.

Even so, he did as the man said, and it was surprisingly cosy once he was out of the wind. 'I'm Dylan,' he said. 'Thanks very much for your hospitality.'

'So, what made you choose this salubrious establishment, tonight?' The man's eyes positively shone with interest towards his new visitor.

'Oh, Trip Advisor said it was one of the best doorways around.' Dylan's laugh was over loud, his state of drunkenness dulling his internal volume monitor.

Fergal's face screwed up in confusion. 'Eh?'

'Sorry, life, the universe, and everything ganging up on me.' His eyes were growing heavy, his lids drooping, the weight of alcohol and sleep dragging them over his eyes. Nausea washed upwards from his stomach as the floor appeared to move from underneath him.

He snapped his eyes open and swayed, disorientated. He leaned into the solid shoulder of Fergal. 'Oops, might have to stay awhile longer.' He righted himself and stuffed the pillow behind his head against the wall. 'This is shit, man.'

'Yeah. I wouldn't recommend it, to be honest,' Fergal said, patting Dylan's knee. His nails were grimy and long, like witch's talons. They reminded Dylan of something. What was it? He tried to dredge up his thoughts in a coherent order. It was something to do with his stylist. He snapped his fingers. 'That's it, the Wicked Witch of the West. She is deffo green underneath that makeup. 'S'not fooling me.'

'Me, neither,' Fergal said, equably. He took a swig

from a bottle that he slid from his voluminous trousers, before it disappeared again as fast as any magicians conjuring trick. Evidently, he had little intention of sharing it anytime soon. He smacked his lips together, snorted, and rubbed his sleeve across his nose.

Dylan tried not to grimace as he leaned away from his new soul mate. 'Thing is, my girlfriend, who only just became my girlfriend, dumped me. Plus, I was on track to be a singing sensation, but I found out it was all based on lies, and now I don't want to be one, even if I could, which I probably couldn't, 'cause I'm crap, and everyone has been laughing at me for believing I was good.' He directed his thoughts at Fergal, who gave every indication of listening carefully. 'But I don't know what's left, if I don't have my music, or Scarlett.'

Fergal nodded sagely, stroking his wiry beard. 'The answer is not at the bottom of a glass, you know.' Once again, his bottle appeared and disappeared just as quickly.

Dylan grinned in the darkness. 'Do as I say, not as I do,' he mumbled, quoting one of his mother's favourite sayings. It was just as well that the thought of drinking anymore alcohol made his stomach turn over. In fact, he'd probably never drink again. 'I'm just drowning my sorrows, I don't think I have a problem, although listening to Scarlett, you'd think I'd signed up for every vice going. She didn't even give me a chance. I thought ...' He screwed up his face, trying to remember what, exactly, it was he'd thought, in his moment of inspiration.

Alcohol amnesia was the problem. He'd read about it in one of the magazines that Anya bought to strew around the pub, pretending that the pub was hip and happening, instead of sad and depressing. He tried to clear his head by taking a deep breath, but it just made him dizzy. 'I thought she wanted me, regardless, but it seems she doesn't want me because I am a handsome, almost-famous dude. Women are so contrary.'

'Sounds to me like you should go and see this contrary woman and see what she does want.'

'I know, but she just upped and left.' He paused. 'I suppose I was a bit cross with her.' He wiped his eyes, which were weirdly prickly and wet. He was really tired. God, he wished he was in his bed. Maybe he'd stay a while longer, out of courtesy, then head off home, once he established where the hell he was.

'I've been given a chance to become something, but I have a feeling my stupid pride and my anger over Scarlett might stop me from doing it.'

The old man nodded. 'Don't let pride get in the way of what you want in life.'

Dylan noticed the man was mostly just regurgitating what Dylan was saying, by way of an answer, but he took his words on board. He was too tired to work out anything, anyway. He just needed to sleep.

He fell into a fitful kind of dozing, letting the old man's tales of missed opportunities, wrongs that had never been righted, and talents that had never reached their full potential, wash over him. He shifted position when his arms got too cold, or his bottom too numb, Fergal's words mingling with snatches of strangely erotic Scarlett dreams.

A sudden jump in his nervous system woke him out of his sleep, when he thought he was flying into Scarlett's open arms, only to drop into a bottomless canyon at the last second. He struggled upright, wondering where on earth he was and why he was so cold. His watch said five fifteen. In the morning? What in God's name had happened?

His panicked eyes did a double take, when he spotted his sleeping partner. Jeez, what had he done?

He put his hand to his head, as foggy memories of the previous night crystalized and he remembered that his sleeping partner was a drunk old man. He thanked God that he hadn't turned gay overnight - though, he liked women far too much for that. Besides, he didn't imagine his first foray into changing his sexual preference would have been with a wild-haired tramp, doing it in a doorway.

Dylan shifted his body, intending to leave the sleeping man to it, but Fergal was, unsurprisingly, a light sleeper, and he instantly jumped up in a panic of activity. 'Time to go, son. Street cleaners will be around soon, and if you linger too long, the school kids will spit on you as they pass by.'

Dylan hoisted himself upright, mumbling out his thanks to Fergal as he gathered his wits about him.

Fergal bundled up his stuff, securing it all with a

bungee clip before throwing it over his shoulder. 'If you need a proper bed, or food, you can go under Whitefriars Bridge, you know. They'll look after you there. Take care and God bless, son.'

As he scurried off, Dylan watched until he disappeared down a side street. 'God bless you, too, Fergal,' he said, hollowly. He flopped back down on the cold step and reflected on the old man's words: missed opportunities and wasted talent. He hadn't come up to muster so far, losing Scarlett and deciding to jack in the one thing he was good at. And sleeping rough in a doorway was hardly the way forward. It wasn't exactly up there with the great achievements of the world, was it?

No, he decided he wouldn't be like Fergal and spend the rest of his life blaming everyone else for his mistakes and weaknesses.

He stumbled along the street, feeling giddy, his throat as dry as a kipper in a smokehouse. But at least he knew where he was going. He was going to give it his best shot at being the superstar Mac expected him to be, and he needed to fight for the woman he loved. So far, he'd done very little of either, had just felt sorry for himself. It was time to do something positive, and he might as well start right then.

He staggered along until he found his bearings and headed towards Scarlett's apartment block, trying to remember as best he could which one it was. All the flats looked the same, though, and he cursed that he'd written down her address on his wrist instead of somewhere more permanent. It hadn't mattered at the time, but right then it was the single most important thing he'd ever written in his life.

In his fuddled stupor, he checked both wrists, just in case the address was still there, but even he wasn't slobby enough not to have washed for that long.

He passed a few people going to work and took stock, noticing that some of them actually veered away from him. He had to look a mess. He probably didn't smell too good, either. And thinking about it, his head was pounding like a tiny man was drilling a Kango hammer into his ears.

He looked longingly at a bottle of milk on someone's step, wishing that thieving came easy. His eyelids felt like they were carrying an elephant apiece on top of them, and he could imagine how Atlas must have felt with the weight of the world on his shoulders. Bone weary wasn't the word. It was no good, he would have to go home for a shower and some rest. True love and grand gestures were all very well, but if he turned up looking and smelling like Shrek, he might not even get through Scarlett's front door.

Reluctantly, he headed home. At least he had more of an idea where she lived, as there was a river on one side of the apartment block he was confronted with, and he'd definitely seen water through her window.

Remembering their first kiss in her flat, he groaned. What a bloody fool he'd been, since. But all that would change once he'd had a quick nap and some food. God, but what he wouldn't give for a full English to be conjured up in front of him.

CHAPTER TWENTY

Scarlett had bought a newspaper every day since she'd run out on Dylan and was scouring that day's version, praying that the fuss over her and Axel had died down. There had been one article about the brother's early childhood, and another one about drugs and the effects they had on the body, where they'd helpfully included a before and after picture of Sky, which Scarlett knew to be photo-shopped. Sky looked half-dead in both images.

Her mangled heart turned over as she traced the image of his face, remembering the good times and blocking out the bad. The pain of missing Dylan added to her already burgeoning heartache, and she wasn't sure how much more she could take, while still functioning as a human being.

The doorbell rang, and she flinched, wanting simply to be left alone, but she wearily hauled herself to her feet and pulled open the front door, to find a pale Axel standing on her doorstep.

She dragged him inside as quickly as she could, although she hoped the journalists had grown sick of stalking her. It wasn't as if there was anything left that they didn't know about. 'Axel, what's wrong?'

'I had to come and tell you in person, that it was nothing to do with me.'

'What wasn't?' Even as she spoke, dread filled her – it had to be bad news for him to come out to see her.

‘I’ve been really grateful for all the support you gave me. My mum is speaking to me again because of you, and the strongest drug I take is Paracetamol. I just wanted you to know that.’

‘Is that why you came?’ she asked, although it was unlikely he’d hauled himself all the way across London just to tell her that.

He shook his head, his gaze shifting, not quite meeting her eyes.

‘Sit down, I’ll put the kettle on. I’ve been calling you for weeks. Have you changed your number?’ She filled the kettle, although a sudden urge to open a bottle of wine hit her as she took in Axel’s nervousness.

He moistened his dry lips, rotating his mobile around in his fingers, clearly agitated, but he nodded. ‘Couldn’t stand them calling me all the time.’

Scarlett knew the feeling well. ‘What’s happened?’ She pushed Axel gently on to the chair – mostly because he looked like he’d fall any second, anyway. She felt decidedly wobbly on her own legs. ‘Tell me. Just come out with it,’ she said, as his mouth moved silently.

‘Some television journalist has written a book about Sky. He seems to know everything about him. Everything.’ His words came out in a rush, and he shook his head as if he couldn’t believe, himself, what he was saying.

Scarlett breathed a sigh of relief. ‘That’s not too bad, is it?’ He was always in the news, anyway. ‘Anyone could have found out what he was like …’ She trailed off on seeing Axel's stricken face. 'Stuff about me? But I didn't do anything.'

'Not as such, although they do mention your airline job, and the claim that you were involved in his drugs, in some way. You were mostly living with him - they just assumed.' Axel scratched his head, looked at the ceiling and the floor as if he'd find his next sentence better constructed in the cream carpet.

'Tell me, Axel.'

'They detail his lovers from when he became famous - practically date line them. All of them.'

'All of his lovers?' She frowned. He hadn't had any other lovers once they started dating, apart from a one-night stand, which had sent her to hell and back before she'd managed to forgive him. His lovers? What did it mean?

She mentally ran through photographs of the women he'd been seen with, trying to remember if any of them had acted overly friendly. A conveyor belt of beautiful women rolled through her head, morphing into one gross, designer-clad, fake breasted woman. 'You mean when we were an item?' She knew what he meant but it still didn't make any sense.

Axel nodded briefly.

She shook her head. It couldn't be true. She scrutinised Axel's face, but he showed nothing beyond his own discomfort.

Casting her mind back again, to any likely scenarios, she came up with nothing. Biting her lip, she recalled how often he'd been away. When it boiled down to it, she really had no idea what Sky had got up to, when he wasn't with her. But he'd loved her, and that love had protected them from intruders in their life. It didn't make sense. He'd needed her, depended on her. 'He loved me,' she blurted out as if Axel was trying to deny it.

'He did, Scarlett. You were his rock, his normality when he lost the plot.' He smiled tightly, the truth hitting Scarlett as Axel fidgeted, looking as if he wanted to bolt – but he knew his brother better than she did. Was he really saying that she was just a safe haven to return to, when he'd finished playing fast and loose? He couldn't be, he just couldn't.

She blinked in confusion. They'd been so happy together before the drugs took hold. She smiled weakly, waiting for some words of comfort, but Axel's face contorted and crumpled. He looked as if he was about to cry, and Scarlett had to remind herself that he'd been to hell and back, too.

If Sky had seen fit to cheat on her, it wasn't Axel's fault, she reminded herself, and there'd be no point in shooting the messenger. She ran a hand over her face, giving herself time to compose her features, needing time to think.

Axel's eyes were bleak when he finally looked at her. 'There's one more thing.' He took a deep breath, and Scarlett knew a killer line was on its way. 'One of his lovers has a child. She says he knew all about the little girl.' He took one look at Scarlett and stood quickly. 'I'll make that tea, I think.'

Scarlett's world blurred at his words. Her furniture swam before her eyes as she held on to the table to stay upright and bile rose in her throat. She gagged and thought she might be sick, but she swallowed down her nausea, almost unable to take in Axel's words. Almost. Deep down, she knew it to be the truth. The biographer would have checked his facts, knowing that he could be sued if he printed lies.

She had one last try at dissuading herself, staring at the carpet in the way Axel had, hoping to find the answer. 'What if it's just a story? You know how stupid rumours start? Most of his posturing was for show. None of it was real, was it? I mean there was always someone bleating to the press, but that happens when you're a star. Anything for fifteen minutes of fame by claiming you'd slept with Sky Angel.' Her voice rose to a panicked whine, and she heard her own desperation, denying it against the obvious facts. 'We need to put them straight, whoever they are. That's slander.' She looked at Axel, waiting for his plan of action, but Axel wasn't defending his dead brother, and the only action he looked capable of, was falling over.

He stared fixedly at the mugs of tea he placed on the table, looking forlorn, before his sorrowful eyes met hers. 'Mum has met her, Charlotte, the little girl. It's given her comfort.'

Scarlett's hand flew to her mouth as she tried to deaden the anguished cry. 'No, no!' She sank to the floor, shaking her head. 'How old?'

'She's three now.'

'Poor mite,' she whispered, even as she tried not to choke on Sky's treachery. She covered her face with her hands as she rocked on the floor. 'Can it be true? All that time, all that grieving. The total bastard.' She looked up at Axel as she wiped her nose and her eyes with the back of her hand, still hoping that he might come up with a better story. One she could deal with.

Axel just took a few stuttering steps towards her and patted her back, clearly out of his depth. He returned to the sofa, heaving out a breath, then another breath as if he was about to hyperventilate. His discomfort at her anger was tangible, and she knew she needed to give him an opt out.

'Thank you for letting me know,' she said quietly. 'I appreciate it. Forewarned is forearmed, and all that stuff.' She let out a shuddering breath as she took in the realization that anyone could read all about her and Sky, anytime they wished. the biography would lay her wide open, in glorious black and white, forever.

She needed to read the book.

She could never read the book.

Axel rose. 'If there's anything else I can do, feel free to get in touch.'

'Thanks, and keep in touch.' She staggered to her feet, weary and totally numb.

Axel stroked her hair, the gesture awkward. 'Will you be …?'

'I'll be fine, really.' She walked into the hallway, anxious for him to leave so she could lose herself in the new grief, one that was alien to her: summoning up a hatred of someone she had spent years loving.

She opened the door, and as Axel bent down to kiss her on the cheek, a bright light flashed in her face. 'Oh, do me a favour, will you?' she yelled in the direction of the unseen photographer.

The camera flashes went into overdrive, as the unseen men made the most of their photo opportunity.

Shit and double shit, she thought, as a figure lumbered up the steps. Was there anything left to go wrong?

A camera flash lit up one side of Todd's face as he reached the top step, and she groaned.

Looks as if that's a yes, then. 'Come in, Todd.' She turned on her automatic smile, even as she cried inside, her re-adjusted thoughts of Sky trampled on before she had time to sift through them and accept that her version of their life together had been a figment of her imagination.

She eyeballed Todd, not in the mood to be civil, even though she knew he would demand attention, and she would have to acquiesce to keep on the right side of him. By the look on his face, as she let him in, he already knew about the book.

'I'm guessing that was the brother.' He jerked his thumb towards the retreating Axel as he walked confidently along the hallway into the sitting room.

Scarlett nodded unhappily. 'Don't tell me you've already read it.'

'Don't be silly. I don't read gutter-press books. You look dreadful, by the way.'

Scarlett blanched and lifted her hands up to her cheeks, wanting to retreat to her bedroom to put some makeup on as the air stewardess in her kicked in. Instead, she glared at Todd, sensing the bullish mood he'd arrived in and already knowing the way their conversation would play out: he'd try to make her feel cheap so he could retain the upper hand and manipulate her. She needed to keep her wits about her, when all she wanted to do was curl into a ball and howl.

She discreetly blotted her eyes with her sleeve and bit down on her lip, determined not to let Todd be privy to her emotions.

'So, you were living with the great Sky Angel. You're a dark horse.'

Scarlett eyed him warily, saying nothing.

'It's true, then, all of it?'

She pursed her lips wishing she could tell Todd to mind his own business. 'I've no idea what's in the book, Todd, I haven't read it.'

'The general gist of it, though. Yes?'

'I guess so, apart from the implication that I had anything to do with his drug taking.'

Todd's grin was malicious and sly. He finally had something on her, and she knew he'd use it to his advantage. She hated herself for thinking she needed to keep him sweet. If he were a decent man, he would be kind to her. But he wasn't a decent man, and she steeled herself, knowing he'd enjoy his moment and drop the bombshell he was clearly preparing only when he was good and ready.

'Would you like a cup of tea?' she offered, wondering for the first time exactly why he had visited instead of phoning.

'Yes, please, unless you have anything stronger.' He took off his jacket and threw it casually on the sofa., the gesture itself seeming threatening as it hit the grey suede of the cushion. He was not a man in a hurry.

Trying to remain calm, she hovered over the kettle, waiting for it to boil, her mind racing through the possibilities. The most likely scenario was that he was angry for not knowing about her relationship with Sky, but he would probably pretend it was some other reason. She would have to tread carefully, because he was acting way too calm.

'Here we are.' She placed two cups of tea on the low table and sat down on the single armchair, rubbing her hands together.

'I checked through your CV at work, the bit where it asks if you've ever been dismissed from a job. That bit?' He smiled encouragingly, as if willing her to remember.

Scarlett groaned inwardly. What a nasty person he was. 'Yes?' She kept her face neutral.

'It seems that you were.'

'Was what? Dismissed?'

Todd nodded, his supercilious smile nauseating her.

'I wasn't. It was suggested that I changed jobs because of my relationship with Sky. Roger from Luton Airport put in a good word for me.'

'But you broke the rules and neglected to tell us about the situation you found yourself in. You were questioned by the police, I believe.'

'Look, Todd, what is this all about? What do you want me to say? Are you waiting for me to plead for my job, or do you want some kind of grovelling apology from me?' She glared at him, tempted to tell him to shove his job up his large arse. She really was in no mood to listen to his pompous ponderings.

His smile was tight, and he inclined his head as if it was her job to discover why he was there.

She stayed calm and waited, even though she wanted to kick him out of her flat and her life, with a resounding slam of the door.

He eventually reached over into his jacket pocket and pulled out an envelope, smoothing down the space next to him on the sofa with his other hand. 'Come over here and read this.'

She stared at the letter as if it was a live hand grenade, as he stroked the grey suede of her sofa. The last thing she wanted to do was to sit next to him, but he patted the patch of soft suede again and smiled up at her, and she knew he wouldn't pass the letter over to her unless she did as she was bid, so she rose reluctantly and sat next to him.

'That's better.' He patted her knee, and she tried not to flinch. 'This is a letter offering StarJet the opportunity to merge with a bigger airline.' He pulled out a thick, cream piece of paper from the envelope. 'We'd acquire G4s, too, which, as you know, would be far superior to our aircraft. We've negotiated with them for quite some time, and finally the deal has been done.'

'What has this got to do with me?'

'We'll need a base manager, and we'll have to recruit more cabin staff. I'm offering you the job.'

'Oh.' She was surprised and touched by the offer, but as he passed the letter over to her, his thumb brushed hers. He held the letter for a second too long as he stared into her eyes. 'Would you like the job?'

If she hadn't been so close to crying, she would have laughed in his face. They both knew he was asking for so much more than her acceptance, and she swallowed nervously. 'If I don't take the job offer?' Her fingers trembled, and she let go of the letter.

Todd sighed heavily as he refolded it, tucking it back into his pocket. 'Why don't you take a week, or so, away from work? We won't call it suspension, and we'll pay your basic salary. Have a little think about your options? I'll be meeting with the board at the end of the month, so I'll need your answer by then. If it's yes, we can take off for a couple of days together, to … talk about your new position. If it's no, then I'm not sure I can save you. You know how we take exception to any kind of adverse publicity.' He drained his mug, picked up his jacket, and pushed briskly to his feet. 'Sky Angel's biography is in all of the shops. Everyone who reads it will know everything there is to know about you. It might not all be pleasant, either.' His oily smirk was knowing and smug. 'But we'll cross that bridge when we come to it.'

Scarlett stood up, too, and folded her arms protectively across her chest. Todd took a step towards her, his smile wide, showing pointed eye teeth and reminding her of a wolf about to attack. He drew a circular pattern across her bare arm with his finger, trailing up to her shoulder. 'I think we'd get on pretty well, if you just gave it a chance.'

She was catatonic with horror as she took in his meaning, only rousing herself when he stopped touching her arm. She swallowed, her mouth dry as dust. 'Thank you for the offer – I'll think about it.'

'Don't think for too long. I don't know how long the offer will be open.' He inclined his head once more, the thin smile stretching slightly.

Her palms itched to smack it off his face, but she simply said, 'I'll show you out.' She opened the front door, half expecting the flash of cameras once more, but all was silent.

Todd turned at the top of the step, leaning forward, and catching her unawares, he grabbed her arms and kissed her fully on the lips.

He pushed his tongue inside her mouth, and she put her hands on his chest to shove him away, unable to hide her revulsion, or bear such an intimacy. His hands were like steel bands around her arms, though, making the move ineffectual, and she was forced to endure his unwanted intimacy for several long moments.

'I'll wait to hear from you,' he said, when he finally broke away from her.

She closed her eyes to block out his face, trying not to gag. Yeah, when hell freezes over. She slammed the door closed, wiping savagely at her lips.

CHAPTER TWENTY-ONE

Dylan had slept for three hours, showered and eaten, and had stepped out of the door with a new zeal, intent on finding his true love, even if he had to beg her to take him back. First stop, though, was the corner shop, where he bought a box of supersized painkillers, a bottle of water, and a very expensive, albeit sad and wilting, bunch of red roses.

He popped the pills and drank the water, feeling better immediately, his night of booze and rough sleeping a distant memory, apart from the crick in his neck and the vague worry that he might have fleas. Despite that, he had banished his self-pitying thoughts and was on the up again. He just needed Scarlett back in his life to make it all perfect.

He didn't seem to be having much luck, though, wandering around the small block of flats where she lived, peering up into windows and clutching his flowers. Growing desperate, he worried he just might have to start singing in the hope she'd hear him and throw open her window rapturously, like Juliet.

He ran through the quotes of Romeo and Juliet he'd learned at school, even considered yelling, But, soft, what light through yonder window breaks? up at a random window, or two.

Or was that a line from Shrek?

He worried at his forehead in confusion. His quest was starting to feel hopeless. He could wander around for hours, and Scarlett could be high above the ocean, serving caviar to rich passengers, while he was making more of a prat of himself than normal.

As he meandered in and out of patches of green grass, and around sapling trees and vandalised waste bins, losing the will, a movement caught his eye.

It was little more than a lucky break that he recognized the man standing on the step of one of the flats.

However, his relief turned to wariness when it sank in that it was the obnoxious Captain Carrington he'd spotted. He was even more perturbed, when the guy leaned towards Scarlett, who stood on the top step of her apartment, and he watched in horror as Scarlett put her hands flat on his chest, seemingly enjoying the exchange of saliva.

Hardly able to believe the scene, Dylan's jaw fell open as he lost hold of the flowers and they tumbled to the ground.

As Captain Carrington bounced jauntily down the stairs, Dylan took a step forward, ready to smack him in his stupid, self-satisfied face, but he stopped himself, clenching and unclenching his hands into fists, as realization hit. Scarlett must have played her part in it. She was a grown woman who could make her own choices, after all.

The hangover he'd thought he'd recovered from, suddenly returned with a vengeance, as his stomach roiled in revulsion. He staggered over to a bin like a drunk and threw up into it, retching and gagging as his shiny, positive thinking world once more turned shabby and tainted.

He sat on the ground until he'd recovered enough to haul himself upright, and simply stared at the door that kept Scarlett from him. She was probably doing a happy little dance of love, or sliding down the door in ecstasy as she relived the wonderful sex she'd shared with her new man - memories that only someone truly in love could appreciate. It was a love that excluded him, though, and Dylan wasn't sure he could deal with that.

He bit his lip, trying to make it hurt more than the pain that reached into the core of his soul, making him retch again, but the heartache won, big time, rendering him incapable of movement. He felt as if he'd been felled, like a tree having its roots chopped away, losing any stability he thought he had.

Staring helplessly toward Scarlett's apartment, he hugged his arms around himself, knowing he should try and man-up over it, accept it as part of life. Except, even as he willed the pain to disappear, he knew it was only just getting started.

Scarlett had managed to swap him with ease, ironically to a man who she'd said she didn't even like. They had both misjudged each other, by the look of it.

Dylan turned away in disgust. At least he'd had the honesty to stay true to what he wanted - although, in truth, he couldn't imagine why Scarlett would choose such a man as Captain shitty Carrington. And it hurt, more than he would ever have thought possible.

After one last glance toward her front door, he picked up the roses scattered around the bin and threw them into the stream, watching as they floated away and took his dreams with them.

CHAPTER TWENTY-TWO

'And he kissed me outside my own front door as if it was a done deal.' Scarlett recounted the story of Todd's surprise visit, to Louisa, the horror of it still physically sickening her. They had already discussed Sky and the new revelations at great length, to the point where Scarlett felt more capable of dealing with his death and betrayal. Knowing that he hadn't been true to her seemed to have laid the constant shadow of Sky to rest; he wasn't worth the anguish.

She tried to smile at Elsa who sidled over, calmly lining up her teddy bears on the windowsill before giving them a stern talking to, wagging her finger at each of them in turn.

Scarlett wondered what terrible misdemeanour they'd committed to deserve such a telling off. 'Poor teddies,' she whispered to her sister.

'You should hear how she harangues her dolls. It's terrifying. Has me standing to attention, I tell you.'

'Born teacher, I reckon.' Scarlett grinned, as Elsa, apparently forgiving the teddies, held up pieces of broken biscuit to their stitched mouths and made nom-nom noises.

'You should have kneed him in the nuts,' her sister said, steering back to the topic of conversation. 'I told you to watch him, didn't I?'

Scarlett couldn't even bring herself to tell her sister how he'd thrust his tongue into her mouth; she seemed fascinated enough, as it was. 'It was truly gross. I could handle him before, but now he has something on me, I don't know what to do. I'm pretty sure he's blown this entire story up out of nothing to try and control me. I really don't think the board will give a stuff that I omitted to tell them about Sky. It's bad enough, finding out that Sky was a lowdown, lying rat, without being held up to ridicule by anyone who cares to read the book. I can't believe how gullible I was.' She grabbed her wine glass once more and took a hefty swig. 'And I miss Dylan so much. Why did I storm off, the way I did? My stupid sense of pride. What a mess.'

The ready sheen of tears washed over her eyes again as she recalled Sky's absolute betrayal. She'd grieved for a man who'd only existed in her mind. The real Sky was a philandering liar who hadn't deserved her loyalty and love. He'd had a child that she knew nothing about. How could such a huge secret have been kept from her?

Her emotions bounced all over the place, as she missed Dylan and hated Todd and Sky in equal measure. 'What am I going to do?' She gulped at her white wine and turned to her sister.

'Do you really want an answer to that question, or are you just thinking out loud? Because if you are asking my opinion, I think, firstly, you need to get hold of Dylan to apologise, and secondly, you need to find a new job.'

'He should apologise to me. He was so horrible.'

Louisa shook her head. 'You are your own worst enemy, sometimes, Scarlett.' She refilled her own wine glass and Scarlett's, wincing when her gaze skimmed toward the clock. It was still only five o'clock, and they'd drunk a bottle between them. She rummaged in the food cupboard and then opened the fridge door and peered inside. 'The best I can come up with is some mini Cheddars and a chunk of Red Leicester.'

Scarlett nodded and gulped back more wine. 'Great … lovely. Have you seen Dylan, at all?'

'No, I don't see him in the park anymore. Haven't seen him for a month, or so.'

Scarlett's face fell. 'Me, neither. I keep circling the lake in the hope of bumping in to him. I even bought a pair of cute welly boots.' She sighed and took another slug of wine. 'He's moved out of his house, too. He said he was going to, because it was a tip and he didn't want me to have to stay there.' She gulped back more tears.

'How do you know he's moved?' Louisa asked.

'Bit of random stalking,' Scarlett said, giving her sister the closest thing to a smile she could manage. 'That only leaves Southwold and the pub, and everyone there probably hates me. And if he's going to tell me what a cow I am, I'd rather he did it without bystanders. I've been humiliated enough recently.'

'Why don't you just phone him?'

'Because.'

'Because, why?'

'Because I blocked him and then deleted his number.'

'You are a stubborn idiot sometimes.'

This time she couldn't raise a smile, at all. 'I know.' Her voice was small as she shrugged. 'He's in all the newspapers and gossip magazines. He's probably forgotten my name by now. He'll have moved on to dating rich, nubile beauties - and I'm still not sure I could bear to go through all that stardom shit again, anyway.' Her voice wobbled with disappointment. She missed him so badly.

'He's not Sky, Scarlett. He's a different man. A good man.'

'I know. He said that. And he said I was beautiful, and he was really sincere about wanting me forever and I disappeared out of his life at the first sign of trouble.' She bit her lip as tears spilled over her lashes.

'Come on, love.' Her sister pulled her into her arms and stroked her hair. 'You'll get through this. You're stronger than you think.'

'I know I will, but I don't want to, I just want him to want me, like he used to,' she wailed.

'Then, at least find him, to see what he thinks. Give him a chance to make it right.'

Scarlett brightened a bit. She sniffed and wiped her eyes. 'Do you think I should? I need to sort out the job thing, too. I've phoned the agency, but they only have a vacancy in Liverpool at the moment.'

'Liverpool? But that's a world away.'

'I know. I've collected a few business cards on my travels - someone else might be recruiting. I can't believe that bastard Todd suspended me and then acted as if he was offering to save me.'

'Steer clear, Scarlett. He sounds like a nasty piece of work.'

Elsa seemed to finally notice her aunty was upset and brought a pink teddy and a teaspoon over and sat the teddy on the table next to Scarlett's wine glass. 'This is Sparkle, and it's time for her tea,' she said seriously. 'To feed her, you crumple up a biscuit, like this.' She broke off a small piece from a Digestive into her hand. 'And then you put the crumbs on a spoon to feed her.' Glancing over at her mother, she whispered, 'If she doesn't eat it, just brush it on to the floor. It's not too messy.' She nodded reassuringly at Scarlett and pushed the spoon at her. 'It will make you happy again, Sparkle Bear, too, 'cause she likes biscuits.'

'Thank you, Elsa.' She drew her niece into her arms and hugged her tightly, needing the comfort of a warm body. She rested her cheek on her hair, until Elsa squirmed out of her reach to pull a fresh biscuit out of the packet. 'I'll just get you started,' she said, as she took a large bite of another biscuit and passed the rest to Scarlett.

Scarlett smiled as she took the half eaten biscuit and began crumbling.

Louisa patted her sister's arm and left her to it. 'Very therapeutic.'

Two minutes later, she came back into the kitchen carrying her open laptop. 'Good old Google.' Louisa set the laptop on the kitchen table. 'Okay, Dylan is on tour.' She exaggerated the last two lines and widened her eyes.

'On tour?'

'Well, I use the words loosely. He's in Highgate this weekend, in Camden next Saturday, and ooh, quite the gad about … in Birmingham the Saturday afterwards, as the warm up for the Bitley Boys. Ooh, I've heard of them.' She stabbed at the screen. 'Look, he has a website and a twitter feed, and everything.'

Scarlett glanced over at the screen, and her heart turned over as Dylan's face smiled back at her. She wanted to be pleased for him, she really did, but it hurt so much to see him reaching his goal on his own. She pressed her lips together, trying not to break down again. 'He didn't waste much time, did he?' She turned away from the computer screen in the hope that the image of Dylan wouldn't become embedded on her mind forever.

'Let's go and see him, Scarlett - tomorrow, in Camden. I'll come with you, yeah? You're not working, so maybe that bastard Todd has actually done you a favour. We can get dressed up and make a night of it. Elsa can go to her dad's.'

Scarlett nodded, too afraid to speak in case she blubbered again, but finally, she had a reason for her heart to keep on pumping blood around her body. She would go and see Dylan and try to make everything right.

Louisa pushed the cork firmly down into the bottle of wine they'd been drinking. 'No more of this, and you'd better get a good night's sleep. You look like crap.'

'Thanks very much.' But Scarlett smiled for the first time in ages and a tiny seed of hope started to grow.

CHAPTER TWENTY-THREE

Scarlett checked out her clothes: black shorts and thick tights, pixie boots, an emerald green silk tunic that hugged her breasts and hips, and a long black cardigan in case the whole outfit was a dog's dinner and totally inappropriate. She layered black eyeliner on her eyes and slicked vampy-red lipstick across her lips. She wasn't sure what had bought about the change in her sense of dress, but she liked the way it made her feel: sexy and a bit alternative.

She knew she was dressing for Dylan, but she was unsure whether she hoped to seduce him, or if she was trying to get him to see what he was missing. Louisa's look of approval gave her the confidence she needed to pull it off, but even so, Scarlett was ridiculously nervous.

They arrived at the venue, which looked more like an old hotel than a concert hall. The foyer was the size of a church, and she was surprised to see how many young women were queuing up to hear Dylan sing.

'It seems he's already made his mark,' Louisa said, eyeing the gaggle of excited women heading for the cloakroom.

Scarlett gravitated towards a large poster of Dylan, which dominated the wall. It was bizarre seeing such a sanitized image of Dylan sporting tight black jeans and a designer leather jacket. His tousled hair had been tamed, his generous smile replaced by a moody glower that made him look sulkily gorgeous, even if it did make her want to laugh. It was a bit too 'put together' for her liking, but still, she itched to trace her fingers over the image, remembering his skin on hers, his kisses and his loving words.

His forthcoming gigs had been listed underneath his picture, and Scarlett scanned the calendar of events. By the looks of it, he was the warmup act for the all-girl band The Pretty Monsters for most of the winter, and a spike of unexpected jealousy hit her. They were already quite famous, and were indeed very pretty, rather than the monsters she would've preferred. Three out of the four of them had their various arms and legs intertwined with Dylan in the photo, and Dylan was laughing down into the face of a far-too-pretty redheaded 'Pretty Monster.'

She sighed. Here we go again with the jealousy - and he's not even mine anymore.

The venue had been set up more like a cosy pub than concert hall, and as Scarlett grabbed an empty table, Louisa, balancing a bottle of wine with two glasses on a round tray, spotted her. As soon as they'd seated themselves, the room darkened and Dylan strode on to the stage to a fanfare of music, his old guitar still welded to him.

He waved at the audience, mostly made up of women, and perched on a chair in the middle of the stage. It seemed absurd to Scarlett that the man who'd become so familiar to her, whose bed she had shared, whose body she had loved, was now, no more than a man across a room, singing to strangers.

His face captivated her, as she took in the nuances of his jaw, his cheeks, his beautiful eyes that had looked at her with such longing. She wanted to run to him and throw her arms around him, beg him to love her, pray that she wasn't too late.

Except, he wasn't the same Dylan anymore, was he? And she had hurt him more than he'd deserved.

His voice cut through her thoughts as the whole room stilled and he became a whole lot more than background noise.

Scarlett hung off his every word and glance, unreasonably hurt when he introduced a song she'd never heard before.

'This is a song I wrote a short while ago, when I was feeling pretty low. I spent an evening with an old man who made me see that you have to make your own choices in life. For some reason, it makes me want to drink, which is weird, because the old man was an alcoholic. I think it just reminds me of a time I would rather forget.' He picked up a bottle from the floor next to him. 'Cheers.' He took a long swig then began to strum.

Scarlett focused on his words. A time he would rather forget? It was their time together - it had to be. And he was telling anyone and everyone. He must have really hated her for how she'd treated him.

Cringing, she shrank down into her seat, wishing she hadn't gone to the concert, but the strains of his song soon occupied her mind. It wasn't a downbeat song, at all, but abstract and positive. Proof, if any was needed, that he had moved on.

She stared, as he took another slurp of his drink and some of it dribbled down his delectable chest, and it hit Scarlett that he was a bit drunk – which was upsetting as much as it was surprising. He'd always insisted that he would never drink to excess, especially if he became famous.

He moved straight on to his next song, sweet and slow, making Scarlett's insides curl with longing. He sang steadily, captivating the audience, even when he did little more than speak.

'This is one of my favourite songs,' he said, and the audience collectively sighed in agreement before he'd even started singing it. 'Quite simply, it has special memories for me.' He took another glug of beer from the bottle that'd been replaced by a backstage hand – twice. His mouth twisted in concentration, as he quickly retuned one of his guitar strings and started strumming.

Scarlett recognised the notes immediately. It was the song she considered theirs. She'd been there at its inception, listening to it over and over as Dylan played it with fabulous monotony. He'd sat on her sofa, strumming the tune, mouthing the words, nodding at a brilliant rhythm, or frowning over a line that wouldn't fall into place. Only then did she appreciate the single-mindedness and the sheer talent of the man who had pursued her with bewildering, yet dogged, determination.

She couldn't take her eyes off him, as he sang about waiting for too long and dying from the pain of needing to be with the woman he loved. It was haunting and heartrending, and the audience was with him all the way, willing the last few bars of the song to finish perfectly.

'So, I think it's true; I've more than fallen for you.'

Rippling applause greeted the last chord, and Dylan twanged his guitar once more for effect while grinning. 'I'm going to take a little break now,' he said, and the audience clapped harder. He certainly was the man of the day, it seemed, if even leaving the stage merited a round of applause.

More than Scarlett's emotions wobbled at the sight of Dylan. Her whole body seemed to have turned into jelly as she realised the song was for her. It wasn't too late after all. He still loved her. She half rose to go to him, before she realised it would be inappropriate to interrupt the show. She sat down again and stilled, unable to take her eyes off him as the spotlight panned over him and he sauntered towards one of the tables, where a woman stood up, grinning and clapping furiously.

Not quite understanding the scene unfolding in front of her, she frowned in confusion, as the woman grabbed Dylan, threw her arms around his neck and kissed him full on the mouth to another round of clapping from her friends.

Dylan's hands dropped to the woman's waist, barely touching as the kiss played out. Scarlett gasped in shock, sitting down heavily on the nearest seat, as pain snaked its way around her body, piercing every cell, until she thought she might collapse.

The woman was the unmistakable ex from Southwold – Kate – her hair shorter, flickier, flirtier. Scarlett instantly hated it.

Another act started playing, as Dylan deposited himself next to Kate and her gang. Scarlett, in a dark, daze of misery, stared blankly. It seemed he had moved backwards, then, rather than forwards.

Undeniably the star of the show, Dylan seemed able to do no wrong where his fan base of doting girls was concerned, and he definitely seemed to be enjoying the attention. He slung his arm across the back of Kate's chair, as she laughed up at him, hanging off his every word.

The shock of it all ripped through Scarlett like a knife. It had been so fast, his transformation into a bona fide popstar. The Dylan she'd thought she knew had gone forever, and she needed to accept it.

In fascinated horror, she leaned in closer, as Kate threw a possessive arm over Dylan's thighs, leaning her elbows practically on his crotch as she chatted across to her friend on his right. No doubt, Dylan had a fine view of her cleavage, Scarlett noted, as he stroked Kate's hair in a distracted way, like he had a cat on his lap. However, jealous as she was, she couldn't help but notice how little of his heart and soul he seemed to be putting into the action, and her despair gave way to a righteous anger.

How dare he throw her away so easily, when he'd

tried so hard to make her love him? And he didn't even seem to be suffering, at all – proving that his feelings for her ran no deeper than the shallow stream outside her home.

She stood up, determined to leave, but the roaming spotlight flashed into her face, at precisely the same time that Dylan glanced across the room.

As his gaze landed smack-bang on her, he did a comical double-take, his head swinging slowly around as his brain seemed to take a minute to register her appearance. The easy smile that she had been fantasizing about fell into place, and he jumped up, his arms opening wide, unbalancing Kate who almost fell in a heap.

His lips moved, as their eyes locked. She could clearly see him mouthing her name, and she cursed under her breath. She didn't want to speak to him – there was nothing left to say.

With her handbag in hand, she lurched towards the foyer, leaving Louisa behind, but as she reached the door, he caught up with her, barring her escape.

'Scarlett? Is it really you?' Suddenly uncomfortably close, the sheer familiarity of Dylan confused her, the phrase, so near, yet so far springing to mind.

'Yes, I came to see you, but it was a mistake. I should have stayed away.'

'Scarlett, Scarlett, you came to see me?' He put his hand up to her cheek, smoothing her hair away, holding her head as he stared at her, his eyes beseeching. 'You have no idea what it's been like.' His eyes fixed on her face as if he wanted to embed her image in his brain.

'I have every idea. In fact, I saw how tormented you've been, only minutes ago.'

His brow wrinkled. 'What, the songs?'

'No, Dylan,' she said patiently. 'Kate. I saw you kissing her.' She suddenly roused herself from the trance his eyes had put her in. 'Didn't I say this was how it would end: you getting drunk and going off with random women?'

She twisted from his grip pushing him away but Dylan grabbed her arm again.

'She's not a random woman, she's Kate – she doesn't count. She just shows up to support me, and she was doing the kissing, not me.' His eyes showed his confusion, as she tried to leave. 'Why are you leaving when you came to see me?'

'I've seen enough, thanks.' She raised her arm snatching it away from Dylan's grasp.

'No. you've got it all wrong.' He waved towards the concert hall. 'I'm just trying to get on with my life.'

'So I see. You're doing a grand job – with your drinking and womanizing. So, don't let me interrupt you.' She tossed her hair and lifted her nose in the air, trying to play the haughty, wronged woman, while in reality, she knew he'd done no wrong. She was just desperately jealous of Kate.

Dylan ran his fingers through his hair, his eyes flashing as irritation kicked in. 'Are you for real? Once again, you're drumming up excuses to walk away. You can't cope with me because of your stupid drug-taking ex.'

'My what? How dare you?'

'Tell me this isn't about him, and your life before I met you, skewing the way you think? You had a crap upbringing, and your sister's husband walked out on her when Elsa was tiny. You think it'll be the same with us, so you take me out of the equation, to save you from being let down again. You think I'll be the same as Sky ....'

'And it looks as if you're shaping up nicely for the job.' She bit back at him her own eyes flashing fury and contempt.

He ignored her comment, catching her again around the waist and walking her backwards, up against the wall, his legs in between hers. 'It's because of you that I'm in this state.'

'Leave me alone.'

'No. I'm sorry, Scarlett, but for once, you're going to listen to me.' He took his hands off her waist, but his legs straddled hers, and she'd have to climb over them if she wanted to escape. 'Can we rewind a little here, leaving aside Sky? You left me, remember? Yes, I was angry, but couples have arguments. It's the reason making up was invented. Couples weather the storms - they don't just run away. I had to assume you wanted nothing more to do with me. And what - I'm supposed to stay single while you get to shag your rich Captain?' His mouth turned down in distaste.

The heat drained from Scarlett's face. 'What?'

'I saw you with him.'

'When? What do you mean?'

Dylan closed his eyes as if his patience was being pushed, and sighed. 'I saw you kissing him, outside your flat. I came to find you, hoping you'd see sense.' He framed her cheeks in his hands again, his gaze intense as he opened his eyes and fixed them on hers.

She forced herself to turn away, unable to risk him hypnotising her again with his piercing stare.

'Goddamn it!' He glared at her and slapped his palm against the wall beside her head. 'For fuck's sake, Scarlett.' He sounded defeated as he shook his head slightly. His grip relaxed and he sighed. 'What the hell do you want from me?'

Scarlett pushed herself away from the wall, but as she tried to leave, Dylan's knee pushed between her legs, and he pulled her into him and kissed her, hard and long. 'Tell me this does nothing for you, and we'll call it a day.' He gave a strangled groan, and her body leaped into life as he lowered his lips to hers. She wanted to kiss him back, as he fired up her body once more from its temporary hibernation. She allowed herself a moment of luxury, tasting his lips, feeling his thigh press against her groin, heat gathering in her pelvis before she pulled away.

She was helpless in her desire, but physical attraction didn't make a relationship. She should have ended it, once and for all, when she'd walked away the first time, before they found themselves on another path of self-destruction as history repeated itself. Besides which, Dylan was half drunk, so his reactions might not be typical of how he felt when sober. And what would the next step be, discovering his choice of drugs by the residue left on the toilet cistern, just like Sky?

'Dylan, you're on in two minutes.' A roadie beckoned him, crooking his finger, as if he hadn't even registered that Dylan was in the middle of a passionate clinch. Or maybe the roadie was just used to such sights that he didn't even think it rude to interrupt.

Dylan raised his hand, acknowledging the man, but he still kept Scarlett close. 'Stay, just stay until I've finished, and we can talk about this.' He didn't wait for an answer, just hugged her briefly and left.

He was right, Scarlett thought, as she watched him return to the stage. She wouldn't allow anyone to get close enough to make her happy, because that would mean they also had the power to make her sad. She was a rock and an island, she'd thought, and that was the way it would stay. Dylan would achieve his dream - indeed, he was already on the way to being the superstar he wanted to be - and she'd be happy for him, but he would do it without her. She was wrong for him.

She was wrong for any man.

She traced his face on the poster once more and, pulling out her phone from her pocket, she dialled Louisa's number. It was time to call it a day.

CHAPTER TWENTY-FOUR

Scarlett dragged her suitcase to the door and took a last look at her flat, before pulling the door closed behind her. She'd left a bottle of champagne and some flowers for the newlyweds, who were renting it from her. She prayed they'd find more happiness than she had in her safe little haven, and hoped that, one day, she'd be able to return to it a better person.

With her car packed to the gunnels, she headed off to spend a last night with Louisa and Elsa, to say goodbye, mentally preparing herself to be upbeat so that Elsa wouldn't realise that she was leaving.

'Hiya. I thought it was your car I heard.' Louisa opened the door before Scarlett knocked and ushered her inside, slopping coffee down the woodwork and over her floor from the mug she clutched to her chest. 'Oh, bugger, coffee everywhere.'

Scarlett laughed, as Louisa swiped at the spilt liquid while fighting off Buster, who seemed to think it was his duty to clean it up. 'You just can't leave your caffeine fix, can you?'

'Come in. The kettle's on, although I wish it was drinking time. I feel as if we should celebrate your new start by cracking open a bottle.'

Scarlett's smile was wan. As much as she tried to put on a brave face over her new job, she would rather it had turned out differently. 'Weird, isn't it? I've travelled all over the world, but I've never been to Liverpool, until now.' She tried to inject some enthusiasm into her voice, knowing that she was failing badly.

'It'll be a great adventure, and your new flat overlooks e Mersey. How cool is that?'

Scarlett loved that her sister was being strong on her half. 'At least I'll never feel lonely, with all that to-ing d fro-ing on the damn river. It's worse than the M25 on ank Holiday Monday.'

Louisa looked momentarily sad. 'You'll soon make nds, and you never know ...'

Scarlett raised her hand. 'Don't. Don't even think it, let ne suggest it. I can't manage a pet in my job - have ible with pot plants, for goodness sake - so what nce do I have with a man?' She bit back the ready rs. 'I'll be fine on my own, really I will.' She opened arms, as Elsa hurled herself at her legs.

Aunty Scarlett, are we going out to the park, or a é?' It was just another day for Elsa, as Louisa had cided not to tell her that Scarlett was moving away. r sister preferred to believe Scarlett would find a job ck in London in no time, at all.

'We can go out later, if your mum wants a break from that chattering you do.' Scarlett tried not to let her ind wander back to their trip to the park on that fateful y when she'd bumped into Dylan, although he seemed loom larger than ever in her thoughts, and it was so uch worse since all connections had been cut.

'Think positively,' Louisa said, reading her mind.

'I am. It's just a bit hard, with my being so crap at relationships.'

'You will go for these gorgeous rock stars. What about trying an accountant, or an office worker?' Louisa smiled gently to assure Scarlett that she was teasing as she thrust a mug into her sister's hand. She led her through to the sitting room. 'At least you got that revolting Todd out of your hair.'

'Yeah. Though, I wish I'd managed to do more than just resign. Didn't even get a chance to wipe his breakfast roll around the toilet bowl, or put laxative in his tea, or one of the other great wheezes that regular stewardesses do, to exact revenge on pervy pilots. Mind you, it was nice to see him grovelling, trying to get me to stay.'

'And he gave you a payoff, knowing how badly he'd treated you.'

'Ah, yes, the Golden Handshake of silence. Oh, well, it's all history now, and I am one-hundred percent committed to forgetting all about Dylan, although his ugly mug does seem to be everywhere nowadays.' Her grimace softened. 'No, it's not fair to say that. He was – is beautiful.' She swallowed. 'What time did you say we could start drinking?'

Louisa rose from the sofa. 'I've got two bottles chilling, just say the word.'

Scarlett spluttered into her coffee. 'It's eleven o'clock in the morning. I'm not that desperate.'

Elsa came running in from the Conservatory. 'Come and see my television.' She pulled at Scarlett's arm.

'Why? I've seen your television before, and it's a very pretty one. I'd have loved a pink Disney telly when I was your age.' She stroked Elsa's hair absent-mindedly and turned back to Louisa.

'Not the television, the man in it. Come see.'

Scarlett's stomach swooped. She knew exactly who she was going to see on the screen. Her knees wobbled, and she wondered how Dylan had the power to do that to her, even from the screen of a TV.

Louisa gave her big eyes as she stood up, throwing a longing look at the fridge. It would probably only be minutes before that first bottle was cracked open.

Louisa took hold of Scarlett's hand, as they both stared at the image filling the screen – a close-up of Dylan's face.

Although it hurt Scarlett to see it, she breathed out a sigh of relief. 'It's just an advert for his debut album, I guess. It's national television, though – he is doing well.' She stared some more, as the image faded, and a song she didn't recognize but was unmistakably one of Dylan's started playing in the background.

The TV audience clapped furiously, as a tall, gorgeous, jean-clad Dylan walked confidently across the room and sat next to a well-known TV presenter.

Scarlett gasped, squeezing her sister's hand tightly. They both sat down, staring at the television.

The pretty, but botoxed presenter, clasped her hands together as she welcomed Dylan, trying to make her immobile mouth mobile in what looked like an effort to match his broad smile. 'So, Dylan Willis,' she said facing the camera, 'the new darling of the music world, has come to sing for us. Welcome, Dylan.'

Dylan nodded to the presenter. 'Great to be here.'

Scarlett moved closer to the television. She'd missed hearing his soft voice with its slight Suffolk brogue. And his brilliant wide smile - she'd missed that so much more. 'His eyes are a deeper blue than they used to be,' she said clasping her hands together.

Louisa threw her a puzzled look. 'If you say so.'

'They look it to me. Much darker.' She inched even closer to the small television, kneeling on the floor.

Louisa glanced at Scarlett. 'I know I'm asking a dumb question here, but as you are so clearly still in love with Dylan, why didn't you wait for him when we saw him at that concert?'

'Because he kissed another woman, and he was drunk. I can't go through it again, not like I did with Sky.'

'You saw him kissing another woman, right?'

'Yes, you saw it, too.'

'And he saw you kissing another man? Todd, right?'

'Yes.'

'You didn't want to kiss Todd, did you?' Louisa's gaze fixed on Scarlett, demanding an answer.

Scarlett's lips twisted. 'I guess. I never thought of it like that before.'

Louisa shook her head, her eyes saying it all.

'Okay, so maybe I was overreacting. And, yes, I know Dylan isn't Sky, we've been through that.'

Louisa threw her hands up in despair. 'What, then?'

'Watch Dylan, Mummy. Concentrate,' Elsa scolded.

They all focused on the screen again, as Dylan shook his newly tamed curls, leaned back, and crossed his long legs in front of him, cowboy boots extended. He looked as cool and comfortable as if he chatted with famous people every day, which he probably now did.

'Sexy new image, eh? He looks like he's showing the ladies what they might be missing. But what the hell have they done to his hair?' Louisa squinted toward the screen.

The on-screen Dylan narrowed his eyes, when the presenter produced a large photograph of himself with Beanie and Scrappy-doo, singing in a rundown side street.

'Dylan made his mark singing in pubs, and before that, for many years, he was destitute, playing in the grimy streets of London to make a living. At his lowest point, he had to abandon his dog, and things were pretty bleak.' The presenter turned to Dylan, who raised his eyebrows, clearly surprised by her summing up of his youth. 'You've come from that … to this.'

Another photograph appeared on a huge screen behind them: of Dylan drinking champagne in a dark suit, a bow tie carelessly undone around his neck. He stood next to a bejewelled, dark-haired woman sheathed in red silk, a controlling hand on his shoulder as if claiming possession.

'Who is she?' Scarlett's nose almost hit the screen. 'God, how cheap. They're playing the rags to riches card.

I happen to know he was well educated and his parents own a bloody massive house by the sea.'

'Why let the truth get in the way of a good story, as they say,' Louisa said.

Scarlett bit her nails, sensing Dylan's reticence to play along with the image they were trying to paint.

'It wasn't like that,' he began, but the presenter ran roughshod over his words as the camera panned out to the audience.

Scarlett squealed and jumped up from the floor. 'Look, it's Mac, looking like a proud parent. And he's holding hands with Anya.' Scarlett stabbed at the television, down on her knees once more. 'And look, there's Stanley. You remember - the one with the drink problem and the bad clothes.'

Stanley seemed to realise the camera was panning out to him and stuck his thumbs up. He smiled, showing pearly-white-veneered teeth, so bright that the camera lights made them look luminous.

'Look at his teeth. Dylan will have paid for those.' She had little doubt of that. 'Oh, Dylan, you are such a darling.'

Louisa shrugged, obviously not having a clue what her sister was talking about.

Scarlett felt her entire being soften as she watched Dylan, until Louisa elbowed her, her smile frozen, as the camera zoomed in on one particular person, focusing rather too noticeably on her deep cleavage.

'No. Oh, Dylan, not her again, please don't tell me you

and Kate are now an item.'

A gothic-looking Kate, all dark-ringed eyes and black clothes, blew Dylan a kiss as the camera panned over her.

In return, he smiled goofily and gave her a little wave.

'Dear God, it's true.' Scarlett didn't even feel defeated, just accepting. 'I knew it, anyway, so I don't know why I'd dismissed it in my mind.'

'She was the one at the concert we went to?'

'The one he kissed, yes.'

'We've just been through this, Scarlett. Kate was the one doing the kissing, and the poor bloke was so fed up, he'd had a few beers.'

'Yes.' Scarlett's voice wavered. She was starting to wonder if she wanted to blame Dylan for her own inability to commit to him.

'And since when did you have such a right to take the moral high ground on drinking alcohol? I seem to recall finding you slumped against the front door one Christmas, when your friends just dumped you and ran.'

Scarlett threw herself into a chair, but she smiled at the memory. 'I still can't smell Pernod without wanting to throw up, since that Christmas Eve.' She flung her arms theatrically in the air. 'Oh, I don't know. I don't know what I think anymore.'

A burst of music from the television had them both riveted again, as the presenter shouted over the noise of whistling and applause. 'Let's give the ladies what they've been waiting for. His latest song, Please Believe You're Beautiful. Ladies and gentlemen, we give you

Dylan Willis.'

Dylan walked on to the stage, scooping up his guitar on the way. A fug of dry ice blew up in front of him, as he raised his guitar and started playing. Coloured lights flashed up by his feet like he was in an outdated Michael Jackson video, and he jumped backwards. He frowned down at the unexpected addition, like he'd walked on to the wrong set, but once he started singing, it was as if all of the props fell away, and it was just Dylan and his music: how he liked it, total concentration on the song and his guitar.

He used the same battered guitar he'd brought to her flat, Scarlett noted – the same one he'd played at his parent's house in Southwold, and on the 'grimy' streets of London. She longed to touch it, as if it might conjure up Dylan, bring him magically back to her, like a genie's lamp with a wish still intact. She bunched her hand into her mouth until her knuckles whitened, praying he wouldn't make a mistake, but he was more than perfect. At least, in her eyes, he was.

Louisa sat, open-mouthed. 'Bloody hell. He's good, isn't he?'

'Yeah.' Pride rose up in Scarlett's chest, even though she had no claims to him, anymore. A lump formed in her throat, and she turned to her sister, her voice strangled with emotion. 'What am I going to do? I loved him, and I let him believe he could love me. And then I let him down.' She tried to moderate the wail in her voice as Elsa glanced up in alarm. 'I was such a fool, worrying about Todd and my job, when I should have been concentrating on Dylan.'

'Don't be hard on yourself. You've had a really tough time with Sky, and Dylan turned up like a bolt out of the blue.'

'And I should have loved him more. Instead, he's gone off to love Kate. Her and her stupid big tits.'

Elsa's eyes rounded, and her mouth fell open. Her eyes darted to her mother as if to see what she would have to say about such a statement.

Louisa put an arm around her sister and hugged her. 'I'm sure he's not in love with this Kate. He barely knows her, right?' she said.

Scarlett laughed bitterly. 'He knows her, all right. She was at the pub in Southwold, the one time I went there, and she was determined to dredge up their history together. She probably saw her chance and took it.'

Gnawing at her knuckles, Scarlett tried to gauge Dylan's reactions to the ever-waving Kate by staring at the television, as if it would flash up the status of their relationship.

As soon as the song ended, he bowed and blew a kiss to the audience, who whistled and clapped, even once he'd left the stage. There was no doubt that he'd been a raging success.

She sat still, staring at the television, drained of emotion. She huffed out a breath and put her thumb and forefinger to the bridge of her nose. 'About that wine in the fridge and starting a tad earlier than we meant to?'

‘Glass, or bottle?’ Louisa asked, heading for the kitchen.

Scarlett plonked herself down on the sofa. ‘Bottle, I think, don’t you? One each?’

‘Definitely.’ She joined Scarlett on the sofa, waving a bottle in each hand. ‘Plan of action?’

‘I don’t have one,’ Scarlett said miserably. ‘I’ve left it too late.’

CHAPTER TWENTY-FIVE

Scarlett hovered around the control office, hoping to be stood down. She'd been called out on emergency standby and had waited for five hours, while her passengers made up their mind about where they wanted to go, or even if they wanted to go anywhere, at all. It certainly gave credence to the term Hurry up and wait.

The whole crew would be out of hours soon, if they took much longer to make up their minds, and if the trip was farther than Europe, there'd be no point hanging around, as a new crew would have to be called out. The situation was farcical, but Scarlett had soon grown used to such situations. The passenger was always right, so long as the money flowed from their wallets to the coffers of the airline.

'The booking has just come through, we're good to go,' the Ops guy said, putting down the phone.

Damn it, Scarlett thought, having mentally prepared to return to her flat, even though she'd do little but stare at the boats until bedtime, once there.

Having spent yet another sad evening on her sofa, drinking wine, miserable and forlorn in her little eyrie of a flat, she'd decided that she'd had enough. The move to Liverpool hadn't worked out, and she was lonelier than ever, so after a lot of deliberation, she'd made a new plan. She had accepted an offer to move to a different airline, based in Moscow and she felt more upbeat than she had in ages, having negotiated a deal where she'd work two weeks on then two weeks off, so she'd be able to commute to London and return to her flat, and a semblance of her old life.

Louisa would be over the moon, and once she'd got back in the swing of single living again, it would be as if nothing had changed. Dylan wouldn't be part of it, of course, but she'd accepted that, although her heart still ached whenever she thought of him.

She snapped back to the present, as a wodge of magazines were slapped down in front of her. She picked them up, to place them on the tiny coffee table on the aircraft, sending a weak smile to the ground handling agent. 'What was the problem?' she asked.

'Bigwig passenger, apparently. Too busy to turn up on time. You know what they're like.'

'Tell me about it. Sometimes, I think a certain kind of passenger keeps people waiting just because they can,' Scarlett agreed, as she ran through the printed catering sheet, checking that ice, milk and other staples were due to be loaded.

'Not sure if there's just one, or two passengers at the moment, but the flight is going to London, then on to some godforsaken airport in the arse-end of nowhere. That's where you'll stopover. Hardly any catering. Couple of bottles of bubbly, and some caviar – a few sarnies thrown in for good measure. Okay?'

Scarlett sighed, losing the will to sparkle for anyone, let alone Champagne-swigging good-time passengers. 'I didn't know it was going to be a stopover.'

'Sorry, but you know the drill: always be prepared, and the passenger is always right. They want to put the aircraft on standby until the morning, in case it's needed. Doesn't seem worth it to me. Might as well have got a cab down there. But, hey, it's their money.'

'True.' She sighed and re-adjusted her bun, making sure any loose tendrils were tucked away. 'Right, I'm outta here. I'll hook up with Pete on the way. He's watching repeats of Homes Under the Hammer in the VIP room.'

'Give him this, will you? Weather's turning shit later, so you might have to re-file.' He slid the flight plan and passenger details across his desk, and she tucked them under her arm as she picked up her overnight bag.

Pete, the captain, yawned and stretched as Scarlett unearthed him, several empty coffee cups and discarded biscuit wrappers on the table in front of him. 'We're on, then? Shame, I was looking forward to an early pint and a kip.' He prodded the first officer who dozed in an armchair. 'Come on, mate, the transport's waiting.' He pressed his uniform cap firmly down on his head and picked up his flight bag, as a white minibus pulled up outside.

They were soon ferried out to the aircraft, where they were told the passengers would arrive in thirty minutes.

'Unbelievable. Keep us waiting for hours, and then it's all, when are we going?' Pete always seemed happiest when he was moaning about miscreant passengers, so no one bothered to comment. 'Better get the old bird fired up. It's bloody freezing in here. Put the kettle on, Scarlett,' he said mournfully.

'Will do, but I've still got the safety checks to finish.'

She checked that the hot water urn actually had water in it before turning the power on, and quickly made them all a drink, afterwards turning her attention to the fire extinguishers, oxygen bottles and life jackets. She straightened the headrest covers and laid out the complimentary magazines and newspapers, glancing around the neat cabin with satisfaction. She tried to be positive, but it was hard to dredge up her old enthusiasm for work, and had recently taken to frequent sighing and wondering why she didn't just find an easier job.

'Passengers in five,' the ground guy shouted up the steps.

'Okay.' Scarlett sighed again, as she opened her compact mirror and scrabbled around in her bag for her lipstick. She slicked on a generous covering of Sunset Shine over her pale lips and dotted a touch of foundation under her eyes, which seemed to be permanently ringed with dark smudges.

What had happened to the bubbly, smiling girl she used to be? Her lips had become permanently set to a default of miserable lately, and her eyes, which used to sparkle with interest, seemed lacklustre and pained.

She tried out a smile, anyway, her lips feeling as if they were made of cement that had already set. Still, she could pretend as well as the next depressed air stewardess, and once she'd fixed on the smile, she was determined to make it stay.

She forced the two bottles of champagne into the ice bucket, twisting and pushing them down, smiling wryly as she spotted the familiar golden coloured labels of good quality champagne. Back in her old flat, she'd knocked back Cristal with Dylan like it was cheap Cava, a time when she'd hoped her life was blossoming again, after such a long depression.

An image of Dylan sprang up, all long legs and tatty clothes, sprawling across her pristine carpet, pretending to enjoy the caviar she fed him. She shook the memory away and focussed on the job in hand, praying the champagne would chill down quickly. Someone in catering should have been on to it much earlier, she thought with annoyance. Instead, it looked as if they'd turned up, dumped the whole catering order in her tiny galley, and scarpered as quickly as they could. It was not the way VIP airlines expected to be treated, and she'd be having a word about it when she returned.

She picked up the caviar box loaded as standard and pulled out the various ingredients. The jar of caviar was tiny, but it would probably be okay so long as there were only the two passengers, although the odds of them wanting it were probably slight. She placed it in the fridge and checked that the rest of the kit was in there, ticking the items off against her catering list.

A covered tray sat precariously on the draining board, and she picked it up, intending to put it in the cold storage. She had no idea what was under the foil, and pulled back an inch to peek beneath, recoiling as the contents gave off a pungent smell. Bugger! Had it gone off?

She whipped off the foil, half expecting a spicy Indian dish, but sitting on the tray were triangular sandwiches, precisely cut with the crusts cut away. A familiar waft hit her as she sniffed and peered closer. Marmite. Seriously? It really was: Marmite and cucumber - and something else.

She lifted the edge of another sandwich. It looked like banana and .... What the hell? She sniffed again, confirming that it was what she'd thought it to be: peanut butter. She knew only one person who ate peanut butter with banana, and Marmite with cucumber sandwiches.

Her mind slid back to the summer days she'd spent in Southwold with Dylan, happy for the first time since Sky's death, not knowing that, within days it would come crashing down again. Surely her passengers couldn't include Dylan?

Her mouth dried. No, it wouldn't be. The odds had to be a million to one.

'Pete?' she shouted, intending to ask if he'd checked the passenger details.

'Yes, passengers are here. We need to get a move on, or else we'll miss our flight slot.' Pete called through the flight deck door.

It was too late to find out.

Her heart lurched.

A car pulled up to the bottom of the steps, doors slammed, and she heard the tread of footsteps as her passengers headed up the stairs. Her breath hitched in her chest until she felt dizzy with nerves.

An oriental lady, with a sleek bob so sharp she could cut herself on it, peered around the cabin. 'Hi. Okay to come on board?'

Scarlett exhaled. 'Yes, of course.' She almost added Thank God, as her pounding heart slowed down, but then a man's voice carried above the din of the right engine firing into life, as a car door slammed.

A guitar, followed by a flash of white teeth and a mop of unruly hair, set her pulse racing off the Richter scale.

Dylan stamped his feet and shook the damp from his hair. 'Ah, Scarlett. Gloomy old day, isn't it?' He stuck out his hand, and she held out her own, automatically, ignoring the trillion volts of electricity that shot through her arm, as he enveloped her hand inside his. 'Ooh, clammy handshake.' He wiped his palm down the front of his jeans, grinning at her.

She was totally lost for words, not that it would have mattered with the way her tongue seemed to have stuck to the roof of her mouth.

Dylan stared, as if waiting for her to speak. 'Yes, well,

good to see you, too.' He ran his fingers through his hair, and she could only gape at the unlikely vision in front of her. He hitched his thumb towards the petite lady. 'Meet Natasha.'

Natasha's smile was stiff as she stood by the galley entrance, waiting to be invited inside the main cabin. The damp weather didn't seem to have dared touch her hair, and she looked immaculate and totally in control, right down to her tiny feet encased in spiky heeled Louboutin's.

'Scarlett is an old friend of mine, aren't you?' Dylan turned his sunny smile towards her once more.

She opened her mouth, but once again, nothing came out.

'She doesn't say a lot,' Dylan assured Natasha. 'I think she's a bit socially challenged,' he whispered in Natasha's ear, loud enough for someone in Paris to hear. 'Okay to sit here?'

Natasha looked slightly confused, as Dylan led her to a window seat and helped her to sit down. He chucked his rucksack on the opposite seat and propped his guitar next to it, rubbing his hands together. 'This is fun, isn't it? I've never flown in such a tiddler.'

Scarlett gawped at him. How could he be making small talk so casually, while she was shocked to her core to see him? She was aware that her eyes were as big as saucers and that she was acting like a love-struck fan, but her usual sangfroid had done a runner in his presence.

She breathed deeply and set her shoulders. She could

deal with this. She was a professional.

Nevertheless, her gaze was drawn to Dylan once more, her eyes thirsty for him. So, his guitar and battered old rucksack were still part of his props, were they? They were so dear to her that she wanted to stroke them, her fingers itching to feel the smooth wood of his guitar inside its case. Instead, she glowered at Dylan, resentfully, wondering why the hell he was on her aeroplane, anyway?

'Of all the planes in all the world,' she muttered under her breath as she dragged her gaze away from him and tried to focus on the job in hand.

Her stomach lurched when she realised she would have to leave the safety of her galley to secure his guitar for take-off. Worse still, she'd have to talk to him and serve his annoyingly perfect girlfriend.

She swallowed hard as panic set in.

'Scarlett, pull the steps up.' Pete hollered from the flight deck. 'What are you waiting for?'

For a second, she contemplated making a run for it, straight down the steps and across the tarmac, not stopping until she reached her car. But sanity won the day, and she pulled up the steps until they fitted snugly into the fuselage. She checked the safety catch, casting a last, wistful eye over her escape route as she did so. There was no way around it. She'd just have to do her job.

'Excuse me.' She swallowed the word Sir down. She couldn't go that far in the call of duty. 'I'll have to secure your baggage.' She picked up the rucksack and placed it in the overhead compartment, turning to pick up his guitar case, but Dylan beat her to it, jumping to his feet.

'Leave it to me. Where do you want it?' His hand closed over hers as he lunged for his case. Their eyes locked, and the moment froze as their fingers touched. Dylan removed his hand, so, so slowly, one finger at a time as they stared at each other.

'Scarlett …'

'Seats for take-off, please.' Pete's voice coming over the PA system forced her to act and she quickly shoved the guitar into the toilet cubicle, slamming the door as the engines revved.

Dylan's smile drooped. 'Nice.'

She gave him a weak smile before falling into her seat and strapping in with trembling fingers, as the aircraft soared into the sky.

While waiting for the aircraft to level out, she peered at him through her lashes, reacquainting herself with his face, noting the shadow on his jaw and the tired lines around his eyes. Maybe life wasn't being as kind to him as she thought.

Her heart twisted when his smile came alive for Natasha, and a white-hot shaft of jealousy flooded her body when he patted her hand. She wanted Dylan's smile all to herself, and those finely-boned fingers she remembered so well touching her skin, not the flawless Natasha's.

Natasha laughed a pretty, neat laugh, as he whispered into her ear, bringing Scarlett straight back down to earth. He had someone new. Sure, he did; he'd be a man in great demand.

She felt excluded and voyeuristic, as she watched their exchange from her solitary position.

She wondered briefly if he'd broken Kate's heart and momentarily felt sad for her. But her own pain was all too raw, knocking at her ribs and demanding attention, for her to dwell on Kate's fate for long.

The double chimes from the flight deck signalled that it was safe to start the service, and she unbuckled her safety belt automatically, going through the motions of pulling out food and scooping fresh ice into the ice bucket. Her fingers fluttered over the disgusting sandwiches, and she looked longingly at a bottle of Cristal, wondering if a good slug from it might help. Apart from the fact that it would get her the sack, she'd need a magnum of it, at least, to get through the next hour.

She pondered the possibility of asking Pete to tell her passengers that the weather was too choppy to serve food. The Ops guy had said the weather was going to be bad, after all, so it could feasibly be true.

Across from her, Dylan parodied pouring a drink with his goofy grin in place, and she moistened her sawdust-dry lips with her desert-dry tongue. My God, he was actually enjoying seeing her discomfort. Was the whole flight some kind of set up? Was that why he'd ordered Marmite and peanut butter sandwiches, to let her know that it was him? He was simply playing with her, showing off his status and wealth.

She wouldn't have thought he would be so cruel, but it seemed that he was. Was he trying to let her know what she was missing? If that was the case, then she could be just as petty and show him what he was missing, too.

She undid the top button of her blouse and picked up the sandwiches, shimmying over to him. 'Would you like some refreshment?' She leaned over, thrusting out her breasts, so he could get a good look at her cleavage.

'Ooh, what are they?' His fingers hovered over the tray, and he grinned up at her. He seemed to be really enjoying her embarrassment, and she wanted to smack him in his stupid, grinning face for it.

Determined to hold the upper hand, she put as much huskiness in her voice as she could get away with, without laughing. 'I believe the selection is Marmite with cucumber, and peanut butter with banana.'

Dylan's gaze dropped to her breasts. 'Great, my favourite. I'll take two. I've missed them – Marmite sandwiches, I mean.'

She almost dropped her tray. The man was shameless.

He took two sandwiches, his gaze returning to Scarlett's face, pasting an innocent expression on his own.

She chose to ignore his comment. 'We also have caviar, which I believe was ordered with the Cristal, although I won't serve it if it is not to sir's liking.' Scarlett wiggled her bottom inside her tight skirt as she trotted off to get the champagne. It was all of half a dozen steps away, but she sashayed for all she was worth.

Dylan turned toward Natasha. 'Champagne again, Natasha?'

Natasha nodded, but didn't lift her gaze away from her sheaf of paperwork, or so much as glance at Scarlett, or Dylan.

Rude cow, Scarlett thought with glee.

Dylan held both flutes and watched closely as Scarlett poured the sparkling wine into the glasses, his gaze flicking briefly up to her chest again. He placed a glass carefully on the table next to Natasha, who smiled tightly.

And Dylan had accused her of not saying much, Scarlett thought. His new woman had evidently got him on the run if she didn't even feel the need to make polite conversation.

'I have champagne wherever I go now, you know,' Dylan said conversationally. 'Cristal, Krug. I could practically clean my teeth with Moet, I've got so much of it. It's a bit of a treat for some people, I believe.' His eyes twinkled, and she saw the beginning of a grin twitching at the side of his mouth.

She didn't know why he was smiling. There was nothing funny about being stuck with each other in a metal tube at twenty-thousand feet. 'That's great. Bully for you, and your liver.'

Dylan glanced toward Natasha's papers, which she was covering in red ink. 'While Natasha is busy, why don't you pull up a chair, metaphorically speaking of course, as these babies don't move.' He patted the seat opposite. 'We can have a natter about old times. For example, I'm wondering why you moved to Liverpool. These aircraft are really small. Didn't you say your old airline was a twelve seater and some were configured with bedrooms?' He waved his glass around, indicating the small aircraft.

Scarlett eyed the seat opposite warily, wondering how far she needed to consider that the customer was always right. No, she didn't want to sit down opposite Dylan and confess that she'd moved to a lesser airline, basically because she didn't want to be blackmailed into sleeping with the odious Todd.

She struck a pose, her tray in one hand and a bottle in the other. 'I have things to do, sorry.' She placed the bottle on the table. 'Help yourself. If, that is, you still do things for yourself?'

'Aww, I was looking forward to you doing it all for me. I seem to recall you were good at taking the lead.'

Her eyes widened. She couldn't believe he was playing such a game – in front of his girlfriend, too. 'Stop being a wanker, Dylan.' The hissed words were out before she had chance to stop them.

Natasha's head shot up, and she raised two perfect eyebrows, glancing at Dylan. 'Unfinished business?'

'No, we're done, thanks.' Scarlett grabbed his plate, including the uneaten sandwiches, and flounced off to her galley, horrified that she'd sworn at a passenger, even if it had been Dylan and he totally deserved it.

She stuck her head inside the flight deck. 'Pete, would you mind putting the seat belt sign on a bit early? I'm not feeling too good.'

'No problem, Scarlett.' He flicked a switch, and the seat belt sign illuminated.

Scarlett secured her galley and sat down, fighting the urge to glance over at Dylan. Who had she been kidding? He had no need for her anymore, and she'd just shown how pathetic she was, trying to tempt him with her body. One look at Natasha should have told her that Dylan had moved way out of her league. She could probably have taken all her clothes off and hung upside down off the aircraft wing, and he still wouldn't have noticed.

Chewing the inside of her cheek until it hurt, she had to stick her tongue against the roof of her mouth to stop herself from crying.

CHAPTER TWENTY-SIX

They landed with a whoosh of airbrakes, as a sudden crosswind bounced them onto the runway. Scarlett was gratified to see Natasha grip the sides of her seat, her knuckles white, her eyes wide and scared. Just as quickly, she felt guilty for thinking mean thoughts. She seemed a perfectly nice lady, after all, and she doubted Dylan would've been with her, otherwise.

She smiled over at Natasha and mouthed, 'It's fine.'

Natasha gave her a wonky smile in return, and Scarlett warmed to her, despite the jealousy still raging in her heart.

As the aircraft came to a standstill, Scarlett peered through one of the windows. Rain hammered against the fuselage – the weather had turned, as anticipated, and once again she wasn't prepared for it.

Forcing the door open, she drew in a deep sigh, fighting against the wind, as needles of rain stung her face and plastered loose strands of her hair to her cheeks. 'Wow, it's really horrible out there,' she said, retreating into the relative safety of the galley. 'Oh, looks as if your transport has arrived,' she added, as a white, stretched Limousine pulled up to the steps, its windscreen wipers going ten to the dozen. 'This is for you?' she asked Dylan, wanting to laugh at the ostentatious car.

'Yep, looks like it,' Dylan agreed.

She grinned at him, expecting him to be mortified at travelling in a flashy Limo, but he didn't even crack a smile. He certainly had changed.

'Do you want to hang on a minute? I can't let you disembark without someone escorting you to your car. Health and safety, and all that.' She shrank away from the onslaught, as she looked out for the ground staff.

'Oh. You could do it, couldn't you?' he asked.

Scarlett glowered at him. 'I don't have a coat.'

'Again? You really do need to organize yourself.'

'I was in a rush. I was called out at six o'clock this morning for a flight that didn't leave until eleven. Some people apparently only think of themselves.' She really shouldn't have been accusing her passenger of being selfish, especially when she had a feeling Dylan was winding her up on purpose, but she couldn't help it, even if she was playing into his hands.

'Ah, hazards of the job, I guess.' He inclined his head as if a good idea had just occurred to him. 'Do you have an umbrella, maybe?'

She gritted her teeth. 'Don't push it, Dylan. Ah, here's the ground girl.' She smiled brightly at Natasha, as she collected her bags and hovered around Dylan, his rucksack slung over his shoulder.

He stood aside, allowing Natasha to disembark first, holding her elbow as she braved the weather and the steps. 'Easy does it, they might be slippery.'

Another hit of pure jealousy almost floored Scarlett at his caring gesture. She tried to paint on a smile, but she knew Dylan had seen the pain in her eyes. He gave her a troubled glance, and she slid her gaze away from his.

Just go Dylan, just leave, she pleaded, silently.

He stood at the top of the steps, running his fingers through his hair. 'Scarlett ...?' Her name hung in the air between them, the concern in his voice clear.

She remembered how tenderly he used to say her name and had to turn away, in case her eyes gave her away. She pretended to tidy up her galley, picking up glasses and unused plates, only to put them down again. Finally, she glanced over to the door. The white Limousine had gone, taking Dylan away forever.

He didn't even say goodbye, she thought, watching the exhaust fumes dissipate in the rain. Her eyes widened. 'Wait, wait, you forgot your guitar. Shit.' She rushed to the tiny bathroom and pulled his guitar out, knowing already that she was too late. She slumped down onto a seat, cradling the guitar case as the whole, surreal situation overwhelmed her.

Placing the case on a seat, she unzipped it and took out his guitar, running her hand over the mellow wood, taking in the nicks and old stickers. She liked that he still took it everywhere with him, even though he probably had much better ones to hand since his rise to stardom.

She plucked at the top string, trailed her fingernail over the rest of them, once again back in Southwold, imagining his eyes scrunching up as he tried to find the right words, the right chords, for the soul rending song that was now his signature tune. Impulsively, she clutched the guitar to her chest as the ache in her heart winded her with its ferocity.

Footsteps hit the stairs and she snapped her head up, dashing at her eyes awash with unshed tears.

Too late.

'Hey.' Dylan once more appeared at the top of the steps, his ready smile vanishing as he took in her distress. 'Scarlett.' He was by her side in seconds, kneeling next to her, taking her hand, smoothing her hair away.

'I thought you'd left?' She jumped up, thrusting the guitar at his chest, her fake smile back. But hope surged through her body at his touch, his words, the expression in his eyes.

'Scarlett. Tell me.'

The urge to sob into his arms, abandoning herself to his kindness almost overwhelmed her, but she swallowed it down, even though she wanted to unburden her soul. He had a girlfriend, the career he'd always wanted, a life without her.

She pulled herself out of her fluffy world of redemption. 'It's fine. Nothing to report here.' She quickly wiped a finger under her eyes for tell-tale mascara stains and summoned up a smile. 'So, you've come back for your guitar?'

'No, I'm travelling on to Suffolk on this aeroplane. I just wanted to make sure Natasha found her way to the terminal. Didn't you know?'

At the mention of Natasha, she straightened her back and stood. 'Oh, yes, I'd forgotten.' She stared dumbly, her mind empty of rational thought.

'Scarlett, about Natasha.'

'We really don't need to discuss your relationships, Dylan.' She exhaled with relief that she hadn't made a fool of herself by confessing her feelings to him. Hopefully, she could manage to play the game for another hour, or so, before he left her forever.

When his gaze didn't leave her face, she found her cheeks heating up, wondering if she had, after all, given herself away. 'I haven't spoken to the flight deck since ... since I found your guitar.' She returned his stare, unblinking, thrusting her chin upwards. She was fine. She could do this. 'I'll tell them we're ready to go, shall I?'

He let the guitar drop to one of the seats, hands brushing his jeans. 'Sure, I guess.' His Adam's apple bobbed, as if he was trying to work up to a speech - a speech she doubted she'd want to hear.

Sweeping past him into the flight deck, she pulled the steps up once more, her mouth drying when it dawned on her that they'd be alone - together - with nowhere to run.

CHAPTER TWENTY-SEVEN

'Are you going to stay fastened in that grownup highchair until we land again?' Dylan shouted over the din of the engines, as they took off once more.

Scarlett turned her head away, stared out of the window, but Dylan knew she was just pretending she hadn't heard him. It was his one chance to talk to her, though, and he didn't intend wasting it. The aircraft levelled out, but the Captain didn't switch off the seat belt sign, and he wondered if Scarlett had asked him not to.

He unbuckled his seat belt, anyway, and walked over to her, working on Scarlett's theory that the customer was always right, and that she was unlikely to throw him off the aircraft.

Her lips compressed into a thin line, and she gripped her seat as if she expected it to catapult her up in the air.

'It's not turbulent anymore, Scarlett.' He hunkered down next to her, nerves kicking in. He couldn't afford to mess up again. 'Come on, Scarlett, sit with me.' She folded her hands tightly in her lap, and he recognized the signs: she was angry with him - or maybe even with herself. Either way, he knew he had his work cut out.

Surprising him, she unbuckled her seat belt and stood. 'Coffee?' Her voice quivered, and it gave him hope.

He watched as she gathered drinking paraphernalia together, guessing she wanted an excuse to move away from him. 'Yes, please, one sugar.'

She rolled her eyes. 'It hasn't been that long.'

Blimey, he thought, she really is in a bad mood.

She rounded on him again as she stirred sugar viciously into his mug, whipping up a veritable whirlpool of coffee. 'So, you've turned into a Limousine kind of guy?' She gave him a brittle smile, and he gave her a knowing look, right back. If she wanted to fight, he could handle it. It might even be fun.

'For your information, they just keep turning up. I don't ask for them. I think someone must have done a deal with the agency, and I get the crap end of it. My Nan nearly died of fright when I rocked up in it the other week. She thought the Mafia was coming to get her, and the driver wouldn't get out of the car because she lives in a dodgy area. I suppose there would be some good money to be made if you managed to jack a Limo up onto bricks and nick the tyres.'

He sat back in his seat, as she handed him a coffee, his gaze trailing over her body, deliberately provocative. 'You look good, considering.'

'Considering what? No, don't answer that,' she snapped as she sat down opposite him, nursing her own mug of coffee. Her brow furrowed and her lips tightened once more.

God, she was cute, and he couldn't resist teasing her, just to see her chin jut out and her eyes flash that beautiful sea-green that he'd missed so much. 'I don't know why you're mad at me. You were the one who walked out, remember?'

'Yeah, like I really wanted to do that.'

'You didn't? Then, why did you?'

'Water under the bridge,' she bit out, her lips compressing again. She glared at him. 'Actually, things have really moved on for me, recently. I've got a job in Moscow. I rented out my flat when I got the job in Liverpool.'

'Really, you're moving to Russia?' He already knew she'd moved out of her flat, but Moscow came as a shock. Still, he wasn't daunted. He knew she'd missed him, but just tried to remember not to let on.

He was, however, intrigued by her performance earlier, when she'd seemed determined to shove her breasts and her very lush bottom at him in that sexy uniform. Very nice it had been, too. He just wasn't sure of her motivation - maybe he'd ask her about it, later. Snapping his gaze away from her breasts, where it'd had wandered of its own free will, he forced himself to focus on her face.

'Moscow, yes. How could I stay at StarJet after everything that happened?'

'What happened at StarJet?'

'I was suspended over the Angel Brothers thing. Pictures of me half naked and visiting a known drug felon don't go down well in the corporate airline world, for some reason.'

'I saw someone brought out a biography about the Angel Brothers.'

'Yes. Stupidly, naive me thought they were taking

photos and dredging it all up again because there was a story they thought should be told. Turns out it was a good publicity stunt for the book. They probably paid the newspaper a fortune to publish that load of garbage.' Her chin jutted out again in that adorable way, but the hurt she carried was clear in her voice and in her eyes.

He wanted to smooth away her anger and kiss away the pain she tried so hard to conceal. 'I tried to find you - at StarJet. All they would say is that you left.'

She turned shocked eyes toward Dylan. 'You tried to find me?'

'Yes. I nearly hit the obnoxious Captain Carrington. Why were you kissing him, Scarlett? You didn't sleep with him, did you?' Dylan's possessive streak was always close to the surface, and he tried to moderate his voice, even as it pained him to ask her. He really shouldn't have brought up the topic so soon, but the words were out and done and so had to be dealt with.

'I've told you, he was no more than a colleague.'

He pressed his lips together, determined not to lose his cool. 'So, why were you kissing him?'

She had the look of a cornered mouse in her eyes, and he prayed she wasn't about to lie to him. He was pretty sure he'd know if she did.

Scarlett closed her eyes and swallowed, and he knew she wasn't lying when she finally spoke. 'He offered me an ultimatum, which was basically get promoted, or suspended.'

Dylan breathed out in relief. It wasn't as bad as he thought, but she still hadn't answered his question. 'Scarlett, will you just tell me why you were on your doorstep kissing Captain fucking Carrington?'

Her eyes flashed once more, the scared mouse gone. 'Not that it's any of your business, but the deal he offered me included sleeping with him. And I wasn't kissing him. He forced himself on me.'

'What?' Dylan's body heated up in anger, and he clenched his fists. 'I should have smacked him while I had the chance, the slimy bastard. You should have kneed him in the balls.'

Scarlett laughed. 'That's just what Louisa said.'

'So, that's why you left StarJet?'

'That's why I left and moved to Liverpool. It was the only job I could get at short notice.' She turned puzzled eyes in his direction. 'Why did you come to find me at StarJet?'

'We can talk about that later,' Dylan said as he glanced at his watch, checking how long he had left with her.

'What later is this, then?'

He ignored her question. 'You know these things are really good - Apple watches.' He tapped his watch. 'I'm amazed at the things they do. Natasha has one, too.'

'I noticed, and actually, I think matching watches are really tacky.'

Dylan broke into a grin and suppressed a guffaw.

Scarlett's lips compressed even further until she looked like she wanted to punch him. Good. She could get all her anger out before they landed, with a bit of luck. 'Matching watches?' He laughed harder and slapped his thigh. 'Priceless!'

'I don't see what's so funny.'

'Do I look like a matching watches kind of person? Seriously?' He laughed some more and wiped his eyes. 'Oh, I love that. I must tell Natasha that one.' He caught his breath and patted her knee. 'No, it was another freebie. You wouldn't believe the stuff they dish out to you, once you make a name for yourself. You don't even have to promise to wear it, or eat it, or anything. Things just turn up, like those blasted Limos. Anyway, some television agency sent me two watches, so I gave one to Natasha … who just happens to be my PA.'

'Oh. She's not your girlfriend?'

Scarlett's face was a picture. She looked relieved and contrite, all at the same time. She must have been dreaming up some really nasty hexes on poor Natasha. He loved the way she tried to compose herself, shifting her bottom in her seat and straightening her shoulders.

His mouth twitched. 'No, don't be daft – she's far too scary and efficient.'

Scarlett smiled thinly.

'No, I have a different girlfriend. She's very feisty. A bit of a pain in the arse, if I'm honest, but she keeps me on my toes.'

Scarlett's fledgling smile dissolved. 'Oh, I see.'

'So, all is good, with you?'

'Why are you doing this, Dylan? We said all we had to

say months ago.' She tilted her head away from him, but he could read the truth in her eyes.

'You said all you had to say. I didn't get a look in, once you'd made up your mind.' He sighed as he turned toward the window where squares of green grass whizzed by, far below. They must be nearing the private airstrip Natasha had located earlier. 'I suppose I'm being mean because I'm pissed off with you, and I want you to get an inkling of how much hurting I did over you.'

'Well, I hope this makes you feel better because I feel like crap, too–since you showed up on my aircraft. You win.' She hugged her arms around herself and Dylan felt a slight twinge of guilt. He wasn't done yet, though. It would soon be time to put Plan B into operation, and he prayed it would put things right between them, for good.

CHAPTER TWENTY-EIGHT

They landed once more, with no more than a whisper of wheels and a hiss of air brakes, as Scarlett opened the passenger door slowly and with reluctance. This was goodbye she knew, but she wanted to hold on to the moment for as long as she could, wishing that she'd been more accommodating, and upset that Dylan mixed up her emotions to a point where she couldn't think straight.

As she turned to him, summoning up a goodbye smile, she was surprised to see the same reluctance mirroring his eyes. He'd picked up his guitar and rucksack but then dumped them both back on the seat wrinkling his nose, as if a thought had just struck him. 'Do you think I could have a quick word with the captain?'

Scarlett frowned, but she nodded. 'I'll just check, but I imagine it will be fine.' She was used to passengers wanting to pass on their thanks, or ask a question, but her heart was heavy as she pulled open the flight deck door to ask Pete if it was convenient. 'He's a personal friend, so I know he's not a threat or anything,' she added. The only thing he'd ever threatened was her tranquillity.

She moved to one side, allowing Dylan through, but in the narrow confines of the galley, his arm brushed her breast as he manoeuvred past her.

He flinched. 'Boob graze. Sorry.'

'It's okay.' She smiled wanly, upset that he felt it necessary to apologise for touching her, and troubled by the zing of awareness that rushed through her body.

As if he could read her thoughts, Dylan raised his hands in surrender. 'Sorry, for saying sorry.' He lowered his hands. 'Oh, God, I'm just making it worse.'

'It's okay.' She smiled up at him and for a second it was as if the distance between them melted away.

They gazed at each other for a heartbeat before Dylan broke eye contact. 'I'd better …' He jerked his thumb in the direction of the flight deck.

'Yes, the Captain's name is Pete.' Her smile was professional once again although her heart pounded unreasonably.

She made a show of tidying the cabin and putting away the provisions, wishing for once that she could eavesdrop as Dylan talked to the flight deck. She knew that, once he left the aircraft, she'd only ever see him through a TV screen, Dylan clearly having made a better job of moving forward with his life than she had.

The thought almost broke her, but she tightened her resolve as he returned from the flight deck, irritatingly upbeat, his captivating smile back in place. She'd be glad to see the back of that, too, mostly because it made her heart flutter too much.

'Where's your flight bag, Scarlett?'

'In the cupboard. Why?'

Dylan pointed to the small stowage area. 'Here?' He opened the cupboard door. 'Ah, yes, same bag. I remember it well.' He hooked it out of the cupboard. 'Coat? Oh, no, I remember, you were in a rush.'

'What are you doing, Dylan?'

'Just taking you somewhere for a chat. I've cleared it with your boss. He said you've been a miserable cow since you started, and anything that might cheer you up, is fine with him.'

'He did not!'

'Go and check, then?' He winked at her, still positively fizzing with cheerfulness.

She wanted to refuse, prolonging the agony was pointless, but a bigger part of her wanted to go along with him, irritating as he was.

Pete popped his head out of the flight deck door. 'If we're not needed tomorrow we'll be positioning back empty. Give us a call if you don't want a lift, it won't be a problem.' He winked at her and she wondered what on earth Dylan had said to him.

The tiny prefab that passed for a terminal building was a short walk away, and Scarlett was relieved to see the lights of a BMW coupé flash when he pressed his key fob.

'Here we are. No stretched Limo here, no siree, absolutely not.' Dylan slung Scarlett's bag into the boot, along with his guitar, and opened the passenger door, before climbing into the driver's seat. 'Right, off we go.' He flashed her a grin as he changed up through the gears and roared through the country roads.

She settled into her seat, both confused and slightly peeved by his cocky manner. Glancing at him sidelong, she tried to understand his motives. She breathed in his familiar scent as she took another long look, getting side-tracked by his curls and his so familiar profile. 'This is a long way to go for a little chat, isn't it?'

Frowning, he glanced at her briefly before concentrating on the road again.

She smiled weakly, wondering what she'd said to upset him. 'What's wrong?'

'Scarlett. Can we call a truce, here?' He took his hand off the steering wheel and offered it to her, but she didn't take it, and he quickly folded his fingers around the gear stick. 'Suit yourself.' His tone was gruff, and he huffed out an exasperated breath.

She took in the long fingers, the clipped nails, the fine hairs on his hand. He glanced at her again, following her gaze, and offered his hand to her once more.

'What's going on here, Dylan?' She folded her arms to make sure she wasn't tempted by the proffered hand. He'd told her he had a girlfriend, hadn't he? It hurt her to even sit next to him, knowing he belonged to someone else, so why would she want to hold his hand?

She flicked her hair over her shoulder and stared out of the window.

'Maybe it'll keep awhile.' Dylan sighed loudly, and when she looked again, his hand was back on the steering wheel.

'Where are we going?' she asked politely - the least she could do was remain civil.

'Wait and see.'

His smile had all but disappeared, and she closed her

eyes, wondering what he wanted from her. And what did call a truce mean, exactly?

As he drove quickly through the narrow, winding roads, Scarlett vaguely recognized a few village names that told her they were heading for Southwold. She didn't know what Dylan's agenda was, but she wasn't in the mood to play his games, at least not until he stopped acting as if he had the upper hand in everything they did. Which was even more annoying, because he did have the upper hand, being in actual possession of her body, and spiritual possession of her heart.

They managed a few polite words, until Dylan pulled up outside his parents' house. Dylan, all hearty and gung-ho climbed out, leaving Scarlett to sit in lonely solitude. With a sigh, she climbed from the car, slamming the door for effect before she stomped up the pathway to join him.

A golden Labrador bounded through the hallway as soon as Dylan opened the front door, and he caught the dog's head in his hands as it licked him and bounced around. 'Hey, Custard, how are you, girl?'

He pranced around with Custard for a while, and Scarlett felt like an interloper: the spoilsport with a miserable face at a private party.

Dylan laughed as he dodged Custard's chasing and head butting frolics. 'Look at her. Anyone would think I hadn't seen her for days.'

'When did you last see her, then?'

He put his head on one side. 'Hmm, let me think.

About eight hours ago.'

Scarlett frowned. 'How can you have?'

Dylan didn't answer as he stepped into the house. After putting food out for the dog, he picked up a key from the coat stand. 'Let's go. Mum will be home shortly and we'd be obliged to stay for a cup of tea, which would turn into staying for a glass of wine, which would then turn into staying for dinner. Don't worry, you'll meet her soon enough.'

'I will?' Scarlett's confusion grew by the second.

He cut through her thoughts, all cheerful and encouraging. 'Yeah, she's looking forward to meeting you. I told her you were nice, which wasn't a lie, so much, just a bit of a deviation on the truth.'

'But I can't ... it's not right.'

'Chill, she's a schoolteacher. She understands badly behaved people.'

Her frown deepened, and he sighed. 'Someone has to teach you how to be a trusting person.' He shrugged. 'I thought it might as well be her.'

'Thanks, I think,' she said, it being the easiest option.

'Right, I'm hoping the old pink fleece has been washed since the cat gave birth on it. We can take a walk down memory lane.' Scarlett paled, and he grinned. 'It was quite romantic last time we were here, wasn't it? I seem to recall it was the first time we made love. Oh, and the last time, too.' He pulled a sad face, his head tilted to one side. 'So far, anyway.'

His persistent perkiness was exhausting, and

Scarlett's tiredness and irritation was winning hands down, over his animated enthusiasm. She blinked wearily. 'You've lost me, Dylan.'

'Oh? It was one of those nights I thought you'd remember, but hey-ho, just me taking a trip down memory lane, then,' he continued cheerfully.

'Okay, Dylan, I admit I was rash and unfair on you. Can you give it a rest now, please, I'm a bit worn out?' She pinched the bridge of her nose, acknowledging a low-level headache brewing across her forehead.

'Let's take a walk, then. The fleece?' He held out his mother's jacket, and she took it from Dylan.

Scrunching it up, she held it to her cheek, as memories washed over her. She felt perilously close to tears.

'Not sure you'll want to wear it, if it holds distasteful memories.' His smile was wry, gently teasing.

Scarlett felt her mouth wobble. She wasn't sure how much more of Dylan's banter she could take.

As if he sensed she was at the end of her tether, his voice softened. 'Would you like to freshen up first? We can go to my new house.' He held out his hand.

'You have a house?'

'I do, and I'd love you to see it.'

'Okay.' She took his hand gratefully, as if it were an olive branch of friendship.

'If madam would like to come with me?'

He tucked her fingers into the crook of his elbow, and they walked together, close enough to bump hips, but still metaphorically miles apart.

They walked down the hill, and Dylan stopped in front of a large house that looked as if it had recently been re-vamped: all slanting glass, stainless steel, and exposed brick. 'What do you think?'

'This is yours?'

'Yup. Wanna take a look?'

'Oh, my God, it's beautiful.'

'I know, I love it.' A grin spread across his face. 'I spend as much time here as I can – I'm determined not to fall prey to the tempting sins of the flesh, or those other addictions you warned me about so many times.'

She grimaced. 'Was I that bad?'

'You did go on a bit, but I suppose you had your reasons.' He motioned for her to walk ahead of him up the pathway.

Remembering the feisty girlfriend he'd mentioned, she hesitated. 'I won't be treading on anyone's toes, will I?' She would happily step on every one of the woman's toes, if it would bring Dylan back to her, but thought it best not to tell him.

'Nope.'

That certainly sounded rather definite and final, although Scarlett was pretty sure the feisty girlfriend would have something to say about that, especially when she found out that Dylan had shown an ex-girlfriend around his new home.

Dylan turned the key in the lock and ushered her in. She took in the huge hallway and lantern light ceiling, which allowed blue sky to flood in, stunned that Dylan owned something so spectacular. An open plan kitchen, shining with state of the art gadgets, had been built in on one side of the house, with the longest run of windows she'd ever seen on the other, overlooking the sea.

She whirled around, taking in the expanse of space, her arms flung wide, not knowing what to look at first. 'This is the most fantastic place, ever.'

'There's a wonderful view from the roof. Would you like to see it? It's even better at night, snuggling down with a blanket and a glass of wine.' His eyes crinkled at the corners as he folded his arms, as if enjoying her enthusiasm.

She smiled back, breathing out as their eyes locked. Was he suggesting what she thought he was suggesting? Was it possible he still wanted her?

She hesitated, almost too afraid to ask the question. 'Would you like me to see the view?'

His soft smile widened, and his arrogant attitude seemed to melt away, leaving behind the old Dylan she knew, gently mocking, yet completely sincere. 'I would very much like you to see the view. It's up on the roof, of course, or else it wouldn't be called the roof view.' He took a step towards her, and then another one, until he was inches away from her, his eyes searching. He nudged closer still, his fingers brushing her cheek. 'Love the uniform, by the way. Incidentally, I meant to ask, what was that performance all about on the aircraft?'

Scarlett sensed her cheeks beginning to glow, but still tried to brazen it out. 'What performance?'

'All that bottom wiggling and breast thrusting.'

'I don't know what you mean?' She giggled involuntarily.

He rolled his eyes. 'What, do I look stupid?'

'I was mad at you, and I wanted you to know what you were missing.'

'Loved it. Can we have a rerun later, please?' Dylan's grin didn't fade.

'Is that every man's secret fantasy - a woman in uniform?'

'Absolutely. What's the point in going out with a hostie if I can't have my very own fantasy played out?'

Confusion swamped Scarlett all over again at his words. Had he just suggested they get back together, or had he, by some terrible coincidence, met another stewardess on his travels? She was hardly going to ask him and risk being ridiculed all over again.

She watched indecisively, as he pulled a bottle from the fridge and snagged two glasses from a cupboard.

'After you.' He waved in the direction of a set of wooden stairs, and she climbed up in front of him, aware that he was probably clocking her bottom in her tight skirt. Unable to help herself, she wiggled just a little bit, throwing him a cheeky smile.

Reaching the top of the stairs, all thoughts of impressing him with her rear vanished, as a vast swathe of blue sky and sea greeted her. 'This is paradise, Dylan.' Once more, she whirled around, taking in the spectacular scenery, visible from every angle. Even the tops of the houses on the high street were on view.

'The roof terrace was the main reason I bought it.' His smile was wide, as they leaned over the balcony rail.

For a long few moments, Scarlett watched the people below and the boats in the distance.

Finally, Dylan sat down and beckoned her over, and she took a seat beside him, her nerves jangling.

He poured out two glasses of sparkling wine, allowing the bubbles a moment to settle before topping up each glass. He passed one over to her, and she took it with trembling fingers.

'Cristal, of course.' He inclined his head.

'Of course.' She raised her glass and took a sip.

Dylan followed suit. 'Here's to us.'

Scarlett inclined her head. 'There's an us?'

'I hope so.' He put his glass down. 'I took on board all of that stuff you said about drinking and drugs, and I decided not to drink alcohol unless you were with me. But I started to feel pretty desperate for a drink, so I figured I'd better try and find you. It took a lot longer than I expected.' His lips twitched and his eyes sparkled.

'And that's the only reason you found me?'

'Yes, absolutely.' His smile broadened as he raised his glass and took a sip. 'Cheers. I've been waiting for this.'

She frowned. 'Not sure that finding a drinking partner was what I had in mind when I said it, but still. How did you find me?'

Dylan placed his glass down and faced Scarlett. 'It looked like you'd gone to ground, so I had to hang around at the park until your sister came by with that delightful little daughter of hers and that rather slobbery dog. Otherwise I'd have to turn teetotal by default.'

'She didn't tell me.'

'I asked her not to, in case you did a runner again. But she did happen to mention that you missed me desperately and regretted storming off.'

'I'll kill her! So, that was why you were so damned smug on the aircraft.'

'That, and the fact that I'm pretty wonderful and only a fool would turn me down.'

'Don't get cocky on me again, Dylan Willis.'

Dylan reached over to Scarlett and took hold of her hand, his thumb rubbing across the back of it. 'I've missed you so much, and I'm so sorry for being an idiot over the Harrison thing.'

'That's okay. It's been okay for ages, really, I just let my stupid pride get in the way. I was never sure why you were so cross about it, though, to be honest.'

Dylan squeezed her hand. 'It's a man thing. We have to be seen to be able to succeed on our own merit. I nearly gave up a couple of times, though. I'm telling you, it can be the loneliest job in the world. I needed you to keep rooting for me and tell me how great I am. I need someone I can trust to be on my side.'

Scarlett laughed. 'And tell you how great you are?'

'What? I am great, aren't I?' He frowned, as if an alternative opinion wasn't possible, although his lips quirked.

Scarlett raised her eyebrows, but whispered, 'Yes, you are great.'

'But the whole deal hasn't been great. That lonely in a crowded room thing caught me out from day one. I soon discovered that celebrating on my own is more depressing than having nothing to celebrate.' Dylan paused, his eyes fixed on hers. 'Can we put all of this behind us, do you think?'

Scarlett was choked by his words. She hated to think he'd been lonely, too, while she'd been missing him. 'I'd like that more than anything,' she said, her throat constricting.

'Don't cry.' He swung off his chair and knelt beside her, taking her hands in his.

'I'm not.'

Dylan wiped her cheek and held up his damp finger, showing the evidence.

'I've not been sleeping well. I'm really tired.'

'Ooh, what a feeder line.' He stood up and took a step backwards. 'And I'm supposed to ask you if you'd like to go to bed, am I?' He put his hand on his hip, hamming it up.

Laughter bubbled up through her tears. She wiped her nose and cheeks, trying out a smile, and held out her hand, her voice small. 'Yes, please.'

'Come here, you silly thing.'

He gathered her into his arms, and she sniffled into his shirt, silently thanking the heaven and stars that he'd come to find her. The awfulness of the past months washed away in his embrace and she finally believed that she was allowed to be happy.

Dylan smoothed her hair away from her face. 'You look done in, so I think a repeat of the rooftop experience can wait until the weather is a bit kinder. Would you like a little nap? I can show you the bedrooms.' His eyebrows wiggled just the slightest touch at his suggestion.

'I don't feel quite so tired now,' she said.

'Aha! So, it was just a ruse to get into my bed?'

'No, I can just as easily ...'

He silenced her with a kiss, one that held promise of more, but he pulled back before it could go any further. 'Just give yourself a break and quit while you're ahead, okay?'

She nodded once more and allowed Dylan to kiss her again, melting in to his arms, remembering how wonderful it was to be kissed by him.

Eventually, Dylan drew away. 'How about we both have a little lie down? I'm pretty tired, too. I was up at five.'

'Really? Why?' She stared up at him through her spiky, tear-drenched eyelashes.

'I had to drive up to Liverpool to hire an aircraft, which literally cost me my whole fortune, just to have the most beautiful air stewardess I have ever seen, bring me back home again.'

'No way.' Her mouth dropped open in shock. 'You did that for me?'

'Once I'd found out where you were, I wasn't going to

lose you again. Although, to be fair, Natasha did most of the sorting out. She's so scary no one dared to refuse any of her demands. She flew up to Liverpool yesterday to make sure you were on the flight.'

'So I have you to thank for my early morning call out.'

'Sorry.' He grinned.

'Do you know, I wondered why you didn't have any baggage. I reckoned you were just a busker boy at heart and probably stuffed a spare pair of shreddies and socks in your rucksack.' She gazed at him as the enormity of what he'd done sank in. 'Oh, Dylan, that's the most romantic thing ever.' She welled up once more and swiped at her eyes.

'Blimey, this being tired business certainly does get to you, doesn't it? Come on.' He took her hand and led her back down the stairs and into his bedroom, another vast space with the most amazing view of the sea.

She sat on the bed as tiredness overcame her. It felt more inviting than the fluffiest cloud ever and she had to resist the urge to just flop down on the duvet and rest her eyes. But she wanted to be in Dylan's arms, wanted him to make love to her. She needed the proof that none of it was a dream.

Dylan poked his head around the door. 'I'll fetch your bag out of the car. Don't go away.'

'I won't.' She stretched and took off her jacket and skirt. Then she took off her blouse, enjoying the freedom from its confines. She scanned the room, spotted a tee-shirt thrown over a chair and slipped it over her head, inhaling the delicious scent of Dylan.

Laying back on the bed, she couldn't resist throwing back the duvet and crawling beneath it. She was so tired. If she could just close her eyes for just a moment ... brush her teeth ... maybe have a shower when Dylan came back with her bag.

***

Dylan found Scarlett fast asleep when he returned. He'd nipped to his mum's house to tell her that Scarlett was staying, in case she thought it prudent to turn up with a casserole, or one of the many little treats she was forever bringing him. He knew she worried about him, but he had Scarlett back where she belonged, so, hopefully, she'd never have to worry again.

Initially, he was a little bit put out to find Scarlett out for the count in his bed, like Sleeping Beauty, when he'd envisaged a passionate reunion. However, watching her eyelids flicker as she breathed steadily, knowing that she trusted him to keep her safe while she slept, made him swell with love for her.

He smiled on spotting his overlarge tee-shirt on her slim body and for a second, he wondered if waking her under the guise of demanding it back would be a bit off. No, he could wait. He was just happy that she was safely in his bed.

Overcome with tiredness himself, he shucked off his boots and socks, enjoying the sensation of air and freedom. He wiggled his toes, looking longingly at the shower room adjacent to his bedroom, but it would be too noisy, and he didn't want to wake Scarlett.

Instead, he crept over to the bed and eased himself next to her. He wouldn't presume anything, but he didn't think she'd mind if he simply held her in his arms. He folded her into his body, and she murmured and snuggled into him. Her hair was soft and fragrant next to his cheek, and he breathed in the scent that was Scarlett. He'd missed it for too long.

His body, tired as it was, responded to the proximity of her warm, femininity, and all he could think about was making love to her. He had to dredge up chord changes and song lyrics to take his mind away from images of her pliant body responding to his caresses.

God, it was difficult. He eased himself away from her before his desire became too bothersome and, kissing her cheek, allowed his own eyes to close.

CHAPTER TWENTY-NINE

'Oh, no, Scarlett, we need to get up. It's seven o'clock.'

'No! Should I be at work?' She jumped up and sat on the edge of the bed blinking at her surroundings. 'Where am I?' She whirled around, colliding with Dylan, who instantly reached out for her. 'Dylan.' Her smile was wide, and she collapsed back on the bed, twisting to look at him as he fell backwards beside her, his head hitting the pillow with a thud.

He rolled over to face her. 'Hi. Missed me?'

'I fell asleep. I can't believe I fell asleep when I've waited so long for you.' To make sure she wasn't dreaming, she reached up and drew him towards her with a smile. 'I need you, now, this minute.' She could barely believe that she was in Dylan's bed, lying next to him, after so much pain and unhappiness.

He hovered over her, resting on his forearms as he braced either side of her. 'You did miss me, then.' He gazed at her for a moment, before lowering his lips to hers. His kiss was gentle and languid, but he quickly pulled away, just as Scarlett was getting started. 'This is all very nice, but my parents are expecting us at The Swan in twenty minutes.' Sitting up, he swung his legs over the side of the bed.

She groaned and pulled him back down again, wrapping the duvet around him tightly. 'Nooo, you are all mine.'

'You don't want to meet my parents? That's rather

rude ...'

'No, it's not that. Of course I do. I just want to ... spend time with you.'

'You were hoping to have your wicked way with me, weren't you?'

She angled her head, taking in his face, and pulled the duvet away. 'Yes, but you have too many clothes on. Why are you still fully clothed?'

He shrugged. 'You were asleep.'

'Well, I'm awake now.' She flung off the tee-shirt she'd borrowed and threw it across the room with abandon.

His gaze dropped to her breasts, and he groaned. 'Oh, God, why do you have to be so delicious.' He reached out for her, and she gave him a self-satisfied smile, but he shook his head at the last second. 'Stop. We have to get ready. I can't have my own parents guessing why we're late meeting them for dinner. You'll have to contain that unbridled passion of yours.'

She covered her breasts with the duvet and sat up with a pout. 'If you say so, but I need a quick shower. Hey, you could join me.'

'That would make the word quick totally redundant, and you know it, much as I'd like to take you up on the offer.'

She knelt up on the mattress and sighed loudly. 'Spoilsport.'

'Seriously, though, I am desperate for you.' He kissed her deeply, his hands roaming over her bottom and around up to her breasts. He dropped his head onto her shoulder. 'I can't do this. Take me now.' Sighing, he raised his head and slapped her on the bottom. 'No. C'mon, no time for this. Let's make ourselves pretty. I'm meeting with some of the guys again later, I hope that isn't a problem. I'd hate to have to run down the road after you again – it might be a tad embarrassing in front of my parents.'

'Will Kate be there?' Scarlett asked, her insecurities surfacing once more.

'She might be, but you don't have to worry about Kate. We are ancient history and we both know it. She was my first love, until university did what it so often does. You know the way it goes.' He shrugged.

Scarlett picked up on Dylan's indifference and decided she could call time on those particular insecurities. She didn't want to discuss what he'd shared with Kate, anyway. 'I'll just jump in the shower.'

Dylan groaned once more. 'Don't tell me, I don't want to know what I'm missing.'

She was out of the bathroom in minutes and found Dylan tapping away at his phone with a frown. 'What's wrong?'

'I don't believe this.' He glanced up at Scarlett from the bed, his expression pained. 'You look ravishing, by the way.'

She struck a pose, but he glanced straight back down at his phone, making her feel a little foolish. 'What's happened?' She pulled her towel tighter, when only seconds ago, she'd have happily let it drop to the floor.

Dylan stroked his chin. 'I'm about to be driven to the nearest helicopter launch-pad and flown to London for an awards show, apparently. I need to be there for ten o'clock, because I've been nominated for the best New Kid on the Block award, and Harrison thinks I'm up for winning it. Damn it.' He threw his phone on the bed, glancing up at her once more. 'Dear God, and you look like you do. How unfair is life?'

She shimmied over to him. 'I'm glad that you'd rather stay with me, than attend an award ceremony, considering that only last year you would have sold your firstborn for such an accolade.'

'You come before everything, now.' He stood, and she took it as an invitation to hug him, but he threw his hands up. 'No don't touch me, Scarlett. I swear to God, I won't be able to resist you, and the taxi's coming in ten minutes.'

'Tell them you're not going, then.'

'I can't, it's in my contract. They can sue the arse off me, if I put a step out of line. It seemed like a good idea at the time, but they practically own me.'

Scarlett wasn't surprised. Managers didn't manage musicians for the fun of it.

Dylan ran his fingers through his hair. 'How do I look?'

'What? That's it? Your preparation for an awards ceremony is running your fingers through your hair?'

'I'll put my boots on, obviously.'

'Obviously,' she mimicked.

Hands raised again, he backed away from Scarlett. 'You cannot imagine how bad my pain will be until I return, so you'd better be ready and waiting. Hey, you could wear your uniform and greet me at the door, balancing a gin and tonic on a silver tray for me.'

'You'd better stop with this fantasy air stewardess thing, or else I'll start to wonder if that's the only reason you want me.'

'There are a million reasons to want you, and I'll tell you all of them, on my return.' He pulled on his boots as he spoke. 'I'll cancel Mum and Dad, and tell the lads I can't make it. They won't mind. They see so much of me now, they're probably sick of me. Don't go away, will you?'

The doorbell rang, and he grabbed a jacket, kissed her forehead, and vanished from the room.

'I won't,' Scarlett shouted at his retreating back.

Deflated, she pulled on jeans and a sweatshirt as she prepared for a lonely night ahead. In truth, it wouldn't be much different from any other night, but she'd rather hoped her life was changing for the better. Right then, though, she appeared to be back at square one, apart from there being sand and sea and lots of activity outside, instead of the river Mersey and its never-ending ferry service.

Deciding to go for a walk, she slipped on her shoes, hoping to make a decision about moving to Russia. She couldn't for the life of her see a way it could work with Dylan, if she went. But she still needed an income, and sadly, love wouldn't pay the bills.

In truth, her situation wasn't as bad as she'd painted it to Dylan, because she could move back into her flat in London if she chose, but Dylan's house was in Southwold, and so was Dylan. And when he wasn't in Southwold, he'd be in a top-notch hotel somewhere, being tempted by top-notch women.

Lost in thought, she trudged listlessly along the shoreline. She checked out the beach huts once more, imagining a bright red one named Scarlett, and hoped she'd be in Southwold long enough to see it happen.

In her mind, an unbidden image materialized, of herself and Dylan playing in the sand, with a couple of sunny, smiling, tousled-haired children. Settling onto the beach wall, she allowed her little fantasy to play out in her mind and it hit her that she didn't want to leave Dylan ever again. She wanted to live in his wonderful town with him, and maybe, one day, the miniature Dylan look-a-likes would come along and would grow up as content and positive as their father.

She knew that she loved Dylan, and if they wanted to make it work together, she would have to be the one to compromise. So, what was the problem? She could do compromise.

She smiled happily. Finding some kind of solution had come easier than she'd expected.

She headed back to the house, happier than she thought possible, even though she couldn't quite imagine selling ice-creams, or fish and chips as an alternative career. After throwing off her shoes, now content to be on her own until Dylan returned, she padded into the kitchen, rummaged in the fridge, and poured herself a glass of champagne.

She wandered up to the roof to look at the sea, but it really had grown too cold to sit outside. Her mood dipped again at the thought of the empty nights that stretched ahead of her, while Dylan would no doubt be entertained and entertaining. It would be exactly the same as when she was with Sky. He'd be partying, while she worked, or sat at home, waiting for him to come back to her.

She wondered, fleetingly, if she should expect to be hidden away, so she didn't upset the fans if she and Dylan became an item. How could she have simplified it all so easily? She certainly couldn't afford to give up her well-paid job to be a waitress, or similar, and expect to run her car? And where would she live? What if Dylan didn't want her as much as she thought he did?

The magnitude of the problem overwhelmed her once more, and she had to fight down the urge to leave before it all ended badly again.

Her phone beeped, and she glanced down, uninterested. She sat up a little more enthusiastically on seeing Dylan's name on the screen.

Put the television on, the text read. The remote is on top of the coffee table. Press number five. Now. I finally wrote you a song.

Hurriedly, she picked up her wine and sprinted back

down the stairs, trying to remember if she'd even spotted a television. She found it in a recessed cupboard behind a glass door and stared at the blank screen, before examining the remote, which looked far too complicated to understand.

She finally worked it out and the television burst into life. Proud of her accomplishment, she gave herself a minute to rush into the kitchen and grab the champagne out of the fridge, flopping down on the sofa just in time to see Dylan's beaming smile fill the screen.

He climbed up to a podium, looking self-conscious, still in his scruffy jeans and baggy tee-shirt. He rubbed his right shin with the heel of his left foot, the way he did when he was a little unsure of himself.

After a bit of prompting, he began thanking various people for their support as he waved a small statue in the air. She leaned forward in disbelief. She'd missed his big moment. No! She gnawed on her knuckle, upset with herself and wondering if Dylan would be angry with her.

No, she reminded herself, this is Dylan, not Sky.

The cameras cut to the presenter once more, as the applause died down. 'Here's Dylan's latest song, which he says he perfected on the journey over here. Ladies and Gentleman, I give you Dylan Willis.'

Dylan started singing and Scarlett listened to the words that were written just for her.

'I should never have let you go, I know I should be home, please pick up the phone, I'm sorry, Scarlett.'

She inched closer to the television as Dylan faded

away from the screen, leaving Scarlett feeling hollow and bereft. But her phone rang and she pounced on it like a starving hyena. 'Hi, Dylan, you were wonderful, and I love my song.'

'I changed the last two lines on my way here. I was worried you might run off again.'

'I won't … ever.' She cradled the phone to her ear, wishing it were Dylan she was cuddling. 'Do you think we can make this work, Dylan?'

'Yes, I've thought it all along. It's you who keeps putting a spanner in the works.'

'No more spanners. Hurry home.'

She finished her glass of champagne, spritzed perfume on her body and hair, brushed her teeth, and lay down on the bed, waiting for Dylan.

CHAPTER THIRTY

At four in the morning, she was woken by the throaty cough of an engine outside the house. She blinked in the surrounding shadows, both woozy and disorientated as her brain connected to her surroundings.

Footsteps landed on the stairs in the house, slow and torturous. It seemed forever before the bedroom door finally opened.

Dylan plodded across the room sat down heavily on the bed. 'God, I'm knackered. Are you awake?'

Scarlett heaved herself up to a sitting position and turned on the bedside light. 'I've been waiting for you.' She reached out a hand, and he took it, his movements weary. 'You won, then?' she said, waggling his hand a bit. 'Well done.'

'Yeah, it was a long night. Got a black cab home – it seemed less trouble than the helicopter, which I think was mostly for show. I think they'd have quite liked for me to disembark from a dangling rope straight into the studio. So much of this game is shallow hype.'

'I told you that ages ago.' She watched as Dylan shucked off his shirt, enjoying seeing his long legs as he unpeeled his jeans from his body.

'I'm assuming I'm okay to share the bed with you? I just want to hold you until I fall asleep.'

Scarlett hitched herself up on her elbow, wondering why he asked such a question. Were they not the newly reconciled couple she'd thought, or was he just incredibly polite?

Deciding on the latter, she patted the bed for him to join her.

His gaze fixed on where her breasts peeped out above her tee-shirt nightie. Not so incredibly polite, then. He grinned sheepishly. 'Caught in the act, sorry.'

'I'm sorry that I don't have my air stewardess red lace and silk creation with me, but having been hauled out of my bed due to rogue fire alarms in the middle of the night one too many times, I learned to take serviceable night attire to work.'

'You have an air stewardess nightdress?' Dylan's eyes bulged like they were on stalks.

'No.' She laughed. 'I'm messing with you. Put your tongue away.'

'What an image, though. I'll go to sleep dreaming of that.' He fell back on the bed and closed his eyes. 'I'm worn out.'

'Hmm, we've done far too much sleeping since we met up again, if you ask me,' she said, a little put out that, once more, he appeared able to resist her.

He opened one eye and reached out for her. 'In that case, I don't need sleep, I need you.'

'Then, allow me to finish undressing your tired body and see if we can put a bit of life into it.'

'Yes! Thank you, God.' Dylan spread his arms and legs wide, like a snow angel. 'I'm all yours. Do what you will.'

Scarlett stroked his cheek, considering her next move. She threw one leg over Dylan and hauled herself on top of him, settling herself on his thighs as she unbuttoned his shirt. 'Be a good boy and lie still, now.' She bent forward to kiss his cheek demurely, but he twisted his head and caught her mouth with his. Nibbling her bottom lip gently, he teased it with his tongue, before turning it into a full-blown, deep kiss.

'Hey, that's cheating,' Scarlett said, as her hands roamed across his chest, before pushing his shirt across his shoulders, dropping kisses on his skin.

He groaned.

'Come on, we can do this. You can sleep later.'

'That's not why I'm groaning, silly.'

'Oh. Good, then, I think we can dispense with these.' She pushed her hands inside his boxers and tugged them past his thighs.

'Suddenly, I'm awake, but I'm not sure how long for, so you'd better make the most of me, quick.'

'I don't think it will take long.' She stared pointedly at Dylan's erection. 'We'll have time, later, to reacquaint ourselves with each other.

'Oh, yes, I like the sound of that,' Dylan said, studying her carefully. He pointed wordlessly to the bedside drawer, and she leaned over him and retrieved a condom.

She repositioned herself and gave herself up to Dylan, whose agility certainly belied his statement that he was overly tired.

Afterwards, he stroked Scarlett's hip and the curve of her midriff, whispering sweet words and falling into an exhausted sleep, mid-sentence. He smiled in his sleep as he mumbled 'Was good, wasn't it?' - leaving Scarlett to watch over him, thanking God for giving her a second chance, until she, too, fell into a deep sleep.

CHAPTER THIRTY-ONE

Scarlett awoke to blue sky flooding through the skylight in the hallway, and she rolled over to find a gorgeous man gazing at her. 'Hey there.'

'Hey yourself, beautiful.'

She stretched languidly, pushing her feet down toward the bottom of the bed, pointing her toes and flexing them. 'I love that.'

'You love what?' He continued to study her as if he couldn't get enough of her features.

'Being able to move freely. I hate hotel sheets and the way they're always tucked in so tightly, I lose the circulation in my feet.'

'Brilliant.' He slapped his forehead. 'I just gave the girl the greatest time of her life, and that's the best she can come up with.'

Scarlett giggled. 'It's the easiest way to find out if I'm at work, before I open my eyes.'

'I'll remember that when I'm on tour in America.'

'You're going to America?'

Dylan raised himself up and gazed down at Scarlett. 'Is that a problem?'

'Why would it be? It's your life.' She twisted away from him and dived under the covers, burying her nose under the duvet.

Dylan slid himself down with her, threw his leg over hers, took hold of her arm, and pulled her around to face him, until they were nose to nose. 'It's very dark under here,' he whispered.

Scarlett giggled, already sorry that she'd shown her insecurities. She wouldn't allow her state of mind to ruin the day before it had even got started. 'Why are you whispering?'

'I thought you had to, if you were under the covers, so the monsters don't hear you.'

Scarlett smiled in the dark, loving that he knew how to deflect her moodiness. Her heart burst with so much love that she had to contain the words from spilling out of her mouth. She was too scared it would burst the bubble of happiness they floated in.

As if Dylan could see the cogs of her brain turning, he asked, 'Come on, tell me what you're worrying about, now.'

'I'm not worrying. I'm thinking that arousal problem of yours might need sorting out again.' She rubbed her thigh against his erection.

'I swear to God, that wasn't there a second ago. I blame you.'

She wrapped her arms and legs around him like a clinging monkey. 'I take full responsibility.'

'Then, you will have to fix it. Sorry, them's the rules.' He hoisted himself up effortlessly from under the duvet, pulling Scarlett with him. 'I think we're safe from the monsters now.' His eyes scanned the room, before he smiled down at her. 'Oh, Scarlett, Scarlett, you do things to me.' He pushed her hair away from her face, cupped her cheeks with his hands, and kissed her.

The sex that morning was sleepily tender, the frenetic rush of the previous night's lust having quenched their desperate need for each other, but still, the morning sun had climbed high in the sky before they were ready to tackle the day.

'We should have some breakfast,' Scarlett said, as she eventually made to climb out of bed, but Dylan grabbed her wrist and pulled her back down beside him, his urgency surprising her. His eyes were, for once, grave and serious and set her anxiety soaring. 'What is it?' she asked, searching his face.

'Don't go to Russia, please.'

Her breath quickened. 'Don't go on tour, Dylan.'

'I have to.'

She raised her eyebrows.

He nodded slowly. 'Okay, I get it.'

Was the moment declaration, or decision, time? They stared at each other for what seemed an age.

'We need to sort this out,' Dylan said finally.

She exhaled, relieved. 'We do, but I'm not sure how it can be resolved.'

He kissed the tip of her nose. 'You're forgetting how great I am.'

'How can I forget, when you tell me every minute of the day?' She flicked a corner of the duvet at him and escaped from the bed, before he could demand a repeat of the last few hours.

She showered and dressed quickly, preoccupied with their predicament, but determined not to let it get her down.

Dylan prepared breakfast, his phone tucked between his shoulder and ear, as he caught up with his mother then returned a call from Harrison. Scarlett heard the pride in his voice, as he recounted his awards night to his mother, and the polite way he thanked Harrison for everything he'd done for him. She was so proud of him, and so full of love, she wanted to tell the whole world, but still, their future together was disturbingly vague.

After breakfast, she phoned the airline and wangled two days off, instead of being on standby. While grateful for their understanding, she couldn't help but wish her temporary break from real life could last forever. She and Dylan would both have to make decisions before too long, work out how they would find time to be together. Scarlett desperately hoped that there'd be a solution - she couldn't bear the thought of being separated from him again.

Dylan seemed to tune into her morose mood and suggested a walk along the beach to blow away their worries.

'As long as you're not going to take me fishing,' she replied. 'And only if I can borrow a different coat, instead of wearing the pink fleece again.'

'Ungrateful wench, but that's fine.' He scratched his chin for a moment. 'I tell you what, I just have to pop into town for a while. Will you be okay?'

'Yes, I'll be fine. You don't have to keep checking on me, Dylan. I'm not going anywhere.'

He looked dubious. 'Okay then, I'll be right back.'

He returned before too long, back to his usual upbeat self and waving a carrier bag in her direction. 'A present for you.'

'For me? How lovely. It's not an air stewardess nightdress, is it?'

'Damn, rumbled again.' He winked as he passed over the bag.

'Dylan, you shouldn't have.' She took out a long cream woollen jacket, smoothing down the soft warm pile of the fabric. 'It's … wow, it's amazing.' She checked the label and pressed her palm to her chest. 'Oh, my goodness, Dylan!'

'The assistant from one of those boutique shops in the high street suggested it – it's from the new spring season, apparently. You know my sense of fashion, you'd have ended up in frayed denim, if it was left to me.'

'I love it. Thank you so much.' She reached up and kissed his cheek, before slipping on the coat and preening a bit. 'It'll go great with my boots. Come on, let's go for that walk so that I can show it off.'

They soon found themselves on the beach at the seafront, dodging children and watching dogs of various shades and sizes snuffle and weave their way in and out of legs and buggies.

'I think I need a dog. What do you think?' Dylan asked, as they strolled along.

'How will you look after a dog when you go away so frequently?'

'Not sure, yet, but I feel my house needs a dog, don't you?' Dylan stopped a tennis ball with his foot as it went to roll past them. As he picked it up, a black and white mongrel raced up to them and stood panting, wagging its tail, and Dylan threw the ball far into the sand, waving at the dog's owners as the dog raced after it. 'Definitely need a dog,' he repeated, as he stared toward where the dog skidded to a halt, sending a spray of sand over itself, returning the ball triumphantly to its owners.

'A fluffy, white Maltese puppy,' Scarlett said dreamily.

'No way. A chocolate Lab is the smallest dog I'm prepared to accept.'

They discussed the merits of various dogs, Scarlett playing along, hoping it would show them a way to make a long-distance relationship work. In that moment, though, all she could envisage was inappropriately-timed, static-filled phone calls as they tried to catch up with each other, pretending to be happy, while Scarlett wondered, in every quiet moment, if he was about to confess to an indiscretion.

She really needed to stop thinking that way, but she couldn't picture it any other way. She also fretted that Dylan might decide it was too restricting, being faithful to a woman he hardly ever saw. She didn't know how she would carry on if he decided she was too much trouble.

'When are you going on tour?' she asked him. She might as well start planning for lonely times, see if he'd thought through the effects the distance would have on their relationship.

'End of the month. When do you go to Moscow?'

'I have another three weeks in Liverpool. I've already handed in my notice.'

'Right.'

'Yeah.' She couldn't inject any enthusiasm into her voice.

They walked in silence, Scarlett's spirits dipping. It wouldn't work, she knew it. They'd never manage to see each other.

'It's a long way to Moscow, isn't it?' Dylan's eyes were bleak, the usual full wattage of startling blue dimmed.

Scarlett's lips twisted. 'It's not too far, in relation to, say, the moon.' She tried out a smile, but it was a poor attempt.

Dylan shrugged his shoulders and hunched into his jacket, shoving his hands into his pockets. He seemed to be distancing himself from her already, and she pulled her coat tighter around her body, suddenly feeling cold and empty.

CHAPTER THIRTY-TWO

As they trudged along the sand, Dylan barely spoke, but he glanced over at Scarlett numerous times, confusing her with his introspection.

She bit her lip, waiting for him to speak, fighting against the wind that had blown up as they reached the pier. She squinted into the distance. 'Isn't that your ginger-haired friend?' she said, pointing a finger.

'I don't think so.' Dylan raised a hand to his brow and peered toward where she pointed.

'Well, he's carrying a case that looks very guitar-shaped.'

'There are enough of us guitar-carrying weirdos around to confuse everyone.' He came to a standstill outside the chip shop on the edge of the pier. 'Can we just stop here a minute?'

'Here?' Scarlett looked back towards the beach huts, then at the wooden tables and chairs laid out for outside eating, unable to see any reason why Dylan would want to linger.

'Just for a minute, please.' His eyes darted from left to right, as if he was looking for someone.

'Are you okay?' she asked.

His phone beeped, but he spared it barely more than a glance before he shoved it in his pocket, unanswered. 'Sorry, yes, I'm fine.' He ran a hand around the back of his neck. 'We can carry on now. I was just a bit ... err, a bit out of breath.'

Scarlett wanted to believe him, but she knew him well enough to know that something was up. She wondered fleetingly if he'd spotted Kate, or maybe someone else from his distant past. She hated herself for her thoughts, but guessed it was just another legacy of Sky. Damn him, and his carryings-on. She wasn't sure she'd ever trust a man again.

They drew level with the Under the Pier show, and Scarlett expected Dylan to suggest they tried out a few more of the silly amusements, but he still seemed deep in thought, and they passed by without comment. She felt unaccountably nervous and snuck her hand into his pocket, grateful for the warm fingers that locked around hers. Surely, he wouldn't do that if he was about to impart bad news?

They reached the Clock Tower, and he drew her towards the balustrade so they faced the beach huts set off farther along.

'Here we are.'

Frowning, she gazed toward the sea and the distant beach huts. 'So, here we are, and ...?' she repeated.

Dylan took a step towards her and placed his arms on either side of the handrail, effectively pinning her in place. 'Scarlett, I'm aware of your hang-ups – no, not the OCD one. The one to do with unreliable men, or in particular, me, and I think it's because of Sky.'

'I do not have an OCD problem,' she snapped, too unnerved to be quiet. 'And I do trust you.' She wrinkled her nose as she spoke, aware that she was lying.

Dylan gave her a look that said he'd go along with it, despite the fact that he obviously wasn't buying it. 'So, because of all of these problems ...' he said, his voice deadpan. A muscle in his jaw pulsed as his lips set in a grim line.

Scarlett's stomach swooped with dread as she studied his granite like features. She took in the serious eyes and met his gaze, steadying her nerves to prepare for the death knell that would end her world. Clearly, he too had thought through their long-distance problem and made a decision. He pushed his hands into his pockets, but pulled them out again, glancing toward the sea and then up at the sky. He swallowed and shuffled his feet, opened his mouth as if to speak, but no words came out.

As she watched him in horrified silence, her mind closed down, as surely as if she'd put her hands over her ears and started singing la, la, la.

'Scarlett, are you listening?'

'No.' She shook her head as she reached out to him, clutching at his sleeve, suddenly nauseous. 'Don't, Dylan, please don't say it. We can try and make this work - somehow. Can't we?' Terror gripped her as she gazed into the beautiful blue eyes that she loved so much.

'Just, let me have my say, will you?' He cleared his throat as if suddenly sure about the words that wouldn't come moments before. 'Scarlett, I want you to know that I will never deceive you, or risk what we have between us. I said it once before, but you left me, anyway, so now

I want to seal it with something more than words. So, that you know.'

His gaze remained locked on to her face, and the unbearable thrumming that had filled her head cleared. 'What?' She heaved out a shuddering breath of relief. 'So, that I know what?' Was it good news, after all?

Dylan didn't have the chance to answer before the loud twang of a guitar interrupted their moment.

From the crowd stepped Curly Ginger and two other band members, their guitars slung low.

'Dylan, what's going on?' Scarlett asked, as Curly Ginger handed Dylan a microphone.

Dylan grinned at Scarlett. 'I'm going to sing my love to you.' He brought the microphone up to his mouth and spoke into it. 'Testing, testing, one-two-three.'

Scarlett's eyes widened. 'Here?'

'Yup,' he said.

'Please, don't,' Scarlett begged, but a smile of relief hovered around her lips.

'Too late.' Dylan's voice reverberated into the microphone.

The wee-wee men peeing on the flowers were suddenly of no interest to the tourists, as they gathered around Dylan and Scarlett with curiosity, settling in to enjoy the impromptu show.

Dylan began to sing, his voice rising above the noise of the waves as he threw his arms wide, exaggerating his gestures and showing off to the audience. 'I know everything will be all right, as long as I have you in my sight.' He crooned to a mortified Scarlett, as her cheeks heated to an unprecedented temperature from being placed in the spotlight.

A woman pushing a buggy, her child clapping to the tune, shouted out, 'Who is she, then, is she famous?'

'Dunno. She's hot, though.' The young man who'd replied sidled up to the railings and snapped a close-up of Scarlett on his phone.

Scarlett reeled backwards, shocked and a little disconcerted. What the hell was Dylan thinking of, drawing attention to himself?

'She's off that baking programme, isn't she?' Another woman moved in closer, her brood of teenagers simultaneously videoing the show on their phones, as if it was up for public viewing - which it indeed appeared to be.

'Yes, it's that Bake Off girl, the pretty one. She has a wonderful blog page full of gorgeous cakes.'

'I think you're right. Isn't he someone, too, though?'

Scarlett tried to stay calm, as Dylan hammed it up like Bill Nighy in Love Actually, almost falling over as his knees touched the ground.

With his legs spread wide, he sang, 'I want the world to know, I love you so.' His overacting was toe-curlingly bad, but the audience seemed to love it.

Curly Ginger grinned from ear to ear, as Dylan turned to the audience, reiterating his love for Scarlett by repeating the chorus.

It was the corniest song she'd ever heard, and she tried

not to laugh, but Dylan's lips were twitching, and she caught his eyes twinkling with merriment.

'Go on, tell him you love him,' a man in a bobble hat shouted, edging his way closer to the action. 'It's that Dylan something, or other. You know, the popstar – I've got one of his songs on iTunes,' he told anyone who'd listen, proud to impart his knowledge.

Dylan, having heard the man, turned to Scarlett, his microphone still on full volume. 'Yeah, Scarlett, say you love me.'

'Dylan!' Scarlett warned.

He lowered the microphone and stepped closer. 'But you do you love me, don't you?'

'Yes, of course I do, you dummy. I wouldn't put up with this sort of crap, if I didn't.' She turned on a smile for the crowd, and they cheered and whooped.

Dylan rewarded them with a flashing smile. 'Tell everyone, then.'

She rolled her eyes. 'Yes, I love you, Dylan Willis.' She leaned forward to kiss him, but he stopped her mid-flow.

'Would you mind just turning to the left a bit and saying it again, 'cause the nice lady over there, from What Now magazine, wants to take our picture.'

Scarlett stared at Dylan, her eyes wild in disbelief. 'What the hell?'

Dylan shrugged. 'It's normal for me now. Sorry.'

'A magazine has paid you to do this?' She wasn't sure whether to be outraged, or flattered.

'Kind of. Natasha phoned them up and asked them to

cover it, so I can tell everyone that you're mine, and I'm yours.'

'Tell me you're joking?' She turned her head, and was met by a video camera pointing at her nose.

'No. How else am I going to pay for that ridiculously expensive flight - where I didn't even get to eat the sandwiches? Plus, the lads'll want at least twenty-five quid each for this.' He patted his pockets as if he was trying to scrape some money together and shrugged. 'Totally skint.' He put his hand on her elbow and turned her towards the camera. 'So, smile for the nice lady, and I'll do the rest.'

'Un-bloody believable,' Scarlett hissed out of the side of her mouth, but she grinned innately at the camera, turning this way and that, grateful that she wasn't sporting the pink fleece.

She gazed in awe at the new Dylan who coped with photo shoots and was confident enough to use them to his advantage.

'There.' He threw his arm around her shoulder, grinning at the camera. 'Is this enough to convince you that I never want to hide you away?'

'That was the most clichéd song the world has ever had the misfortune to hear,' Scarlett said, through a fixed smile.

'Excuse me? I'll have you know, it took me almost half an hour to come up with those words, and another ten minutes to persuade the lads to help me out.'

'And I'm guessing my new coat wasn't quite the spur

of the moment present that I thought?' She peeped coyly from under her eyelashes, as the video zoomed in once more.

'Can't have the crème de la crème of the gossip magazine showcasing images of my gorgeous girlfriend while she's dwarfed by a psychedelic pink fleece, can I? I mean, what would it do to my image?' Dylan laughed.

Scarlett hit him playfully on the arm, but he deflected it, caught her hand, and pulled her into his arms. She smiled up at him. 'I love it, whatever the sentiment, Dylan. And I love you for ... for being you.'

'That's enough, thanks, Dylan. We'll be in touch' The cameraman stuck his thumb in the air and disappeared into the crowd.

'Cheers for that.' Dylan waved and turned back to Scarlett. 'There is one more thing to do, now the show's over.' He dipped his hand into his pocket and pulled out a flat envelope, tipping out the contents into his hand, as Scarlett watched, intrigued. 'I actually have two of these, but it's up to you whether we use them both.' He slid out a flat oblong piece of metal from its tissue paper and laid it flat on the balustrade where there was a gap between the plaques.

Scarlett glanced up at Dylan and down again, frowning at the small metal shape.

'Read it, then,' he said, those blue eyes once more pinned on her face.

'Dylan Willis proposed to his one and only love, Scarlett De Verre, on this pier. Oh.' She snapped her gaze up to Dylan's. What was he proposing?

He smiled ruefully. 'What do you think?'

'I think it's lovely.'

'Great.' He ran a hand around the back of his neck. 'Could do with a bit more than that, though, really.'

'Dylan, what are you asking?'

'Isn't it clear?' He pointed at the plaque again. 'Like, will you marry me? Not now - God, I'm far too busy - but ... you know.' He waved the other square of metal in the air.

'Dylan, that's so lovely, but we haven't been seeing each other for very long, not really.'

'Only because you keep fighting with me. I mean, we first met ages ago, and I'm pretty sure ... I mean, I did track you down and drive all the way up to Liverpool to find you, and ... well, you know what I'm like. I said, the first time I saw you, that ...'

'What's written on the other one?' She interrupted him, amused by his sudden shambolic ramblings.

'Oh, I have to hold on to this one, hoping that you agree to marry me, but if you don't, well, it's no problem. I can just use it as a paperweight, or throw it in the sea.' Despite his words, he unwrapped it from its tissue paper and placed it on top of the other plaque. Glancing at Scarlett, he read out the inscription carefully: 'Dylan Willis married Scarlett De Verre in Southwold, in the summer of two-thousand-seventeen. In love, forever.'

Scarlett read the inscription and shrugged. 'Cool. I've always fancied the idea of an August wedding.'

'Okay. That's good, then.' He grinned, and she grinned back. He gathered her into his arms and whispered in her ear, 'You could be my official groupie. The first and only one that I have sex with, if you act quickly and take the job offer.'

'Is that a proper job title? Only, if I don't go to Russia, I will, actually, be unemployed very soon.'

He nodded enthusiastically. 'Best job going. Although, the salary is crap - paid mostly in kind, if I'm honest.'

'Well, yes, then, I guess. How could I turn down such an offer?'

'Smartest decision you've ever made.' Dylan winked. 'Scarlett Willis sounds so right to me. Absolutely, best decision.' He tucked her hand into his pocket. 'Let's go and buy us a dog.'

EPILOGUE

The London News Live August 2017

The much-loved face of megastar, Dylan Willis was snapped for a different reason today, when he was cautioned by police at London City Airport after slugging a pilot.

The prestigious airline, StarJet, is known to have carried some of the best loved celebrities to their destinations and was booked to take Dylan and his new wife, Scarlett, to Paris.

A StarJet employee reported that Dylan took one look at the captain, standing by the aircraft steps and punched him on the nose. 'It's a total mystery to everyone,' he added.

Dylan's right-hand man Robert Masters, more commonly known as Beanie, had this to offer. 'Dylan's normally a peace-loving man, but there was a good reason for him smacking Captain Carrington one. I've never met the bloke but I'd have probably done the same, to be honest.'

Robert Masters and his long-term girlfriend, Natasha Millar are currently dog-sitting for Bob, Dylan's Labrador, while overseeing the refurbishing and repainting of one of the prestigious beach huts in Southwold, which the Willis's have just acquired.

The red beach hut is being furnished in bright primary colours, causing speculation that there might be a small version of Dylan in the making. We certainly hope so, and we wish the happy couple all the very best.

About the Author

Discover more about Jackie Ladbury at jackieladbury.com or @Ladburywriter

If you enjoyed Air Guitar and Caviar, please consider leaving a positive review on Amazon - every little helps!

And if you fancy visiting Southwold, do check out: http://www.underthepier.com/

Acknowledgements

I'd like to thank my wonderful Write Romantics who have helped me to reach this point and are so much more than a writing group of friends. Also, the Romantic Novelists' Association which kept me going when I was ready to quit. (Many times.) The same thanks go to Fenella Miller and her constant encouragement, Sarah Callejo for being a fab beta reader, and pilot Pete for buying that first notebook for me, all those years ago, basically telling me to put my money where my mouth was.

Much love and appreciation goes to my stalwart friends and family, especially my husband and two daughters, who have nodded sympathetically during my road to publication, whether they understood a single word of my mutterings or not.

Printed in Great Britain
by Amazon